CHINA'S MASTER PLAN

By Shawn K. Lipton

The Trusted Coach, LLC
Seattle, Washington

First Edition

For Nicole and Amelia

Chapter 1

Matthew Barley was not the type who frightened easily. He was supremely confident, rather naïve, and much too self-centered to realize or care about the usual fears that impacted the lives of the ordinary. He made decisions carelessly, with little forethought to the consequences of his actions. His disregard for caution should have gotten him into trouble long ago.

As he furiously threw clothes into his backpack and experienced the discomfort of hyperventilating, he realized that for the first time in his life he was learning how it felt to be gripped by fear and extreme anxiety. The emotion was completely foreign to him, but so intense and real that he wondered how it could be that he had never previously experienced such feelings.

Matthew, though naïve, was not stupid. The problem was that he was of average intelligence, which conflicted greatly with his ambition. He had no desire to climb the corporate ladder and after receiving numerous rejections from the top investment banking firms on Wall Street, he hastily decided to do what a good friend had done a year earlier and go to Beijing, China. His friends and family were not shocked with his decision. It was always assumed that Matthew "knew what he was doing." It wasn't that he was enamored with the Chinese culture or had a desire to travel outside U.S. borders and broaden his horizons; he simply looked at his trip as a way to avoid searching for a traditional job in a depressed U.S. economy … and to get laid. He wondered what had persuaded him to make such a rash decision and still could not comprehend how a seemingly innocuous choice to travel abroad could have gone so awry.

Things had started out just as the rest of his life had, perfectly. He had found work easily, had blended right into the expatriate community, and had started dating the most beautiful woman in China. As Matthew packed, he tried to fill his thoughts with those first three months of his stay in Beijing; he never could have imagined how terribly things would turn out.

Perhaps he was overreacting, he thought. His fear had become so increasingly intense that maybe he was unable to think rationally. He took repeated deep breaths and tried to calm himself, with little effect. Though he had avoided his instincts for the previous three weeks, he now knew he had no choice but to get on the overnight train leaving Beijing, heading north toward Russia. At this time of night, it was the quickest way out of the country from the capital and probably the safest. By morning, when he did not show up for work and the search began, he would already be in Russia and practically home free. In the midst of his panic, he smiled. Who would have thought that Russia, once the cold war nemesis of the U.S., would be considered a safe haven? Matthew was now positive that they realized he already knew too much.

Packing was going slowly. He had already sweated through two t-shirts. July in Beijing is normally stiflingly hot, but this particular summer, temperatures had broken 100-year records. He couldn't understand how he had collected so many things in a three-month period. It wasn't all going to fit, but at that moment all the little mementos and souvenirs seemed important; he really did not want to leave anything behind. He slipped in and out of the gravity of the situation, hoping to convince himself that the conspiracy he thought he had discovered was a self-concocted fantasy. He checked his watch, a Swiss-made Victorinox that his girlfriend had given him at O'Hare just before he boarded his flight to China. It dawned on him that this was the first time he had thought about her in months. He had become so immediately immersed in his Chinese surroundings that it had seemed foolish to maintain the long-distance relationship.

He snapped out of his daydream and realized it had cost him precious time; as he checked his watch again he found that he only had thirty minutes to get to the station. Beijing traffic crawls at a turtle's pace during rush hour, and even at this time of night what should be an eight- to ten-minute ride to the Beijing Railway Station could take twenty to thirty minutes. He was cutting it way too close.

As he finished packing and forced the zipper closed on his bag, he heard a knock on the door. A sweet, heavily-accented English voice came from the hall, "Matthew, you in there?" It sounded more like "Matu, u in dere?," but after being in China for three months, Matt had no problem understanding the most mangled English and especially not from Way Lin: the person who he had spent almost every day with and the main reason why he had so easily forgotten lovely Karen back in Chicago.

Matt's armpits were drenched with nervous sweat and streams of perspiration continued to trickle past his solar plexus as he opened the door for Way Lin. As she stood seductively in the doorway he marveled at just how gorgeous she was. As he slowly and openly moved his eyes from her face down to her perfectly sculptured body, he became aroused. Perhaps, he thought, one last time as a sort of goodbye.

"Way Lin, I thought you were going to Shanghai?" Just before he opened the door, Matt had attempted to hide his pack in the closet and spread the items around the room that he decided to leave behind, but it was quite obvious he was leaving.

"I decide no go, miss you so much." As she said this, Way Lin glanced around the room and added, "Where you go?"

"I am going to take a short vacation to Tianjin to visit a friend from home who is working at the Motorola factory up there. I actually need to leave pretty soon." He thought this excuse a good one and was mildly proud of being able to think on his feet and come up with an answer so quickly. Most of the time she seemed so clueless. With the culture gap and communication problems, she took anything he said, if it were expressed in a convincing manner, as truth. But sometimes when she spoke in Chinese and he caught her off guard, her eyes looked so comprehending and her demeanor, instead of being demure and subservient, was confident and commanding, much like he would expect from a CEO of a Fortune 500 company. It was hard to tell her true nature since Matt spoke very little Chinese and to him she was always the naïve Chinese girl from the country.

"You not say goodbye?"

"I will be back in a couple of days, and of course I would have said goodbye if I knew you were staying in Beijing." It was important for Matt to enunciate everything he said or it would simply fly right over Way Lin's beautiful head.

"Why all your clothes put in suitcase?" She didn't know the word for backpack. "You leave and not come back, foreign ghosts all same."

"Listen, I would love to continue talking, but I have to make a train." Matt only had about 15 minutes; he was worried, but still pretty confident he could make the train since nothing in China ran properly or on time, least of all the trains.

"Matue, you not want take later train and make love with Way Lin first?" She walked over to the bed and laid down, letting the slit from her traditional Chinese red dress fall open, exposing her long, perfectly toned legs. She was confident he would not be able to refuse her. *Who could?* It was the one thing Way Lin knew she would miss about Matthew; he was great in bed.

Matt walked over to her and kissed her passionately. He wanted to as much as she did, but just as her probing hand began massaging his loins and unzipping his pants, he pulled away.

"Way Lin! I can't. I have to make that train." As he said this, Matt realized that this was the first time in his life that he had refused sex.

With this, Way Lin started crying. She tried to maintain her role as long as possible. She knew his knowledge of the project would put its existence in jeopardy, especially if anybody in Washington were notified. She wanted to see just how serious Matt was about leaving, it went directly to the amount of knowledge he had and his level of fear. And besides, she had become so adept at the role of naïve Chinese country girl that sometimes she almost enjoyed it.

"Way Lin, I really have to go." Matt removed his pack from the closet, loosened the straps, and flung it over his back. He hated to lie to Way Lin like this, but if what he knew were true, it was

7

information the Communists would not be willing to part with freely. If he did not escape tonight, he was quite positive he would be executed in the morning. This was more premonition than absolute certainty, a persistent paranoia that he no longer felt able to control. "Come on Way Lin, see me to the station."

Matt reached for the doorknob and simultaneously looked back to Way Lin who had gotten up from the bed and was now one step behind him. As he did this, he caught a last glimpse of Way Lin just as she wrapped a thin piece of corrugated wire around his neck and swiftly brought him to the floor. There was not much of a struggle. Way Lin was much too skilled and Matt was so taken by surprise that he was paralyzed to do anything except look in bewilderment at a woman he thought he knew.

"Goodbye, Matthew. Forever," Way Lin whispered in a perfect American accent as she stood over his lifeless body.

Chapter 2

As the opening bell sounded, the Hong Kong Stock Exchange roared to life like a fire-breathing dragon. Ruled by the mighty Hang Seng Index, the exchange set new records almost daily and had been on a thoroughbred pace for the last three years. Initially, the almost irrational bull market run was primarily fueled by the appreciating prices in the U.S. markets. Hong Kong's exchange was not very different from any other exchange around the world: it included some quality companies and a few industrial giants that could move the indexes, but what really impacted the psychology of the market was what happened in New York the day before. It was common practice among young, gung ho traders to set their alarms for 4:00 a.m. to check their computers for the final numbers on Wall Street, and then sleep for two more hours before rushing to the office to make sure they were in front of their flashing green terminals by 7:00 a.m. The divorce rate was high among traders, as was alcoholism, but in the end, nothing mattered except the insatiable quest for an eight-figure net worth. Seven figures just did not cut it these days on the island.

Recently things had started changing. The U.S. markets had hit a massive brick wall, but the Hang Seng had continued its climb. A few high-tech, China-based IPOs were floated each month on the Hong Kong exchange and were typically greeted with enthusiastic fanfare, not just from the Chinese, but also from bargain hunting, international investors searching for avenues of investment aside from the oversaturated and declining NASDAQ. Most of these companies were small, unheard of Mainland China-based outfits. 90% were situated in Zhongguancun, the Chinese equivalent of Silicon Valley. Zhongguancun, located near the top universities in Beijing, was China's leading incubator for high-tech companies and had served as the engine for China's growing knowledge-based economy. Its center was a short bike ride from Beijing University, a hotbed for young, tech-savvy entrepreneurs. Some of the companies had invented cutting-edge technologies, the likes of which the U.S. had never seen. With the announcement of a groundbreaking technology and a subsequent IPO, these Chinese companies, who like their U.S. brethren were bleeding red ink, would see their stocks rise meteorically.

The current stock of the day was Young Gan Technologies, literally meaning "brave technologies." The stock was priced at $28 per share at the market's open, but closed at $131 per share, making the two co-founders instant USD billionaires. Six months ago nobody even knew the company existed.

Tommy Anderson worked for Asia-Pacific Corporation, a consulting firm that specialized in advising U.S. companies on investing and doing business in China as well as assisting Chinese companies with investment in America. It was the perfect front for his day job as a CIA operative. Chinese companies had become increasingly savvy, flush with extra cash, and anxious to move money out of the communist state. America received the overwhelming majority of the investments. Larger American companies had been investing in China for years, but Tommy's business was primarily from small and mid-sized U.S. companies that had recently started buying into the dream of selling one widget to one billion people. Scared to make the same mistakes that the Fortune 500s had 20 years earlier, these companies relied on consultants like Tommy to assist them with investment decisions. Tommy spent most of his time in Hong Kong and Beijing researching the burgeoning technology sector and meeting with government and business officials. Much of the information he gathered for the CIA was from these business contacts. Landing this assignment was impressive for a 27-year-old just out of the CIA Academy in Langley, but Tommy was ambitious and fluent in Mandarin Chinese, so he had scored the posting. He sensed that he was in the fortuitous position of working on the greatest economic espionage case the world had ever seen, and he relished the challenge.

The latest technological discoveries and subsequent IPOs by unknown Chinese companies had left Tommy baffled. He knew Chinese companies were gaining ground on their American counterparts in technological developments and that most of the employees of the Chinese companies had received advanced degrees from top American universities, but in certain areas the Americans were still years ahead of China and he just couldn't fathom how the Chinese had caught up so quickly.

Pondering these questions, he walked into the Lion Head Pub in the heart of the tourist section on the Kowloon side of Hong Kong. After the turnover to China in 1997, the English pubs remained, but instead of English expat bartenders, the whole place was run by Chinese nationals. Before the turnover, English kids would arrive in Hong Kong, take the jobs the haughty, nouveau riche Hong Kongers were unwilling to do, and make enough money to travel the world. Now newly arrived immigrants from the Mainland who barely spoke English worked the taps—and the English pubs, once a sanctuary from the overbearing bustle of Hong Kong, were now just another example of the remnants of a crumbling English empire.

When Tommy walked into the pub, heads turned—as they did wherever he went in Asia. He was an imposing figure, 6'5'', broad, with greased back blond hair, and a smooth, Scandinavian-pale complexion. Tommy knew he looked good, but came across as engaging and humble, which added to his allure among both men and women. He had been an All-American tight end at Notre Dame and a Chinese Language major. He was actually drafted in a late round by the Minnesota Vikings, but did not have the quickness to make it in the NFL.

He spotted his friend Bill O'Malley at the corner of the bar drinking a scotch and soda. O'Malley worked the Asian tech beat for *The San Francisco Examiner*. "Did ya catch page one of yesterday's *Examiner*, Tommy me boy?" O'Malley was not wasting any time before gloating. His article on the death of Silicon Valley was brilliant and the editors back in San Fran had given it top billing. Even for a veteran like Bill O'Malley, Page One coverage was reason to celebrate.

"*The Examiner*? I'd sooner read the headlines of *The Enquirer* than search the island for the lone copy of *The Frisco Examiner*." Tommy had in fact read the article online and was impressed by it.

O'Malley, a Bronx Irish Catholic, had been in China for five years. The son of a dockworker, he had put himself through St. Johns University by working the graveyard shift as a forklift operator, and then had moved west upon graduation and had found a job as a cub reporter for *The San Francisco Examiner*. He had been out of the Bronx for 30 years, but retained a street-wise edginess as well as his New York accent. He was quintessential Irish in every way, from his ruddy red face, to his bright orange hair, to his love of the occasional drink. Since Tommy's arrival in Asia nine months ago, Bill had served as a good friend and confidant.

"Still trying to act like some old school New England Yankee, always looking for an opportunity to disparage the West?" O'Malley asked. They were both laughing and getting stares from the rest of the bar. Tommy sat down, ordered a stout and had the bartender refill Bill's scotch and soda.

"So what's your take?" Tommy asked.

"My take? You're not wasting any time. You got your pen and paper in hand or do ya want me to speak into a recorder?" O'Malley knew exactly what Tommy was referring to. The mighty Hang Seng. Everyone, from the old men maneuvering tourist-laden rickshaws in the bustling streets of Hong Kong to the top brass in Beijing, was talking about "the market." Tommy was always inquisitive and though O'Malley trusted him he was never comfortable parting with information.

"Hey, whoa!" Tommy moved his hands forward. "Just an innocent conversation among friends, unless of course deep throat is feeding you information again."

O'Malley finished his drink and ordered another round. "OK, I'm gonna tell you my fuckin' take. There's no way in hell the Chinese have the capability or know-how to develop such cutting-edge software. Man, if I were Linksound Technologies I'd clean house and start by giving walking papers to every yellow face in the place." O'Malley was not very fond of the Chinese. He had spent too much time in-country and had become jaded by the whole "Chinese experience." It was common among expats. He was fine when he was sober, but after a few scotches the insults would fly from his tongue with such acerbity that even Tommy would be offended. On more than one occasion, O'Malley's vocal condescending taunts had led to fights and sometimes even a hospital visit.

"What are you saying?" Tommy asked. "That someone in Linksound is feeding information to Young Gan Tech? No way!" Linksound Technologies was a U.S. company that had been developing software that was ultimately introduced by Young Gan. Linksound was said to be close to a major product launch in voice recognition software when Young Gan suddenly announced its breakthrough in the same technology.

"What da ya mean 'No way'?" Bill roared back. "Man, just check the headlines. Remember that scientist who was arrested for funneling secrets from Los Alamos a few years back? And what about the three Chinese arrested at ACC recently. I'm telling you, it's endemic. They're everywhere. Scurrying around like a bunch of fuckin' cockroaches in a Bronx tenement, stealing secrets and sending them back to the Motherland. This shit is happening all the time and with all the Chinese now working in the Valley and other high-tech hotbeds, there's gotta be some economic espionage going on."

"I still say it's impossible," Tommy responded. "Everyone in the Valley is too paranoid to let anything like this happen. Only the paranoid survive. It's the mantra throughout the industry. Man, these guys are scared to death of having their proprietary information stolen. They walk around with non-disclosure agreements wherever they go—cocktail parties, dates, high school reunions—and literally as soon as someone asks what they do for a living, out comes a carefully crafted legal document. Only the most trusted people would've had access to Linksound's top-level research."

"You're missing the fuckin' point," Bill answered back. "There's a forest among those trees, Tommy. Don't just focus on Linksound. This has happened too many times in the last year to be a coincidence. Five times within the last year, U.S. companies have been on the verge of releasing groundbreaking technologies, only to be upstaged by the commies. Man, something big is going on. Something you and I can't even begin to fathom." O'Malley had begun slurring his words, but it took a near comatose state for him to lose his sharpness and lucidity. "It's a conspiracy!"

Tommy continued to push back. "I still say no way. These companies do more thorough checks than the CIA and FBI combined. They check everything: schools attended, friends, drug history, foreign travel. They give polygraphs. The top people are screened relentlessly. It's absolutely sick what lengths a high-tech company will go through to protect their secrets."

O'Malley was not convinced. His instincts were rarely wrong, but he was too drunk and tired to continue the discussion. Tommy, for his part, was worried that O'Malley might break a story that would ruin months of hard work and spoil any hope of busting the ring. "Another drink, Tommy ole boy?"

Chapter 3

Song May Chen (Way Lin's real name) rarely thought about how her life had turned out or the events that had shaped her. She was not the introspective type. But as she awoke, the August Beijing sun, normally unbearable, was especially unforgiving even at such an early hour and she was reminded of the summers spent with her grandfather in Fujian Province. As the school year wound down each spring, she would count the days until she'd be by her grandfather's side listening to stories of the revolution.

As she reluctantly crawled out of bed and began another day of her less-than-satisfying life, thoughts of her grandfather floated through her head and seemed to calm her racing mind and let her escape, something she rarely allowed herself to do. Her grandfather was not originally from Fujian. He was sent there in 1957 by Mao to lead a legion of the People's Liberation Army to Taiwan to overthrow Chiang Kai Shek once and for all. But other than minimal bombing, and most likely due to the U.S.'s support of Taiwan, the attack never occurred. However, Song May's grandfather, Sho Wun Chen, fell in love with the province's semi-tropical countryside and decided to stay and retire there.

Sho Wun, born a peasant farmer in a village outside Hunan very close to the birthplace of Mao, was one of the Communist Party's top military strategists, and he was by Mao's side during much of the Long March. He is still famous in Communist Party folklore as one of the men most responsible for driving the Nationalists from their stronghold in the mainland city of Nanking to their present home of Taiwan. He was a masterful spy who had gained the confidence of some of the top Nationalist generals. Though barely educated, he spoke a standard Mandarin and few could match him intellectually. It was the perfect combination; he had the smarts but not the bourgeoisie background. This kept him out of harm's way during the Cultural Revolution, one of the few high-ranking generals who were not purged.

Song May loved to walk through the fields with her grandfather and listen to stories of the Long March and the long Civil War with the Nationalists. He would weave tales of the brave soldiers: men and women who fought for the revolution and drove the Nationalists from power. Little Song May was enthralled. She remembered clearly that even as a seven- or eight-year-old she felt passionately about fighting for her country and protecting it from capitalist insurgency. While American kids were innocently playing Cowboys and Indians, Song May, or May May as she was called then, was launching World War III against the capitalist pigs. It was the days spent with her grandfather in the fields and on the porch of his country home drinking tea that she decided that she, like her grandfather, would be a revolutionary.

Song May could not remember wanting anything else. But as she walked to General Wang's office for debriefing and information on her next assignment, she wondered how she had become the Chinese Secret Service's top whore. She crossed Chang An Road and gawked at the modern buildings that lined the street and eventually led to Tiananmen Square, and was almost hit by a cyclist. He was about sixty-five years old, riding an old, black bike from the 1950s, and talking on his cell phone discussing an upcoming business transaction. She considered cursing him, but smiled instead, amused at the site of this contradictory old man. She was still occasionally surprised at the changes, especially economic, that had taken place in China over the last twenty years.

If the communists had society, she would be considered a blue blood. Besides her grandfather, Song May's parents were the Chinese equivalent of 60s flower children. They came of age during the Cultural Revolution with such idealism and passion. They were both early volunteers of the village outreach programs that took high school and college students from the cities and sent them to the countryside to educate the peasants in modern communist ideology. It was in one of these villages that Song May's parents met. They were both natural leaders and headstrong. Repelled by each other at first, over many months they developed strong admiration for each other's tenacity, passion, and work ethic. They were indelibly Mao's children. This mutual respect developed into a dependence on each other's skills and eventually nurtured into love. Of course, at that time, love of country and party and undying loyalty to their mission were never to be superseded by selfish affections for the opposite sex.

It was in this revolutionary zeal that Song May was born. From day one, Song May was indoctrinated with the communist party manifestos. Some of the first sentences she spoke came from Mao's Little Red Book, and the only picture she kept in her entire apartment was her at two years old holding the book up in front of her. She had a look of such seriousness and almost fanatical zeal in her eyes that each time she even glanced at that picture she wondered what that little two-year-old was thinking.

After Mao died and the Gang of Four were caught, tried, and eventually executed, the country returned to normalcy. Due to good family backgrounds, her parents both took positions with the party as loyal yet inept bureaucrats. Their passion was gone. At fifteen, Song May was appointed leader of her school's Communist Youth League, the Red Brigade. Soon after, she was recruited by The Ministry of Intelligence to attend a special high school for gifted children. Her parents encouraged her to attend, though they both knew there was no choice in the matter. Besides, even though Deng Xiaoping had introduced economic reforms, they still felt that the best way to ensure a stable life was to become a Communist Party member and rise through the bureaucracy. Song May's intelligence combined with her inordinate bravery led to an invitation to enter a secret training program. By the time she was twenty-five, Song May was a top spy and had been decorated for bravery on more than one occasion.

'Where had her youth gone?' she wondered. Though she understood that she was working on the most important project in the Ministry of Intelligence; she felt belittled by her role as a glorified hooker.

As Song May entered the drab, cream-colored, non-descript building, all thoughts left her and she focused on her meeting with General Wang. As she entered his office, she noted, as she always did, the hypocrisy of the pretension in this public servant's office. It was immaculate. The office was as big as most people's apartments. His 19th century American mahogany desk with a black leather top was the first thing visitors noticed. On his desk were a few papers, a pen, and a picture of the general in full military dress shaking hands with Chairman Mao, a picture he pointed out to Song May every time she entered his office. To the left was his library with expertly preserved books from the Ching Dynasty as well as a glass case holding original swords from the early days of the Ming Dynasty. This opulence would not have been tolerated before the turn of the century, but today it was glorious to be rich in China, even for high-ranking party officials.

The general stood and smiled. His top agent had once again performed brilliantly. "Comrade Chen," General Wang spoke with a thick Beijing accent. He was one of the few old-time military men who was actually born and raised in Beijing.

"Comrade Wang," Song May went through the formalities and casually sat down on the red velvet chair across from Wang's desk.

"Comrade, I assume you managed to arrange the apartment in such a way that it appeared to be a random break-in," General Wang asserted. He was an old school Communist. Though he had been working with Song May for close to eight years, he still spoke to her with the same formality he had when they first met.

"Taken care of. No money or anything of value was left, and no one saw me enter or leave. A standard break-in. In a week we'll bring forward a killer, a peasant from the countryside targeting rich, white tourists. Hopefully the Americans will be assuaged."

"You sound slightly incredulous that the Americans won't believe our little crime. All three murders were brilliantly staged as accidents, no?"

"No, I don't think the Americans will suspect more than they usually do," she lied. "Though I should add that this practice of killing Americans is not something we should make a habit of. Suspicions will be raised."

"Indeed, but we had no choice in this instance."

"If we had been more careful and you had listened to my warnings that the American had seen too much, we could have deported him a month ago as I recommended and the killing would not have been necessary. We were fortunate that he was not that smart or he would have been at the Pentagon's doorstep long ago." Song May had been trained to hide her emotions, but she was sick of toeing the party line and lost her cool briefly as she thought how little respect she had been given regarding her analysis of the situation.

"Comrade Chen," was all the General said before allowing the silence to fill the room for a minute until he continued speaking. "I see your point and agree, but we've only killed three Americans in the last two years and they were all staged as accidents." Wang was peeved and unsettled at Song May's tone; he was not accustomed to such blatant insubordination, but was willing to exercise patience. Unfortunately, he realized that he had to tolerate it since he would allow nothing to stop the wheels from moving forward on this perfectly conceived operation. As he studied her face carefully to see what he could ascertain, he thought of ways he could purge her once she was no longer needed.

"Accident? The Americans are not idiots. They know the party controls the police. Do you really believe they were satisfied with the previous investigations?" The anger had been building up for months, the incompetence of her superiors frustrated Song May to no end. She had felt for quite some time that Wang was slowly losing it and she knew that if this were America, he would have been laid out to pasture long ago.

"Comrade," General Wang relaxed as Song May's emotions got the best of her, "the operation, if I need remind you, has thus far been a resounding success."

"Point taken, but let's remain vigilant. Three American kids killed, all in the prime of their lives, all teaching English in Beijing, and all killed by a random robbery. The Americans are dumb, but not so myopic that they won't see the connection." Song May thought Wang was becoming complacent with the thrill of success. Rumor had it that Wu Bai Ming, the president of the country, was personally overseeing this operation. Continued success could ensure Wang's promotion to the Communist Party General Standing Committee, the highest political body in the country.

19

"Quite right, Comrade Chen." He once again let Song May's outburst pass without reprimand. He simply looked at her as any other overly emotional woman. "We will monitor the situation closely. That will be all."

"General Wang, there is one more issue that I need to discuss with you."

"Comrade, I'm very busy."

"I want to be reassigned. I've been working on my current assignment for two years and it's time for me to move on and to bring new blood in."

"I'm afraid that's impossible, comrade. You are aware of the importance of the program. We simply cannot risk changing the status quo."

"General, I'm currently being underutilized. There are other projects that could benefit from my expertise and knowledge."

"Comrade, may I remind you that you tipped us off to the teacher's discovery. The English teacher is now the only outsider who has access to our finest agents and our facility. He needs to be monitored at all times. The success of the last two years is, in large part, due to your undercover work."

"Yes, General, but a newer agent could, with little experience, do the job just as well. This is an entry-level assignment."

"Comrade Chen, we have no idea how much the CIA knows. They could be planting an agent as our next teacher and you would potentially provide the only link. I'm afraid there is no one more qualified than you and the assignment is too critical to the program."

"Perhaps we should reconsider bringing Americans in to teach."

"That will be all, comrade."

As Song May turned to leave, Wang called out, "Ah yes, Comrade Chen, I almost forgot. We have a new American starting next week. He's supposedly a very handsome young gentleman. I think you will like him." Song May did not respond. She knew the comment about the American's looks was done intentionally lest she forget her assignment.

Chapter 4

The sun was still out and the sky remained blue even at this late hour. Peter Stimpson had seriously considered delaying his trip until after September. The summers were to be cherished in Seattle and by leaving in August he was probably missing out on a good six weeks of perfect weather. All year long, along with the rest of Seattle, Peter constantly talked about how the months of rainy and overcast days were worth the sacrifice for three months of absolutely ideal weather. Today was one of those perfect days that all Seattleites keep in mind as they silently endure each long, dark winter day. From his airplane window Peter had a perfect view of Mt. Rainier; the site of it always left him in awe even though he was born and bred in the Northwest. He hoped he would never grow used to its awesome beauty and powerful presence overlooking the Seattle skyline.

He still hadn't completely come to terms with why he was flying to Beijing; everything had just fallen into place. Less than two months ago, he was sitting at his desk grading finals for his 11th grade English class at the Westerly School in Kirkland, Washington when one of his colleagues stuck an advertisement in his face about teaching English in Beijing, China. On a complete whim and almost as a dare, Peter applied—and got the job. He was not quite sure why he had accepted the position. Was he running away? Did he fear failure? Had he taken a job as an English teacher because it was easy? Or was this the adventure he always wanted but was previously too scared to go after? One thing was clear: it was a way to avoid the otherwise inevitable career in finance working for the top brokerage house in the Northwest.

Peter's father, William Stimpson, was the founder of the firm, and the pressure to be his dad's eventual replacement was starting to wear down even the recalcitrant Peter. It was understood that when Peter was ready, he would enter the family business. Everyone still referred to Perkins Stimpson as "the family business," even though the company, while still private, had over 20,000 employees and offices in 10 states throughout the west. Father and son had an unspoken understanding that Peter would one day join the company, but part of the understanding was that Peter would join the business on his own terms and in his own timeframe. William knew not to push too hard and Peter in turn knew just how much his father would tolerate. In telling his father about the opportunity in China, Peter began with his plan to join Perkins Stimpson in a year, but explained that first he wanted to travel the world a bit and experience living in another country. His father put up very little resistance, besides an almost passing remark about the safety issues of working and living in a communist country. Peter gave his father a timeframe for joining the firm, something William had been asking of Peter for quite some time. They both got what they wanted and no argument ensued. The two had a wonderfully close relationship, each making sacrifices for the sake of the other, but not standing in the way of each other's goals, namely Peter wanting to live his own life and William wanting to groom a successor so that he could retire peacefully. Peter's father wanted what was best for his son and Peter, always precocious, delicately balanced what he wanted with his responsibilities to the family.

Once in Beijing, Peter spent the first few days acclimating to his very foreign surroundings and recovering from a severe bout of jet lag. He woke early and studied the city maps he had bought a few days before leaving Seattle. He decided to leave early and walk to work, having already become tired of the over-crowded public transportation system. He wondered why the language school had not supplied an apartment closer to the school grounds. Though he was only a 30-minute walk door-to-door from the school; there had to a more convenient place. The thought faded as he remembered where he was and embraced the Beijing morning. As he passed Mao Zedong Park, he watched in awe as hundreds of senior citizens moved in unison and fluidly performed each movement of the soft martial art, Tai Chi Chuan. They moved together so seamlessly that it looked as if they were connected in some way or part of an intricate computer animation. The display so captivated Peter that he was unable to take his eyes off the group until they had finished and stood heads bowed meditating, absorbing the energy created from the movements. Peter wished he had his camera, the moment was that perfect.

As he continued east down Fu Shing Road the aromas of breakfast in Beijing filled the air. He began to hear the calls of the breakfast street-food vendors promoting their delicacies and inviting the bicycle riders and pedestrians to stop and enjoy a hearty breakfast. Peter was clueless as to what they were saying, but he easily recognized the universal art of selling. The vendors were lined up in a row for at least two blocks and each vied for his attention and his business. The foods were all foreign to Peter, but the smells were inviting and he had trouble deciding where to start. He saw long, fried sticks of dough coming out hot from a deep wok, steamed dumplings being prepared in bamboo containers, and white steamed buns lined up like soldiers in uniform. Everything looked delectable. The vendors worked tirelessly, simultaneously promoting their specialties, working the woks and steamers like short order cooks, collecting cash and dolling out change, making small talk with their loyal customers, and exchanging jokes with their fellow vendors. Peter stopped and stared at the organized mayhem. As he walked further down the street, he saw scallion pancakes, eggs in a pancake, and more steamed buns.

"Hello!" yelled a vendor in English. It was all the welcome Peter needed. For a buck, Peter bought two buns, more than enough to satisfy his hunger pains. The vendor pointed to the bun and said, "Bao zi, bao zi." Then pointed to Peter. Peter repeated, "Bao zi," and at that moment all commotion stopped as the vendors and patrons laughed in unison, clapped, and gave Peter the thumbs up." He bit into the white bun, which was twisted closed on top with a small hole in the center to let the steam out, and he tasted a combination of ground pork and a variety of vegetables. After wolfing down an egg in a pancake, or Ji Dan Bing as he learned, Peter rushed away not wanting to be late for his meeting with his new boss at The Beijing School for Government Officials.

Upon entering the school, Peter was immediately approached by a scowling uniformed guard who looked more like he should be in a high school homeroom than the People's Liberation Army. He began rattling off in Chinese what Peter assumed were instructions, continuing for two or three minutes as his voice got progressively louder. Peter, in shocked panic, listened intently and tried to comprehend, but he understood barely a word of Chinese. The guard, clearly exasperated, pulled out his walkie-talkie and in a voice more reflecting his age, he spewed out something in what seemed to Peter to be a most deferential tone. In a matter of minutes another guard appeared from behind a closed door.

This guard was quite a bit different from the young one who guarded the door. He looked to be about seventy and was small, almost petite. He had a welcoming face with kind eyes, a wide toothless smile, and the smell of vodka on his breath. He approached the other guard, ignoring Peter completely, and swiftly admonished the youngster. He then turned and faced Peter for the first time, and with arms spread wide and an ear-to-ear grin, he said, "Please," grabbed Peter's arm and led him to the door the man had just come through. He entered a combination, pulled on the heavy metal door, and entered with Peter in tow. He gave Peter about ten forms to fill out and again said, "Please," in a perfect American accent. Peter would later learn that this was one of only five or six English words that the guard knew and certainly the only one that he pronounced correctly. Just as he finished filling out the forms, a man entered the room wearing a western-style suit. His presence was immediately apparent and slightly intimidating to Peter. He was taller, broader, and more handsome than any Chinese man that Peter had previously seen. The man walked up to Peter, introduced himself in perfect English as Mr. Shue, and led Peter to his office. He walked with a military confidence and addressed Peter in a formal manner yet also gave him the feeling that he had run into an old friend.

Mr. Shue addressed Peter, "We are very pleased to have you with us at The Beijing School for Government Officials; your credentials are impeccable."

"Thank you," Peter answered respectfully.

"I assume you had a nice trip to Beijing and are happy with your accommodations?"

Peter wanted to answer truthfully and explain that he had expected a nicer apartment with more modern amenities, but felt uncomfortable doing so, fearing that he would come across as an ungrateful, spoiled American. "Yes, everything is perfect!" Peter answered enthusiastically.

"Very good, let's cut to the chase. There are a few ground rules we need to cover and I will explain them as candidly as I can. You should be aware that the students you teach will, in many cases, become the top leaders in the People's Republic of China. They have been selected to attend this special school and they follow a very rigorous academic as well as physical program. The students you will meet are smarter, stronger, and more ambitious than any student you've taught or will ever meet regardless of country. They were chosen at a very young age to attend this boarding school; they see their parents infrequently, if ever. You are probably wondering why I am being so honest with you about the students you will be teaching."

"Uh ..."

Before Peter could answer, Mr. Shue answered what he considered to be an implied question. "I don't give a shit about your ideology, why you decided to come to China, or if you agree with China's practice of taking these students from their parents to indoctrinate and train them for a future position as leaders of this great country! What I do care about is that you will take your job seriously, work hard, and teach these kids everything you know about America, the culture, the language, family life: the small details that only a child living in America could learn. These future leaders will frequently be dealing with their American counterparts, and I want them to understand their adversaries better than they understand themselves. I know this sounds like you will be helping in the training of government officials to somehow defeat America ..."

Mr. Shue stopped abruptly and stared at Peter as if waiting for an answer. Peter had nothing to say and felt extremely uncomfortable with the silence. Just as the silence became almost unbearable to Peter, Mr. Shue started again as abruptly as he had stopped. "Well that is not the case at all. China will be a superpower one day, sleeping in the same bed as America. We only wish to have officials who deeply understand our partner. I'm aware that this was not fully explained in the job description and if you now decide not to take the job, we will buy a plane ticket and send you back to America first thing in the morning, with our deepest apologies. Are you willing to accept the basic terms of the arrangement?" Mr. Shue was obviously looking for an immediate answer.

Peter, though a bit perplexed and for some reason feeling guilty at the thought of somehow participating in the training of Chinese government officials, could not escape a vivid picture of his hasty return to America and his father's 'knowing' smile. He looked at Mr. Shue and said, "Yes, those terms sound fine."

"Ok, good. Let me go over your day-to-day teaching schedule. I have in my hand 100 lesson plans that you will use for your first 100 days of teaching. Think of this as your version of President Roosevelt's first 100 days in office during the Great Depression." Mr. Shue laughed heartily, amused with his analogy and genuinely impressed with his own knowledge of U.S. history. As Mr. Shue's laughter increased, Peter remained seated and smiled embarrassingly.

For the first time he was able to look around Shue's office, which was quite sparse. Except for a couple of diplomas on the wall, a large picture of Chairman Mao, a sizable portrait of Deng Xiaoping, and a smaller picture of the current president, Wu Bai Ming, nothing else decorated the room. The office looked to have been hastily put together: no personal effects, no papers on the desk, and the furniture looked like it had just been pulled from one of the classrooms, except for the all-mesh, high-end desk chair that Shue was sitting in. Peter thought it could not be Shue's real office. The picture of the current president looked odd. On the lapel of President Wu's's suit, Peter noticed what seemed to be a small hole, but could just as easily have been a pin. Before Peter could take a closer look at the picture, Mr. Shue's laughter ceased and his sharp, black, eyes focused on Peter as he continued speaking in the exact place he had left off as if he had never stopped.

"Each lesson plan will require preparation. These students will challenge you, please come prepared. Do not fear burdening them with large homework assignments as you might have with your students in America. The children will learn more quickly than you can imagine. You were chosen from a list of 100 applicants, which

I found rather amusing and confusing that so many young Americans would want to come to China to teach English. You were chosen because of your teaching experience and your Harvard pedigree. Quite frankly, we didn't have many applicants who were Ivy Leaguers, as you call them," he smiled again, openly impressed with his mastery of the English language. "Why did you apply?"

The question seemed to come out of nowhere; Shue had seemed very disinterested in Peter until this point. Peter was unprepared, but had he known it was coming still would not have had a clear answer.

"I will return to America in one year to pursue a career in finance. I thought this might be my last chance to take an extended trip and experience living in another country. I chose China for reasons similar to those you described earlier. China is gaining in strength militarily, economically, and politically and I wanted to learn as much as possible about this future superpower."

Shue was silent for a moment, openly staring directly at Peter before continuing. "Your working hours will be 8:00 to 6:00 as stated in the contract, with one hour for lunch. You will begin tomorrow with lesson number one. Do you have any questions?"

Peter, anxious to leave Shue's very commanding presence, meekly answered, "No."

Shue stood, graciously shook Peter's hand, and led him to the door where he was met by the old guard, handed to the young guard, and summarily shown the exit.

As soon as Peter left the room, Shue entered the adjacent viewing room and his eyes were immediately drawn to Song May. As much as he wanted to glide to the couch, sit down, and address Song May in the offhand, condescending manner in which he spoke with all other women in Chinese society regardless of their position, he was unable to. Her beauty never failed to intimidate him. Shue was handsome and would be considered so even by Western Standards. He was tall, about 6'1'', which by Chinese standards made him a giant, and his upper body was finely sculpted with a broad chest and nicely toned shoulders. His time spent in the military compound's gym was not for naught. When in the military he wore his uniform as if it were part of his body, and now, donning an Armani suit, he looked just as good as he did comfortable. He was aware of his physical presence and used his outward appearance to his political advantage.

"Any opinions?" he asked of Song May about the newest American teacher, Peter Stimpson.

"This one is smart, sharper than the others, better educated and more observant. I don't know why we are taking this risk; it would be better at this stage to bring in one of our own. There is too much going on in America. Success is upon us, we must minimize risk." Song May had been lobbying to have one of the U.S. operatives return and take control of teaching the students. These Chinese agents spoke English as a native and had been in the U.S. for so long as to be genuine red, white, and blue.

"Comrade Chen, we've discussed this on numerous occasions and the committee still thinks it best to have an American teach these classes. Not just because of the accent, but also because of the ingrained culture, something a Native Chinese could never understand. Besides, when it comes to American culture, the students seem to trust and learn more from a white face. Remember, we have tested this concept at other schools and the results are documented; I can get you the white paper if you like." Shue was tired of this conversation; the decision had already been made. In truth, his opinion and that of Song May mattered little, and no matter how logical or illogical, the plan would not change.

"I've read the white paper, time and again, but don't necessarily agree with it in this instance. Things were easier before, there wasn't as much focus on economic espionage. Times have changed since the end of the Cold War." It was wasted words falling on deaf ears, but she always felt compelled to present her case.

"I assume you're aware of your assignment; you've spoken to the General," Shue changed the subject; Song May's plea had ended.

29

Chapter 5

Tommy couldn't remember the last time he had been lazy. A day when he hit the snooze button five or six times, rolled over, and comfortably fell back to sleep in nine-minute stretches. Even on the weekends, his day was planned out to the last minute. Of course, he would spend Saturdays in the fall watching Notre Dame Football, but after the game he rarely spent time channel surfing, daydreaming, or catching a catnap; he had the utmost respect for time. He was dedicated to his work as an operations officer, which was easy since he absolutely loved his job. Downtime was usually spent doing something productive like catching up on reading, practicing one of three foreign languages that Tommy was fluent in, or simply working on a case that had perplexed him during the week. Casework was how he had spent this particular weekend and as he awoke at 4:30 a.m. on a rainy Monday morning, he was disgusted with himself. After sixteen-hour days on both Saturday and Sunday he had failed to unearth even one dusty little lead to take him closer to breaking the most complex of cases. Though he now knew where not to look, Tommy considered the time spent a waste. It infuriated him to no end.

As he entered the CIA headquarters in Langley, Virginia, Tommy felt a certain secure feeling come over him, the kind most people get when returning home after a stressful day of work. He loved working at the Agency and had sacrificed a number of serious relationships to devote more time to his job.

At 5:59 a.m. he walked down the hall and knocked on the oak doors of the current head of the CIA, George Moreland. Tommy was not looking forward to the meeting. It was not often that he had nothing solid to report to his superiors.

"Tommy, how are you? Have a seat," Moreland was also not one to waste time. This case had been high on his radar for the past month. The President, fearful of a shakeup in the tech sector and its effect on the economy, had recently started to exert a bit of pressure on Moreland to come up with some answers or at least some concrete leads. Moreland knew he had put his best agent on the case, but since Tommy was still young, he often got lost in the trees, missing the forest altogether.

"Thank you."

"Tommy, I would not normally pull an agent from assignment for a stateside briefing, but this case has become my top priority. I need some good news; the White House is breathing down my neck. What have you turned up?"

"Unfortunately, the only positive news I have is that I now know where not to look. I've come up empty in China. Let me give you a brief rundown of the steps I've taken and of course, the details are outlined in the report prepared by Will Richards, the collection management officer working the case, and Jane McBride, the staff operations officer."

"I don't have time to read this fucking book, Tommy," Moreland slammed Tommy's report on the desk. "Give me an overview of the steps taken since you were assigned the case." George Moreland was a tough son of a bitch and intimidated the most seasoned of agents. It wasn't so much his physical presence—he was short, bald, and didn't weigh a pound over 150—but the sharpness of his tongue, his caustic nature, and the speed of his mind. He was an impossible read, calm and encouraging one moment and caustic and acerbic the next. He joined the Marines at eighteen and served three tours in Vietnam; it hardened him for life. Over the years, Tommy had heard that he had mellowed, but from the stories, George Moreland's outbursts would make Mount St. Helens' 1980 eruption look like a dormant geyser blowing bubbles.

Tommy launched in with what he did know. "Over the last year, five China-based companies, which were previously completely unknown to the rest of the world, announced groundbreaking technology, went public on the Hong Kong Stock Exchange, and subsequently saw their stock prices rise to meteoric heights. This, in and of itself, causes no concern. Red flags were raised after U.S.-based companies approached the FBI and CIA claiming economic espionage. All five China-based companies that went public in that period introduced similar technologies that five U.S. companies had been working on for years and were close to product launches."

Moreland had begun pacing; he wanted answers that at this point Tommy couldn't provide. "Ok, I assume we have collected data from the CEOs of all of the U.S. companies involved, what have you learned?"

"Yes, McBride in conjunction with the FBI has had contact with each of them and they have provided us with a list of employees who could potentially be involved with transferring proprietary technology to the Chinese. Most would like to fire all the top executives of Chinese origin, but fear wrongful termination lawsuits, and in many cases a majority of the top programmers and executive management team are of Chinese descent."

"Have you uncovered any information regarding the employees on the list?" Moreland pressed.

"Our search thus far has come up empty," Tommy admitted. "Morale at all five companies is horribly low and the CEOs prefer that none of the employees are interviewed for fear of a mass exodus of their generally most trusted and certainly most skilled workers. We completed standard searches on family background, schools attended, year of emigration to the United States, current ties with China, and similar background checks of all the employees' parents. We came up empty-handed. Besides some minor infractions, the employees on all of the lists seemed to have had quite normal childhoods, were generally at the top of their class throughout school, and attended top universities. We found it difficult to examine a change in spending habits, since many of the employees were already quite well-off due to the respective company's initial public offerings."

"Was there any link among the employees of all five companies? Did any grow up in the same neighborhood, attend the same school? How many suspects have traveled to China and how often? I assume you cross-checked for any type of connection."

"No common thread jumped out, the data is quite extensive and we still need to do a more thorough cross-checking to see if anything pops up. Of course, many of the suspects had done some traveling to China, a few were very recent immigrants, but nothing we've come across has led me to focus on any one particular person. I really have nothing." Tommy hated to admit his lack of progress.

"What about China, Tommy? Have you had better luck on the ground there? I assume you're getting assistance from our other operatives?"

"Our best sources and informants have nothing to report. I am pursuing a couple of good leads, but nothing worth reporting at this time," Tommy sighed.

"Have you come up with anything from the language schools in Beijing?"

"It's a dead end. I have not dedicated enough resources on that front. The connection is too tenuous."

"Anderson, we've learned of three deaths in a two-year period of American English teachers in Beijing, China. All with a similar story. Americans have been teaching English in China since the late '70s and we've never had a single death until now. Coincidence? Who the fuck knows. But we have spies in America who are undetectable. I want you to search every language school in Beijing and connect with every teacher you can. We need to rule out the possibility."

"Will do, sir. I'm on it," Tommy promised.

"Ok, Tommy, I'm very aware of your thoroughness. Please keep me informed of any new breakthroughs. The President is starting to take interest in this case. He's had very little success stemming China's military buildup or its continued weapons and technology transfer to the third world. Just over the last week, this case has become top priority, and quite honestly he's breathing down my fuckin' neck. I need something. What's your plan of action?"

"I return to China tonight and will continue my fieldwork tomorrow morning, and if I have to scour the entire country pursuing leads, I will. We have already asked the CEOs to list the suspects in order of who they believe to be the most suspicious and most likely to act as an agent for the Chinese. We will work with the FBI and track each of their lives one-by-one, from the time they were born to their present-day situations." Tommy was anxious to get started. He had been given a dressing down and wondered if the chief was losing confidence in him.

"Time, Tommy, something I understand you are very aware of, is not on our side. Get back to China as quickly as you can; that's where I think we have a chance to break this thing."

The two men shook hands and Moreland walked Tommy to the door.

Chapter 6

"Where are we going, Mom?" Lee Chen's son Thomas wailed for the fifth time in as many minutes. "I wanna go home."

"Everything's going to be all right, Thomas. We're going to China, birthplace of Mommy and Daddy. We're gonna see Nanny and Papa and your other relatives. You'll be able to play with your cousins all day in the park, won't that be fun?" Lee Chen hated lying to her son. She never thought this day would actually happen, never imagined that twelve years could go by so quickly or that she could love so deeply and unconditionally; she truly never imagined. And now it would all be taken away from her: the center of her life, her reason for being. She knew she had no choice, in truth she had known this day would come.

Why hadn't she escaped? Taken Thomas to some small town and raised him? How many thousands of times had she thought about running, knowing that she would never have the courage to follow through, and also aware that "they" were watching. She didn't know for sure, but she assumed it to be true; it had to be. As she sat with Thomas in her arms, she tried to remember when things had changed, but couldn't recall a specific day or even a particular moment. These emotions, her attachment, happened over time and slowly pulled her in without her knowing or realizing. Had she been aware, perhaps she could have avoided it … perhaps. When she finally stepped back and realized how attached she was to Thomas, it was too late. Her maternal instincts had taken over.

As Thomas got older, Lee Chen's misery increased with each day. The thought of losing him was ever-present in her thoughts, but she never allowed her preoccupations to interfere with her affection and love for him. In recent years, she found it difficult to trust any Chinese person she met, always suspicious, always wondering if he or she was coming to take Thomas away. But her worrying was for naught; it had come down to a trip to Beijing.

"Mommy, what's the matter? Why are you crying?" Thomas asked.

"Mommy loves you very much, Thomas." She reached over and put her hand on his cheek. Why hadn't she at least tried to run away? Why had she been so weak?

She couldn't even remember how many times that her arranged husband, Lee Bing, had warned her. "Don't get too close to that child. It's not your child, we're merely custodians. Lee Chen, this is an assignment." During the last couple of years this admonishment had become a daily ritual. At the beginning things were different. She thought she would grow to love Lee Bing, imagined growing old with him, holding hands while walking through the park together, talking about nothing in particular. However, the relationship she envisioned never materialized, only a professional one; her only comfort was Thomas.

After landing at The Beijing International Airport, mother, father, and son were met by General Wang, treated to the finest of Chinese dinners, and escorted back to the offices of the People's Liberation Army, two blocks from Tiananmen Square. The General turned to the boy, "Thomas, why don't you go out back and play with Uncle Chu. I need to talk with Mommy and Daddy for a while." As Thomas ran off with little resistance, General Wang ushered Lee Chen and Lee Bing into his office. "Comrade Chen, Comrade Bing, welcome home. You have both performed admirably. Your service to the country will not go unnoticed. You and your families will be well taken care of, compensated for your very valuable work. I thank you both."

"Thank you, General," the two said deferentially in tandem.

"We have arranged time for both of you to visit with your families, but I'm afraid your schedule is quite tight. I wish you could stay longer, but your assignment simply does not allow for it. You're scheduled to return to America shortly; we have already arranged new housing for you in San Francisco—fully furnished I might add—and have handled all other arrangements. You and Thomas's brother, one of our brightest prospects, will return to the States within the week. We require you to go through debriefing and psychological evaluations before your return to the States. Very routine. Is there anything else you need from me, any irregularities you need to discuss outside of the submitted reports?"

"What will happen to Thomas? What do you plan to do to him? How will he adjust to life in Beijing without his mother and father? What will you tell him?" Lee Chen tried desperately to control herself, but the frantic questions spilled out.

"Thank you for your concern, Comrade Lee, but we have been through similar cases and are quite adept at handling these situations. Thomas will be well attended to and will adjust just fine; I assure you." The General looked at his watch while rising from his seat. General Wang had feared this reaction from the mother; he had noticed mother and son at dinner and realized Lee Chen had gone beyond her assignment and become attached to the child. Before such an assignment, they scrutinized each agent, putting them through a myriad of tests to avoid this exact situation. The selection committee rarely made mistakes, it had happened only once before now and had put the project in great jeopardy.

"I was wondering what exactly you plan to do, where will he live, who will raise him, how often will we get to see him?" she asked looking to Lee Bing for support, but receiving nothing more than a blank stare.

"I'm afraid, comrade, that the information you seek is highly classified. To release these details would jeopardize our mission." General Wang hoped the conversation had ended. He walked around his desk, opened the door, and gave instructions to the two soldiers guarding the other side.

"Comrades, please follow these soldiers. They'll show you your rooms. We will begin briefing you on your new assignment at oh-six-hundred. You will be well taken care of."

"Where's Thomas? When will I get to see Thomas?" Lee Chen knew the answer before she asked it.

"Thomas has already been taken away; you will never see him again."

"What? This is outrageous, I need to say goodbye! Talk to him, touch him one last time. Thomas, Thomas!" As she tried to run through the door where Thomas was taken, the two guards grabbed and subdued her. She didn't fight; it was useless, she had already lost.

"Comrade Chu, did everything proceed as planned?"

"Yes, General, the boy didn't feel a thing. The lethal injection killed him instantly."

"Very good, Comrade Chu. We may have to delay the flight back to America; Comrade Chen may need some reconditioning work."

"Consider it done, General."

Chapter 7

After his stressful meeting with Mr. Shue, Peter rushed home to begin preparing his first lesson: *Sports in America: The Spectator and Participant*. He spent some time looking through all of the lessons he had been given and found most of them to be quite odd: *Lesson 2: Sex, Drugs, and Rock & Roll*, *Lesson 20: The American Teenager, Relationships, & Slang*, *Lesson 62: Parents & Children in America*. He wondered where in the hell they came up with these topics and how he was expected to prepare Lesson 62, unable to imagine a broader topic. He was expecting basic grammar and vocabulary lessons, maybe some general U.S. history, not in his wildest dreams could he have imagined such bizarre, incoherent lessons.

"How the fuck am I going to teach this shit?" he complained out loud. This assignment was turning out to be more of a 'job' than he had originally envisioned. He thought he was going on vacation, experiencing the culture and customs of a new country, and making a living in the process. Instead he had to deal with some fuckin' Chinese idea of learning "English." Peter wasn't happy.

He looked around his apartment in disgust. Had he taken a step back? A New York City studio would have been considered a palace compared to this dump. He still remembered the day he arrived; the taxi had dropped him off outside a building that looked like it could've been used in a Hollywood movie as an extreme exaggeration of what life was like in a communist country. It was a drab, boxy, coal-soot-laden, concrete block. The concrete was probably white at one point, but China's use of coal as the main energy source had turned it a dirty gray. Caked along every windowsill were long streams of pigeon droppings. Some sills looked as though someone had attempted to clean them, but instead created smears and streaks that a child might mistake for an intricate finger painting. As the driver sped away, Peter had stood there for a moment in disbelief, assuming he had been purposely taken to the worst part of the city and left to fend for himself.

As he fantasized about what his accommodations might look like, a sound that faintly resembled his name pierced the humid air. As the sound grew louder, Peter saw a small, bespectacled man. "Pita!" the man yelled more loudly as he finally came face-to-face with Peter. Peter hoped his name wasn't going to be synonymous with flat, Greek bread for the next twelve months, but he was too exhausted to correct the man's pronunciation. The man grabbed Peter by the arm and led him inside. Peter stopped, pointed at the apartment block, and gave the man an Academy-Award-winning look of disbelief about his new neighborhood. Uncomprehending, the man continued walking, his flip-flops echoing as he walked into the building and up the stairwell. With an obviously weak negotiating position, Peter followed.

The building had eight stories and as they continued past the seventh floor, suitcase in tow, Peter realized by process of elimination which floor his apartment was on. The building did not have an elevator. The apartment was of a similar bland, communist style as the exterior, but looked as though it had been thoroughly cleaned and seemed a bit upgraded, though Peter had no point of comparison. The apartment was furnished with a full-sized bed that was nicely made with a red and navy bedspread, a standard desk with a mesh-backed office chair, a small dresser against the wall across from the foot of the bed, and a small nightstand. The apartment had a bathroom, but no kitchen. Most surprising and pleasing to Peter was the sight of a brand new oscillating fan. Almost as soon as they entered the apartment, the man handed Peter the keys, mumbled some gobbledy-gook in Chinese, and left.

Now as he sat at his desk in his drab apartment, he really thought he had hit rock bottom. He was getting paid jack-shit, living in squalor, and working a job he wasn't sure he wanted, but he wouldn't dare go home before the year was up. He was stuck. Peter rarely wallowed in negativity, but at that moment it felt right and he indulged himself, almost laughing at his predicament.

After a few minutes of self-pity, he turned on a dime and said out loud, "Enough of this shit." That was all it took. He opened his laptop and began working on his first lesson plan. Peter's friends at Harvard were always jealous of his ability to completely immerse himself in what he was doing. He would distance himself from everything around him, not get up to go to the bathroom, ignore hunger pains, and stop only after finishing what he had set out to do. He attacked Lesson 1 with this tenacity until he was satisfied that he was properly prepared for his first day of teaching. He closed his books and looked at the clock. Seven hours had gone by; it was almost 9:00 p.m. and Peter was hungry. He was excited with the work he had finished and either pumped up or a bit punch drunk from the sudden release of tension.

Starting had been the hardest part, but once he came up with a structure, the content for the lesson flowed easily. Peter actually enjoyed it. He realized that he knew, without thinking, most of what he would discuss in class. He began with sports in general, both watching and participating, as an integral part of American culture. Since these students were supposedly extremely smart, Peter decided not to dumb down the lessons, he would teach as if this were a college class. He couldn't fathom that the kids would absorb all of the information or grasp the more abstract concepts, but he was determined to give Shue what he requested.

After an introduction, Peter made a simple outline, sport by sport—starting with baseball and ending with the culture and sport of skateboarding. He started each section with a brief history. So for baseball he would discuss the all-time greats: Babe Ruth, Hank Aaron, Mickey Mantle, Willie Mays; names all American kids would know. He then spoke about the storied teams: the New York Yankees, Boston Red Sox, and Chicago Cubs. He focused the bulk of the lesson on cultural aspects, information not as easily found in a book. He used personal examples, like going to his first Mariners game with his father, waking early and playing pick-up basketball all day in the sun, or hanging out in the skateboard park. Despite the long hours of preparation and the lack of a textbook, Peter concluded that teaching would be both more enjoyable and more challenging than he first envisioned. He was invigorated.

As he left his apartment, Peter had every intention to continue his immersion into the Chinese culture by having a standard combination of meat, veggies, and rice, but after walking a few blocks he noticed a McDonald's and couldn't resist. He decided that tonight he would go out on the town, his energy level returning to normal after a week of jet lag. He had heard of the infamous Chinese dance clubs from the guidebooks and from the few Americans he had met on the street, but hadn't had the energy to check one out. He decided that tonight he would see what the nightlife was like in the capital of the Middle Kingdom.

As he walked into the McDonald's at the cross-section of Chang An and Shin Yi streets, he felt a bit guilty. He had planned on immediate immersion into the culture, mastering the language, and enjoying the food—assimilating. He had bought The Lonely Planet's *Survival Chinese* book and had been getting by with a few words and pointing, but he reluctantly admitted that he longed for a taste of home and Mickey D's would have to suffice.

Wandering the streets of Beijing wasn't as easy as one might expect; hundreds of dangers awaited the unsuspecting. Bicycles passed at a furious clip with no regard for pedestrians or standard rules of the road. Hoards of people appeared from seamlessly empty streets, and an innocent walk down an alley, what the Chinese refer to as a Hutong, usually resulted in a disoriented foreigner. During the daylight it's easy enough to navigate the Hutongs, but at night they become a maze that would put the most intricate Iowa cornfield mazes to shame.

Stubbornly and foolishly Peter convinced himself that he could find his way out of one of these alleys by using his guidebook, but after 30 minutes he gave up and asked … and asked … and asked. He quickly learned that pointing and hand motions were not as effective as he had expected. Finally an old man took him by the hand and led him to the door of Club Spice. Peter followed obediently.

After paying the cover, he quickly found a waiter and ordered a beer. As he slowly sipped his drink and looked around the room, he again found himself both impressed and shocked. The club was huge, with three levels. On the ground floor was a large dance floor of, he guessed, almost 10,000 square feet. Small bars could be found everywhere you looked. Lights flashed from below the floor and sidewalls; Peter was waiting for *Staying Alive* to blare from the sound system. On the second level were three bars scattered around the room and plenty of small tables for drinking and socializing. Club Spice's crowd was mostly Chinese, but some white and a few black faces could be seen mingling freely. The third floor formed a ring around the entire place, like a large running track, with tables seating eight to ten and wonderful views of the dance floor below. The tables were filled with sharply dressed Chinese men in what looked to be Italian cut suits, to Peter's unprofessional eye, and beautiful women, all wearing long, silk, tight, red dresses with slits running down one leg. Waitresses scurried around in black dresses like an ant colony paying homage to its queen, serving dish after dish and filling empty beer glasses. In what seemed like a continuous wave at a baseball game, every couple of minutes each table raised their glasses with both hands and yelled "Gan Bay!" Peter recognized the word. He had studied it in his *Survival Chinese* booklet. The book said that it was similar to the U.S.'s "Cheers!" except that all members of the table were essentially required to finish their beers for fear of losing face.

As Peter turned to find the bathroom, he bumped straight into a Chinese woman. Luckily for her, he had just finished his beer; unfortunately for him, she had just gotten a fresh drink. His shirt was soaked with a Cosmopolitan, her glass completely empty.

"I'm so sorry, I'm so sorry," she said, laughing demurely and embarrassed.

"That's ok; it was my fault. I'm sorry I bumped into you. It's really my fault. I apologize for spilling your drink," Peter said as he looked at his soaked shirt. He was still unsure of how well the Chinese people understood him, so he spoke slowly.

She laughed more loudly now, "You don't have to speak so slowly, my English is okay. Don't worry about the drink, I wasn't thirsty anyway."

"Let me buy you a new one; I won't let you refuse. I insist." It was the first time Peter had looked directly at her. She was stunning. He couldn't help but quickly check her out. Her eyes were almond-shaped, larger than most Chinese, her lips full and pouty like Angelina Jolie, and she had perfectly smooth, cream-colored skin.

She smiled and looked directly into his eyes, a knowing glance; he had been caught.

"It's really not necessary, but I won't turn down a free Cosmo."

As they walked to the bar, Peter one pace behind, he was able to get a better look at China's own Lucy Liu. She had long black hair that rested comfortably about halfway down her back. She was tall, about 5'8", with long legs and a tight ass. Peter was horny. "So what brings you here?" she asked, after they had gotten refills and found a table on the second level of the club.

"Still trying to figure that out. I'm teaching English at one of the schools in the area, but still don't know why I'm in China—it's all still a haze." Peter could not take his eyes off of this bombshell.

"I meant, what brings you to Club Spice? How'd you hear about this place?"

"Oh, well, I heard this was the place to see and be seen, most trendy place in the city. Every American I ran into said it's the best place in town. Am I right?"

"It's okay, there are better places, but this place is good. It's only been open a couple of years, so it's still pretty trendy. Foreigners like it because they think it's a Chinese hangout. So what's your impression so far?"

"It's amazing, never would've ever have imagined a place so hip and cool."

"We're not so backward as you Americans think, we have dance clubs and everything," she smiled.

"No, no I—I didn't mean it that way, I suppose I was expecting something a bit more conservative."

"Stay for a while, it gets better. You'll be writing home to your friends in no time detailing your every adventure at Club Spice."

"Really, and what adventures am I in store for?"

"I'll leave that to your imagination."

"You seem to know the place pretty well, are you a regular Club Spice girl?"

"I've probably spent too much time here over the past year or so, I think I may be a bit sick of the place."

"Why come back?"

"Don't know—best Cosmos in the city, it's close by, and I guess it's comfortable. Are you here alone or with friends?"

"Just by myself, I have only been in Beijing a week so haven't met too many people yet."

"Ok, so you're looking for friends."

"I guess you can say that. Is this a good place to find 'em?"

"Depends on what you're looking for."

"Someone that can hold my interest."

"And what does that take?"

"Good looks, a bit of sassiness, and a sharp tongue. You might do," he quipped.

The waiter had brought another round of drinks and the beers were having their desired effect. Peter was pretty buzzed.

"Don't get your hopes up." She was enjoying the flirting.

"Not interested in Americans or am I the problem?"

"I said don't get your hopes up, not drop all hope. I know the American game, but it doesn't mean I don't like to play it from time-to-time with the right person."

"And what game would that be?"

"It's your game, you know how it works. Why ask a naïve Chinese girl who's still learning the rules what it is?"

"You lost me."

"Yeah, whatever." They were both laughing and having a good time. The conversation was flowing nicely and during the lulls, a playlist of American pop hits from the '80s kept them entertained. Madonna's *Like a Virgin* was currently blaring from the speakers.

"So what brings you out mid-week?" Peter decided to change the subject; she had gotten him off track.

"Bored, my friend didn't want to come alone, but she left as soon as her boyfriend showed up. What about you, what would your students think if they saw their teacher in a place like this?"

"Tomorrow is actually my first day on the job."

"Wow, you're really going to make a nice first impression. Maybe I should cut you off. You don't seem too nervous," she laughed.

"I will be tomorrow, I'm sure. My boss seems like a real ball buster. Do you have to work tomorrow?"

"Six days a week, bad pay, and an incompetent boss. You were doing so well until you brought up work. I'm here to get my mind off the office."

"I'll get your mind off the office."

"Oh, really. What'd you have in mind?" She looked at him quizzically, putting her hand under her chin and leaning against her elbow on the table. She waited for his next line. *What a telegraph.*

"How 'bout we go back to my place?"

She was shaking her head. "American men, do any of you understand subtlety? I lost a bet to myself, I thought this question would've come 10 minutes ago, but I knew it would happen sooner or later. Things aren't so easy in China. It takes a bit more work, unless you wanna pay for it. An offer of a walk home and asking for my number would've put you in the driver's seat. You screwed up."

"Didn't realize I was doing well enough in the first place to screw up." Peter was three sheets to the wind and laughing pretty hard.

"You were holding your own, kept me here way past my bedtime."

"How about a second chance? Any interest in letting me retract that last statement?"

"You know what, I know your kind and I think I have had my fill. We had a nice chat, let's just go our separate ways."

"One minor screw up and I'm thrown to the dogs? Come on, one more chance. Let me take you out to dinner this Saturday. Give me a chance to make it up."

"I don't know."

"One dinner. What harm could it do? If nothing's there, we move on."

"Ok, I'm not going to dock you for one mistake. Tonight was fun and I'm feeling generous and I'm tired. Meet me at 7:00 outside the club's entrance on Saturday and we'll go from there."

"It's a date. How 'bout that walk home?" he pressed.

"Think turtle next time, slow and steady wins the race. I'll take a cab." She stood up and the two left the club together. She shook hands with Peter. "I'm Song May."

"Great meeting you, I'm Peter Stimpson. I'll see you Saturday."

"Yes, maybe," she said as she closed the door of the taxi.

Chapter 8

Peter entered the school at 7:30 a.m. and was still about fifty paces from the old guard sitting behind a school desk when he was consumed by the strong smell of liquor. "I guess, I wasn't the only one tying one on last night," Peter thought. As he approached the desk, the guard belched loudly and said, "Please," in English as he had done the day Peter met him. The liquor smell was combined with mint; the guard had failed miserably at hiding his liquor breath. He smiled, said something else in Chinese, and buzzed Peter in.

Peter was a bit early; he never could sleep after a night of drinking. He guessed the young guard didn't come on duty until 8:00 a.m. and decided that from then on he would show up early every day just to avoid that asshole. He checked the doors of a few offices but they were all locked. He wondered why anyone had bothered, the locks looked like they hadn't been changed since Mao's time and could be opened with a credit card. He didn't have to resort to an amateur break-in; an office at the end of the hall was open and Peter sat down at the desk to review his lesson. He had no idea what to expect for the first day of class, could not really guess what questions the students would ask on the subject, and wondered if they would be able to understand him at all. At 7:55, Mr. Shue walked in.

"Good morning, Peter. How are you?"

"Fine, I'm a bit nervous I must admit, don't really know what to expect."

"I'm sure you'll be fine, Peter. Would you like to meet the students?"

"Let's do it."

Mr. Shue walked Peter to a classroom at the other side of the building. As they entered, 10 male students stood in unison and sang, "Good Morning, Mr. Stimpson."

They remained standing, hands at their sides, feet together in military pose. They looked to be young, eleven or twelve years old, and all had crew cuts and wore the same uniform: white, short-sleeved, button-down shirt and blue pants.

Mr. Shue looked at Peter and then leaned over and whispered in his ear, "Challenge these kids. I leave them to you."

Peter took a minute to look at each student. They all remained at attention, looking directly at Peter and following him with their eyes as he walked slowly from the doorway to the teacher's desk. It was going to be a long day; he regretted the last two beers from the previous night. As he gazed around the room, he had to stop himself from smiling; they all looked alike. He didn't think he would be able to tell one Chinese face from another. They were all well groomed with their military hairstyles, tall, and broad-shouldered. These kids were handsome, clean-cut, and quintessentially all-American boys. It was weird.

He had this class for three hours and then a class of eight girls in the afternoon for three hours. Mr. Shue expected him to use the same lesson plans, but change them accordingly based on the gender of the class. Accustomed to the casual and nonchalant norms in America, Peter quickly realized that his experience in Beijing would be a bit more formal.

He addressed the students, "You may be seated. As Mr. Shue just mentioned, my name is Peter Stimpson. I'm from Seattle, Washington in America. During the last fifteen minutes of each class I will give you the opportunity to ask me questions, things about America that you may be interested in. But for now, I want to get to know all of you. When I point to you, please stand up and tell me your name and a little bit about yourself. Does everyone understand?"

"Yes, Mr. Stimpson," they all sing-songed in unison.

Peter couldn't tell if they really understood a word he was saying. He had addressed them as if they were students who had lived in America their whole lives.

50

"Ok, we'll start in the front row. You," and he pointed to the boy sitting at the far left.

"Good morning, Mr. Stimpson. My name is Christopher Lee. I'm originally from Sichuan Province, but have been living and studying here for most of my life. When I'm not studying, I enjoy playing basketball and tennis, as well as riding my bike. When I have the time, I also like reading novels. Currently I'm reading *The Sun Also Rises*, by Mr. Ernest Hemingway. When I grow up, I would like to be China's Ambassador to the United States so that I may assist in overcoming the barriers that are currently plaguing U.S.-Sino relations. Thank you."

Peter was floored. This kid spoke English and communicated his thoughts as cogently as any student he had ever had in America. It was not possible. "Where did you learn to speak such perfect English, have you spent time studying in America?"

"No, Mr. Stimpson. Since we are all studying to be diplomats and government officials, we have been studying English from a very young age, mostly from American teachers. In order to become a diplomat or high-ranking official, the Chinese government has enacted new guidelines that require each candidate to be able to speak English as well as a native speaker."

"And why do you think it's so important to be able to speak English so well?" Peter wanted to see how well this kid could think on his feet.

"Well, Mr. Stimpson, in the past China has been very isolated and closed-minded. Now we want to join the world and advance our civilization, so we must learn to interact and engage in constructive dialogue with the rest of the world. English is the tool to accomplish this goal."

Again, Peter was shocked. He never imagined that a group of Chinese kids would be able to speak at this level without ever having spent any time in America. He felt his forehead prickle with beads of sweat; he would have to work much harder than he had originally thought. "A very thoughtful and insightful answer. I can see that you've spent quite a bit of time considering this issue. Very well done, Christopher."

"Ok, you're next." He pointed to the boy sitting to Christopher's immediate right.

"Good morning, Mr. Stimpson. My name is Steven Wang. I was born in Xinjinag Province, located in the northwest part of China. My parents moved to the capital, Urumuqui, in the 1960s and became farmers. At the age of three I was brought to Beijing and began studying at The Beijing School for Government Officials. I enjoy playing basketball, just like Christopher, and soccer. When I grow up I want to be Ambassador to the United Nations because as each nation becomes increasingly interdependent, the UN will play an ever more important role in world affairs. Thank you."

"Steven, why and how did you come to this school?" Peter was curious how he would answer.

"At a very young age the government determined that I was of above-average intelligence and they asked my parents if I could come to Beijing to enter a special training program for foreign diplomats. Although my parents were very sad at the thought of me living so far from home, they realized that I would have more opportunities later in life if they allowed me to go."

A canned answer if Peter ever heard one; more likely he was forcibly taken from his parents, he thought, but Peter did not want to get too political, especially his first day on the job. "Okay, Steven, very good. You may be seated."

A stunned realization washed over Peter; he was teaching a class full of geniuses. As each student rose and introduced himself, expounding on his desires to solve world hunger or become president of China or the Minister of Foreign Affairs, Peter, instead of stressing, became excited at the prospect of teaching English and American culture to some of the brightest young men and women in China.

As the last student sat down, Peter began his first lesson. "Okay, who likes to watch the NBA?" Ten hands shot into the air. He would now make the assumption that they understood everything he said, until proven otherwise.

Chapter 9

Afraid that he would get lost, Peter left his house at 6:00 p.m. for the twenty-five-minute walk to the club where he had first met Song May. When not teaching, preparing lesson plans, or reviewing homework assignments, there were very few minutes of each day that Peter did not think of her. He questioned whether he had actually started glorifying her; perhaps she wasn't as beautiful or as sweet as Peter remembered. He had fantasized about her so incessantly over the last week that he now admittedly was unable to separate fact from fiction. He had also been completely smashed, unsure of all he had said to her.

Peter arrived at the dance club twenty minutes before 7:00 p.m., getting lost only twice, but in both cases was able to navigate his way back to a familiar street. He actually could have taken a more direct albeit longer route, but instead tried again to weave his way through the famous Beijing Hutongs. He was enamored with the alleys' sense of history and culture. Besides the Forbidden City, the alleys were one of the only intact landmarks linking Beijing with its glorious past. Surrounding the alleys were the traditional Northern Chinese square houses, with a courtyard in the middle and all of the rooms surrounding the courtyard on four sides. Most native Beijingers were unable to navigate through the myriad of mazes that made up the complicated alley system, but Peter promised himself he would know the alleys inside and out before he left Beijing—as sort of a final test of his knowledge of the city. Though he had no time to learn the language, he decided that he would immerse himself in the day-to-day existence of the city.

Peter was wearing a white-and-blue-striped oxford shirt, a pair of khakis held up with a dark brown belt, and a pair of dark brown Timberland loafers. He looked very New England, a style of dress that would have appeared nondescript on the campus of Harvard, but now felt strangely out of place. Though he was warned of the isolation that most westerners feel when living in Asia, this was the first time Peter felt acutely aware of the stares he was getting from passersby. He attributed it to nerves. It was 7:25; Song May had not yet shown up and Peter was starting to worry. He regretted not getting her number, but before he had a chance to further admonish himself; he saw her.

Song May was wearing a black miniskirt and a white, sleeveless top exposing a perfect midriff. She wore low-heeled pumps that accentuated her shapely legs as she confidently crossed the street, weaving comfortably among passing bicyclists, small delivery trucks, and the ubiquitous red Beijing Taxis. She looked just as beautiful in the daylight as she had in the dimmed, kind lights of the club. Peter was psyched.

Song May had gotten a good look at Peter on the video screen in Shue's office, but that was business. Although she was still technically on the clock, Song May was intent on enjoying herself and was quite pleased with Peter's appearance. He was about six feet tall, she guessed, with blond hair parted to the side and sleepy, hazel eyes. He had a narrow frame, but was in good shape. He looked to be a good athlete, which matched his bio. He was confident, yet fun and not too full of himself. More modest than the others, she thought. She'd had fun with him the other night. Not that anything long-term could ever develop, but she did end up spending quite a bit of time with these Americans and found the experience more tolerable if she actually liked the guy and was attracted to him. She was impressed with Peter's wit, knew he was smart, and overall was pleased with his looks; she couldn't complain.

"Hi, I was worried you wouldn't show."

"Well, I almost didn't come. You really almost blew it, but I promised you a second chance, and after soaking you with my Cosmopolitan, I thought I at least owed you one date." She smiled and brushed her hair back behind her ear.

"Not going to let me live that down, are you?"

"Maybe, eventually." They conversed easily. Peter couldn't tell if he was still in pure lust mode or if he was feeling some type of connection with this girl.

"Well, I know I'm the one who asked you out, but I don't really know where to go. I checked my guidebook for some cool places, but I thought you, being a native Beijinger, would know best," Peter suggested.

"So the pressure's on me, huh?" Song May replied. They both laughed. "I actually thought you might do this, so I was trying to think of a place to go while I was walking over. I know a nice place, quite close to here, that is quieter than most restaurants in Beijing and usually has a three-piece Jazz band playing starting around 9:00. What do you think?"

"Sounds perfect, let's go."

Upon entering the restaurant, Peter immediately felt his whiteness become something akin to a scarlet 'A.' The place was filled with young Chinese men and women nicely dressed, and evidently reveling in their nouveau riche lifestyle. As Peter looked around the room, the faces seemed to look back with annoying stares as if this white man entering the bar had brought an unwanted plague to their quarantined restaurant. Entering with a drop-dead gorgeous Chinese woman didn't seem to help matters, and Peter felt a bit uneasy. He was in a foreign country and was not familiar with the cultural subtleties and idiosyncrasies that he took for granted in America. He hoped to be placed in a corner table and craved a cold beer to quench his suddenly dry mouth. He wondered if Song May could tell how uncomfortable he felt. She spoke with the host who led them to a table located right in the middle of the restaurant.

Perfect!

As they sat Song May asked, "Is this okay?"

"Yes it's fine, I just feel a little out of place," Peter responded.

With this comment, Song May took a look around the restaurant and realized that the two of them had caused some hushed conversation among the other patrons. "You know, I didn't really think about it. Foreigners don't usually come to a place like this, it's something of an, I think in English you say, "underground" or "word-of-mouth" type of place. Like a little treasure. I thought it would be nice for you to experience the true Beijing. It's not a big deal; some of the patrons may not want you here, but in a couple of minutes they'll forget about you. We can go if you like, whatever you want."

Peter felt embarrassed. "No this is great; this is the type of place I want to come to. It takes some getting used to, being in the minority. I really stick out like a sore thumb, but that's my problem and nothing that a beer or two won't fix."

"Ok, let's get some beers," and with that she motioned to the waitress and ordered the drinks. She had a confidence about her that put Peter at ease.

"Cheers."

"Cheers."

They sipped their beers in quiet. As Song May glanced at the menu, Peter took a moment to look around. The band was setting up at the front of the restaurant and the stares subsided. Peter felt much more relaxed, the beer already having its desired effect.

Song May looked up and smiled at Peter, "What do you like to eat? Everything on the menu looks so good to me and then I suddenly realized that I am with an American."

"I'll eat anything you order, whatever you decide, but stay away from the super-hot dishes."

"Okay," and she again motioned for the waitress.

"So how's everything going for you in Beijing, what have been the hardest adjustments?"

"Every day thus far has been an adventure; things that I completely took for granted in the States, are difficult to accomplish. Finding a restaurant and ordering a simple meal takes careful planning and preparation and can be an exhausting pain in the ass. I constantly need to consult my guide books and look up words in my dictionary, though no one seems to understand my pronunciation, map out my course, check bus routes if necessary, and by the time I'm finished planning I'm not even hungry." Song May was laughing at his account, so he continued. "And then after covering every detail imaginable, I still get lost and have to start asking people. I've become a master at using my hands to communicate. I'd heard there were many people throughout Beijing who spoke English, but when I'm lost I never seem able to find them." They were both laughing.

"You must miss your family, and friends, and ..."

"Girlfriend," Peter finished her sentence. He knew what she was getting at and having her ask if he had a girlfriend back home was a sign she was interested, though he already suspected she was.

"Well, I'm not really homesick, everything is still so new and exciting so I'm still on a bit of high just being in Beijing. And about the girlfriend," Peter smiled. "I did have a serious girlfriend, we were dating for about two years. I think I loved her ..."

"You think? That seems kinda strange. You either know or you don't, right?" Song May challenged.

"I guess you're right. I think I knew that she wasn't the one, but the relationship got so comfortable and it was better being with her than alone. I didn't tell her anything about my plan to come to Beijing until I was accepted for the teaching job. Ya know, if I had told her from the beginning, it would've caused a huge strain on the relationship, but I think my plan backfired because when I did finally tell her, she flipped. I mean, really went crazy. She couldn't comprehend why I hadn't shared such a life-changing decision with her. She felt the relationship had come far enough that such decisions should be discussed. I don't know. Anyway, she gave me the ultimatum. If I went to Beijing it would be over and if I stayed she wanted a more serious commitment. So here I am." He smiled.

Song May listened intently. "Americans are so much more honest and direct than the Chinese. In China, everything is interpreted between the lines. Nothing is said directly: not among friends, lovers, or colleagues. It's annoying at times, but sometimes I think Americans make it too easy."

"I like the direct approach, especially when I'm asking the questions. Any man in your life?" Peter asked.

"My turn now, huh? I was in a serious relationship until just recently. It ended badly." *Little did Peter know how badly.*

A couple seconds of silence passed as Peter waited for Song May to elaborate. He was curious to know the details; she couldn't just throw out such a broad statement and not expect to provide specifics. Peter didn't want to pry and was still unclear about proper etiquette in China. He was anxious to find out more, but decided to hold back. The date was going well and he didn't want to do anything to screw it up. Maybe she was giving him a hint not to be so direct all the time. The silence was interrupted by the waiter and the arrival of their food.

"I hope you like everything. I stressed to the waiter not to make the dishes too hot."

"Everything looks delicious," as Peter said this, he unconsciously, as he had done for his entire life, reached to his left feeling for a non-existent fork. He now realized that his frequent visits to McDonald's, Kentucky Fried Chicken, and Pizza Hut hadn't prepared him for an authentic Chinese dinner. He had used chopsticks plenty of times since arriving in Beijing, but that was alone, now he had a girl to impress. He picked up the chopsticks in his right hand and with his left adjusted them to the proper position, and then slowly reached for a small piece of boneless, glazed chicken. Song May nonchalantly looked up. He pierced the chicken with one chopstick ensuring that it wouldn't fall and slowly delivered it to his open mouth. *Success!*

"You're pretty good with chopsticks," Song May said, suppressing a smile.

"Are you making fun of me?"

She was laughing and covering her mouth, which was full of food, "It must be tough to adjust to using chopsticks everyday when you've spent you're whole life with a knife and fork."

"I guess I have no choice but to get used to it." The conversation continued unabated for the rest of the meal, aided by frequent deliveries of Beijing beers. It seemed that what was mild to the Chinese pallet was nuclear to Peter's. By the end of the night Peter was quite drunk and unabashedly smitten with Song May. He insisted on walking her home, ignoring her repeated objections.

"Well, this is home," she said as they arrived at her doorstep.

"Is a second date on the agenda? I think I earned it. No major screw-ups, right?"

"Not yet. You may want to keep your mouth closed; men have a tendency to put their foot in it at the most inopportune times."

"You're tough. Can I have your number?"

"Why don't you give me yours, that'll be easier."

"A girl who likes to have control. I hope you don't expect me to sit by the phone all night waiting for a phone call."

"I'll call you, don't worry."

"Isn't that my line?"

As they said good night, Peter, hesitating only slightly, leaned in and kissed her softly on the lips. She didn't resist.

As he turned to walk away, Song May called to him. "Peter, do you know how to get home?"

"Uh, yeah, I think so. No problem, I should be okay. Good night."

"Good night," she answered back.

Peter began walking, enjoying the cool breeze that had come south from the Gobi Desert, bringing an end to Beijing's worst heat wave in twenty years. He had no idea where he was going, and it would be two and a half hours before he would crawl into bed.

Chapter 10

Scott rolled down his window and showed his badge to the security guard working the graveyard shift.

"Morning, Al."

"Morning Mr. Chen. Like clockwork, as usual. 5:00 a.m. on the dot."

"I guess I'm just an old man stuck in his ways. Maybe one day I'll surprise ya, Al."

"Have a good day, Mr. Chen."

"You too, Al."

On this particular day, Scott did feel old. He couldn't remember a day over the past ten years when he had done something exciting or out of the ordinary, or had even slightly strayed from his mundane, compulsively-planned life. Today was no different from any other. He woke at 4:00 a.m. without an alarm and began his daily routine. Before climbing out of bed, he kissed his wife on the forehead. She always looked so serene and content; Scott wondered if he looked the same while sleeping—he doubted it. He wasn't a good sleeper; he needed very little sleep to function and he normally relented to exhaustion with great reluctance like a tired child fighting to keep his eyes open to avoid being put to bed. As his wife slept comfortably, he prepared for another sixteen-hour day at Sageware Technologies.

He was a product of his upbringing and a stringent program of indoctrination. His methodical schedule was simply how he lived day-to-day. His wife goaded him about it and teased him incessantly, but Scott knew she actually loved the normalcy and predictability of their life: a solid, upper-middle-class, American existence. He married young. On the day he received his PhD from the Massachusetts Institute of Technology in Applied Physics and Computer Engineering, he proposed to his wife. They had met two years earlier one late night in the library. She was finishing her

Master's in International Relations at the Fletcher School of Law and Diplomacy at Tufts in Boston and was currently working on her thesis: "The Disintegration of the Chinese State." She spent much of her time at the MIT main library because her then boyfriend was working for a bio-tech company in Cambridge and his one-bedroom walk-up was close to campus. Scott, usually at the Science Library, was studying at the main library as a way to hide from his classmates, who constantly peppered him with questions. It was raining outside and seeing his future wife, Jane, without an umbrella, he offered to walk her to her car. The next time they ran into each other, coffee was proposed and a relationship ensued.

Before beginning his day, Scott allowed himself a moment to daydream about his life. As he looked at Jane every morning sleeping soundly in bed, he thought about how strange it was that he'd married a white woman. Never had he imagined that he would assimilate so fully and completely into American culture that his soul mate would be a White Anglo-Saxon Boston Brahmin. Her family, one of the oldest Boston families, pressured her unceasingly to end her relationship with Scott, but to no avail. They threatened that she would no longer be welcome in Boston or Newport society and deluged her with statistics about the failure rate of mixed-race marriages, but no amount of coaxing or threatening could stop her from marrying the love of her life. In time, her parents accepted Scott and welcomed him into their tight-knit family. Scott shook his head in disgust thinking of all the troubles the two of them had endured in their early years dealing with Jane's family. If her family ever did find out his true identity, the "I told you so's" would surely drive Jane to insanity.

Before he left the house each day he opened the doors to the rooms of his two children, Eliza and Ethan. He admired them and couldn't believe how American they were, growing up in a blessed country with no inkling of the life their father had led as a child in China. He prayed for them daily and hoped his secrets would never cause them harm or pain. Scott always dispelled the thought as quickly as it came, confident that he was too good to get caught— but at the same time, he was too well-trained not to analyze every possible scenario in his head if the worst should happen. He sometimes wondered what would happen to his family if he were ever discovered. The thought was at times so powerful that he considered discontinuing his work, giving up his double life, and simply being a loving husband and father: a role at which he'd become very adept. The thought was almost a fantasy for him. The reality was that Scott understood all too clearly that he would be hunted down if he ever aborted his mission. Sitting down at his desk, Scott settled in to begin another arduous workday.

Chapter 11

Not one of Tommy's contacts had any information about how these Chinese startups had invented such groundbreaking technology or what role the government played in their day-to-day operations. Tommy knew, just as his journalist friend Bill O'Malley had guessed, that the top echelon in Beijing was pulling the strings and that Chinese agents were working for top technology companies all over the States. What he did not know was how they had gone undetected in this environment of extreme paranoia.

CIA statistics showed a direct relationship with the amount of time a Chinese agent stayed in America and the likelihood that he would turn on his native land. The allure of America was strong and the role of a Chinese agent was thankless.

Chinese civilians living in America were also heavily recruited for economic espionage, but were usually caught before the most sensitive and top-secret material could change hands. In contrast to trained agents, civilians, regardless of country, were simply too naïve about the intricacies of economic espionage to have any chance of continued success. Most cases broke when the civilian spies got cocky. They pulled off a couple of exchanges of information and then thought themselves invincible, considered their American colleagues obtuse, and themselves untouchable. Trained agents did not make those mistakes. They were patient, especially the Chinese. They were able to control emotion and stay calm under intense stress and pressure.

Tommy was certain that the espionage completed thus far was the work of the most skilled professional agents. No amateur could extract enough information to allow the Chinese to produce a product even before the American company who invented it had released its own version. The contradiction was that the Agency spent countless man hours and millions of dollars on both sides of the Pacific monitoring suspected agents. Such widespread infiltration was simply implausible without some red flags flying at headquarters.

As he was instructed, Anderson researched every English school in Beijing and connected with hundreds of teachers, but found no link between the spying in America and the murders of the three Americans. It was a dead end. Adding further confusion, this case was spread across five U.S. companies that over the last year had been beaten to market by a Chinese company with almost identical technology. It was virtually impossible that no leak existed or that no suspects had been identified. The infiltration thus far had been perfect. Tommy pondered these and other peculiarities of the case as he walked into the Lion Head for his bi-monthly meeting with Bill O'Malley.

"Tommy, mi lad, you looking a wee bit parched. How 'bout a lager?" O'Malley's family emigrated from Ireland to America almost 150 years ago, but you'd be hard pressed to find a native Irishman with a better brogue. He actually fooled most Irishmen, with people from the old country often asking what town he was from.

"Give me a Guinness," Tommy answered.

"Ah, a man after me own heart, supporting the homeland."

"Cheers."

"What's been going on?" O'Malley asked. Though neither was ever willing to share too much, Tommy and O'Malley willingly exchanged small bits of information. They had developed a mutual trust and respect common among expats in Asia.

O'Malley went first. "I've been up in Beijing, trying to find a link among any of the Chinese companies that recently went public. Couldn't really come up with anything, I'm still a bit baffled how they did it. I've interviewed a couple of the CEOs who were unwilling to share much as you might imagine. I'll tell you, this story is getting bigger. Even with the correction in the NASDAQ, the Hang Seng continues to rise." O'Malley finished his drink, ordered another, and continued.

"It's gonna get worse. Fear is already setting into the market. I still don't know how the hell the Chinese did it, but I'm positive orders are coming right from the Standing Committee of the Communist Party. No one has any information on this one and fuck I've tried—I've wrung my sources dry trying to get just one shred of proof that there's a connection, or at least a tenuous link among the Chinese government, the sudden explosion in new technology in Zhongguancun, and the downfall of those five U.S. companies. So far nothing, but this story has Pulitzer Prize written all over it. Barkeep, another round."

"There has to be a mole, but it's unprecedented that the Chinese had five moles spread around such diverse companies without someone being discovered or detected. How do you think they've done it?" Tommy questioned.

"You know, I have no fuckin' clue. I'm completely fuckin' stumped. How can the CIA or FBI, or whoever, not be able to definitively identify at least one suspect? It's absolutely fuckin' baffling. I do know one thing; the answer is not going to be found on this side of the Pacific. Something has to give stateside."

Tommy nodded in agreement, but felt there must be something he could uncover in Beijing.

Chapter 12

Song May had decided that after her current assignment she would remove herself from the case. She spent the early morning writing her decision down on paper and then reading it repeatedly—to the point where she could almost recite word-for-word what she had written, ingraining the thought so clearly in her mind and to such a degree that she was completely committed to leaving the project. She knew she would have to be methodical and carefully strategize how to convince General Wang that keeping her on the project would put its success in great jeopardy. She made a list of every contact that she, her parents, and her grandfather had in the upper ranks of the Communist Party and promised to use every connection possible to get reassigned. Her grandfather's contemporaries now had children in powerful positions in the Party, but even with this clout, getting a new posting would be difficult. Anyone associated with the project was convinced that Song May played an absolutely integral part in the mission and that any change would create bad chi. Everyone was so flush with the results thus far that they had become almost frightened to change anything.

In two years she had gone from party girl with James from Colorado, to naïve country girl making her way in the big city with Matthew, and now with Peter, where she was really just being herself. She had become too tired to act and constantly feign a thick Chinese accent when speaking English. No more acting, hiding her English skills, or intelligence, she'd had enough. She tried hard to separate her life from her assignment, but she was burned out. She suddenly remembered Christopher; that did not last long. He was useless as a teacher and was eliminated quickly. She also decided to use her own name. Song May had probably become a bit lazy, but she had stopped caring long ago. Peter had proven to be the most interesting and intelligent of the four. He was closest in age to Song May and she actually did not mind talking to him. They had been together for over a month and had yet to have sex, though she did not think that would last much longer. She was almost treating their relationship like a regular courtship. She had not had a real boyfriend since starting this assignment and she wondered if she just longed for some normalcy in her life. Song May admitted to herself that spending time with Peter had almost become a pleasant diversion and holiday from having to think about her career in the Chinese Secret Service, and with this thought she buzzed Peter's apartment. She had borrowed a car from her parents and was going to take him to the Great Wall of China. She planned to take him to Si-Ma-Tai, a part of the wall that was less touristy than the more popular Ba-Da-Ling.

"Hey, baby," they greeted each other with a long kiss.

She was looking forward to the day and felt her stress melt away upon seeing Peter. "Peter, I've been told that America is one of the easiest countries in the world to drive in. The roads are wide, drivers actually obey the laws, and speed limits are enforced. Is that true?"

"Well, it's not exactly the utopia you describe. Most people speed and there's plenty of road rage, and I won't even talk about the drive-by shootings. That said, in comparison to how people drive in China, the roads in the States are pretty sedate."

"In China, 90% of the people on the road today have probably been driving for less than five or six years and the majority of drivers are male," Song May countered. "Just imagine streets filled with 21-year-old drunk men and you can pretty clearly visualize what the streets are like in China."

"From what I've seen, there doesn't seem to be much respect for pedestrians either," Peter offered.

"That's an understatement. We have more pedestrian fatalities due to auto accidents per car than almost any other country in the world." They were having this conversation leaning against Song May's car, a China-made Volkswagen Fox.

"Well, Peter, how do you think you'll hold up behind the wheel?" She asked the question more as a challenge and Peter knew he had been set up.

"I guess we'll find out. Does this car have seatbelts?" Peter asked jokingly. Song May tossed him the keys and got in the passenger seat. It was Sunday, so the drive out of Beijing was easier and less stressful than normal. Peter drove with extreme caution. As he slowly navigated the streets, taxis weaved in and out with reckless abandon and honked incessantly at Peter who was yielding to crossing pedestrians. He quickly learned that his considerate driving upset the system and did more harm than good. Driving in Beijing was organized chaos.

"My grandmother never rode anything more than a bicycle, but I imagine she would drive just like you if you if she had ever gotten behind the wheel." Song May laughed.

"These guys are crazy; I'm shocked anyone survives."

"The key is to drive just as crazy, that way you earn their respect. It's insane logic, but that's China."

They arrived at Si-Ma-Tai at about 11:00 in the morning unscathed. "I'm impressed, no accidents and only three or four close calls," Song May ribbed Peter.

"Hey, if it weren't for my quick reflexes, we'd be spending the day in the hospital."

As they entered the main gates to the Great Wall, Peter was mesmerized. The wall stretched as far as he could see, undulating with the peaks and valleys that defined Northern China. He stood for a moment taking in the site. It was the first time in a month that he had left the city and for some odd reason, the wall and the lush surroundings reminded him of home. "This place is fantastic; do you know anything about the history?" he asked Song May.

"Not much, only what I learned in school, but I guess I may as well serve as tour guide. A major renovation of the Great Wall began in the 14th century and took over 200 years to complete, but parts of the wall were built in the 7th and 8th centuries B.C. by the warring states, which were trying to protect themselves from northern invaders. During the Qin Dynasty the separate walls were joined

70

together and served as a barrier to the increasing powerful nomadic tribes. During the Ming Dynasty, the Chinese became very isolationist and built huge additions to the wall including garrison posts, watchtowers, and multiple layers. It is currently more than 4000 miles stretching east to west. The wall did help stem attacks from the north, but as the nomads became more sophisticated and demanded trade and the Ming Dynasty weakened, most realized that the wall provided little protection from attack. Today, it's a tourist trap and now you have my download."

Even in this less touristy part of the wall, the peddlers swarmed like gnats, hocking pictures of Mao at the Great Wall, Mao lighters, Chinese masks, books describing the history of the Wall, postcards, anything to make a buck—and they were recalcitrant, repeated no's didn't phase them and once you asked "How much?" it was over; they had you. They began bargaining; offering you deep discounts and walking with you all the way up the wall until they made a sale. The only problem was that if you bought from one, the others identified you as a sucker and went in for the kill: swarming, biting, and pecking at your wallet until all that was left was a driver's license, a few credit cards, and a dilapidated piece of leather that barely resembled something that once carried money. Having Song May by Peter's side didn't deter the Chinese equivalent of the used car salesman. Peter wondered when the communist state had turned into a capitalist flea market.

"Seems like the locals appreciate the business the tourists bring," Peter smirked.

"Most of these former farmers can afford to put a child through college from selling these trinkets," Song May responded.

In between sales pitches, Peter asked Song May about her family and if they were involved in any of the major events that shaped Chinese history.

"You once told me that your grandfather fought alongside Mao during the civil war against the Nationalists. Was he with Mao during the Long March?"

"Yes, he was one of the original 90,000 who began the Long March with Mao and Deng, and was fortunate enough to be one of the 10,000 who survived twenty months later. The fighting was intense and the Nationalists were trying to destroy the Communist Party before it took hold in the countryside."

"Did he ever tell you any stories?"

"My grandfather was an amazing man, a loyal confidant to Mao, and a true communist. I spent hours listening to him tell tales of the revolution. He could mesmerize crowds with his stories. I loved him so much. He died about three years ago; he was ninety-two."

They were holding hands as they walked the Wall, passing guard towers and finally breaking free from the peddlers and other tourists who mostly went only to the front section, took their pictures, and quickly descended.

"I'd love to hear one of his stories," Peter commented.

"Well, I've never told this story to anyone so I trust you not to repeat it," Song May started and Peter nodded. "I bet my grandfather is turning in his grave, just seeing me walk hand-in-hand with an American, let alone telling his stories, but I'll make an exception for you 'cause I like you." She looked at Peter and smiled sweetly.

"The Long March saved the Communist Party. If it had never taken place, China would probably be carved up into a hundred pieces with the Western World still controlling the major cities and ports. Imagine 90,000 people walking together, from all over the country and all classes: peasants, intellectuals, and business owners, all with the same ideology, passionate about their principles and committed to the struggle. It was a powerful group, not because of their weapons—they had few—or their supplies— there were none—but because of their message. Their struggle wasn't easy. In some villages, they were met by nationalist armies with superior weapons using brutal, inhumane tactics. The battles were bloody and casualties great. In other villages there were no soldiers, but the villagers in many cases had already been indoctrinated by the Nationalists and were unwilling to hear Mao's message. My grandfather would spend weeks in villages talking to anyone who would listen. He was an extremely intelligent man who spoke eight Chinese dialects. He passionately explained the principles of the Communist Party and ultimately, in most cases, convinced the peasant farmers to join the struggle. Until the day he died, he was just as passionate, refusing to see or acknowledge the many faults and hypocrisy of China today.

"He was a great spy and was called on by Mao to infiltrate enemy forces on many occasions. Once, about a year into the Long March when they were about two weeks from a village 50 miles outside of Chengdu, the Capital of Sichuan Province in the interior of China, Mao's scouts identified a sizeable nationalist troop buildup. Mao asked my grandfather to enter the village and infiltrate the army. Later he would spend years behind enemy lines as a Nationalist officer gaining the trust of senior officials, but this was his first mission behind enemy lines. During that time, the Nationalists would enter a village and conscript all of the men of fighting age into the nationalist armies. Later the Communists would do the same, but in the early days it was more about spreading the ideology.

"My grandfather entered the village unseen and was quickly given a well-worn, blood-stained uniform, a gun, and a lieutenant to report to. Very few people outside of Beijing spoke Mandarin, so the generals were often careless when discussing strategies, assuming no one could understand. Granddad acted like the ignorant, illiterate peasant, volunteering to feed the generals, prepare their baths, and wash their clothes. As he did this, he listened and learned that the Nationalists were expecting the Communists to enter the village from the west of the city. The east was surrounded by mountains and the Nationalist generals assumed that, since it was late autumn and the mountain region was impassable, the Communists would take the easier route."

Peter and Song May were next to one of the guard towers sitting on the wall. Peter listened intently, but Song May hardly noticed. As she told the story she imagined herself as a little girl again, walking through the fields holding her grandfather's hand and listening to his stories. She missed her grandfather greatly and wondered what he would do if he knew how the Party was underutilizing and abusing her skills. He had been so proud of her successes within the Secret Service.

"One night he secretly slipped from the village, returned to the communist camp, and reported to Mao the information he had collected. Mao and his generals decided that the only way was to send a small force from the west as a decoy and to risk hiking through the mountains on the east to surprise the Nationalists. At the time the nationalist forces were a bit complacent and cocky. They had built up a string of victories, were better equipped to survive the winter, and had support from America. Their complacency would aid the surprise attack.

"The trek through the mountains proved more arduous than anyone had suspected. A cold front from the north approached unexpectedly and brought heavy winds, sleet, and snow. Hundreds of men lost their lives. They were inadequately dressed, their shoes had holes in them, and food was severely rationed. The hike took two weeks and my grandfather could recall every minute of the journey until the day he died. He described the conditions as almost insurmountable, like hiking up Everest in a storm. Some had to turn back, but most continued and developed a camaraderie and bond amongst them that would last until victory in 1949. They attacked at night and completely surprised the Nationalists, killings thousands and forcing an immediate retreat. It was the Communists' first major victory in over a year and turned out to be the first in a series of successes."

Song May spared Peter the pressure of having to drive home. She'd had a wonderful day with him and was worried that she was developing dangerous feelings. She was slightly frightened. She was much too strong and jaded to become too attached, but this one would be more difficult to "take care of" if it came to that. She sincerely hoped it would not. As they pulled up to his apartment complex, she hoped for the question that Peter had been asking about once a week. He was persistent, but not overdoing it. He was trainable, she thought. As she looked at him and admired his good looks, she was almost shocked that she had been able to refuse for this long.

The whole way home, Peter had been pondering the best and most suave way to ask Song May to come upstairs. He had moved more slowly after crashing and burning the first night, not wanting to 'screw up' anything, but tonight Peter could not fathom going upstairs alone. The direct approach would have to do. "Would you like to come up?"

"To your apartment? To do what?" Song May teased.

"Talk," he responded smiling.

"Peter, Chinese women cannot enter a man's apartment without being chaperoned. Perhaps I can call my mother and she can join us."

"I don't think your mother would be too interested in what I have in mind."

"Hmm, you've piqued my interest."

As they walked the eight flights of stairs, they could barely control themselves. They stopped on practically every landing, unable to keep their hands off each other. They both realized that they had waited too long for this. As they entered Peter's apartment, Song May barely looked around. She knew Peter's place better than he could have ever imagined. As they kissed in the center of the room, Song May reached down and began unbuttoning Peter's Levi's. Peter simultaneously grabbed Song May's skirt and began pulling it down. They were undressed in seconds and as they explored each other's bodies, Song May slowly backed up. She let go of Peter, fell backwards onto the bed, and whispered, "Give it to me, Peter."

As soon as he penetrated and started to grind, he knew he wouldn't make it more than a few minutes. As her hips deftly moved in sync with his thrusts and her nails dug into his lower back, he felt himself begin to lose it. Waiting a month had not helped; the anticipation had driven Peter crazy and he was now too worked up. It was too late for distractions. He went full throttle.

"Yes, yes, Peter!" she screamed. "Fuck me, fuck me! Peter."

A moment later, Peter climaxed and continued thrusting until he was almost flaccid. He lay on Song May catching his breath.

As Peter's thrusts slowed, Song May opened her eyes, looked at the ceiling and thought, "Is that it?" She hated having the thought and regretted letting it seep into her mind, but for the briefest of moments she longed for Matthew. Perhaps she had made him wait too long. She would make it up to him.

Chapter 13

Scott woke earlier than usual from a restless sleep and quickly walked downstairs to retrieve *The San Francisco Examiner* from the front stoop. He had been doing this practically every morning since the first story broke of a Chinese company announcing a new patent, groundbreaking technology, or a release date for a product that no one thought the Chinese had the technical know-how to create. His life, though never easy, had been turned on its head. He knew from the day the first story broke that regardless of the trust he had built up over the last ten plus years his life would be scrutinized. He worked in high tech on highly classified products and he was Chinese. After the announcement, he had originally thought that the leaders in Beijing would prefer to be more low-profile and wait perhaps years for a second release, but the reality was the exact opposite. Every couple of months brought a new announcement of groundbreaking discoveries by a different Chinese company followed by a ballyhooed IPO. It had happened five times in the last year and Scott was expecting another front-page story any day.

It was a simple case of greed and hubris for the inept bureaucrats in Beijing. Scott hated checking the Internet for these stories, preferring to read everything in the morning paper. As he walked to the kitchen, he pulled the paper from the plastic bag and looked intently at the front page. Today, his worst fears were not realized. A picture of the Golden Gate Bridge covered three columns with a caption reading: *10-car pileup closes bridge for hours*. Chinagate, the media's designated name for the espionage, was buried on page six with no new announcements. Scott left the paper on the kitchen table and ran upstairs to get ready for work. He had another long day ahead of him.

Stealing company secrets had recently become slightly more difficult for Scott. His greatest asset was his patience, and he knew that the success of the whole project was due to the patience of the Chinese agents who had painstakingly infiltrated U.S. companies around the country. Scott had worked for Sageware for ten years and had been on his current project for about five. He was one of the senior software engineers in the company and was trusted implicitly by everyone, including the CEO David Biddleberry, who started the company out of his parents' basement with a $1000 loan from his uncle. Sage, as most employees referred to the company, had successfully invented technologies for flat screen displays and had various patents related to laptop computers, but had staked the future of the company on its current project. Scott had played a key role in developing the technology, but over the last year, in order to protect against espionage, Biddleberry had split the research and development phase among six different workgroups so that no one group or individual had complete access. Over the past year and with each new story about a Chinese company introducing a seemingly stolen technology, the Valley had become precipitously more paranoid, and Sage was no different. About a month ago, new security controls were put in place and each employee with high-level security clearance had been asked to go through a "psychological evaluation."

Over the last four years Scott had collected enough information on Sage's Nanotubes research to ruin the company. Nanotubes, a tar-like substance that consists of billions of tiny tubes of carbon, would impact countless industries including computing, medical devices, and television, basically taking the place of silicon. Nanotechnology had the potential to revolutionize the computing and electronics industries and Sage was at the forefront. With the new security measures in place, Scott didn't have access to all of the information and research, but with four years on the project he could draw reasonable conclusions based on what was required of his workgroup. Some of the results of the other teams had to be shared, which also helped Scott to draw logical conclusions. Sage was about two months away from announcing its first product, so Scott was in the final stages of information gathering. He often wondered what would eventually happen to his photographic memory. He kept thinking it would just turn off one day and then he would be like everyone else.

From the time he was a child, Scott could read a page of a textbook and regurgitate it word for word even months later. In China he never knew he was special, each of his classmates was gifted. Almost all had photographic memories and the ones who did not had the capacity to study non-stop for hours until they remembered the same material that took Scott an hour. He felt sorry for them. The Secret Service School was both physically and mentally rigorous, but Scott still got a decent night's sleep most nights while those one step below genius had to survive for weeks with less than four hours of sleep per night. Of course, it was these students that seemed to be the most physically gifted and it was Scott who struggled through advanced Kung Fu, spending days practicing nun-chuck moves that some of his classmates mastered in hours. As a child, unable to sleep at night, he would often daydream of being a spy, breaking into buildings and outrunning the CIA. He envisioned a life of adventure. He never would have guessed how 'ordinary' espionage really was. It turned out that his one God-given gift of memorization had become more important than anything else he had ever learned.

On this day, Scott was looking at a computer design of a near prototype of a new, not-yet-released product. He studied the intricate drawing and looked over the code that would be the brains, eyes, and ears of the system. He had been given an update from the other groups and was responsible for finishing his part of the project within two weeks. He sighed, knowing that tonight would likely be another sleepless one as he transcribed all of the new information in his head and translated it into Chinese for his superiors who were anxiously awaiting the information in Beijing.

Chapter 14

Peter constantly wondered why Mr. Shue had chosen these topics to teach and could not figure out why future diplomats and government employees needed to learn slang mostly used by high school and college students. When he inquired, Shue seemed to give him the standard response.

"We need to fully understand the mind of the American and what better way to truly comprehend that mind than by learning all the variables or stimuli that went into making an American who he or she is. It's culture! We don't want to just understand history and geography. We don't need an American teacher for that. Present-day culture needs to be taught since it is ever-changing and by learning how Americans live from children to adults, how they interact with their peers and parents, how they entertain themselves through sports, music, TV, and relationships, that will help us truly understand and be able to work with our American counterparts, government to government, CEO to CEO, and general to general." Shue ended every one of his soliloquies with, "Does my answer satisfy your curiosity Mr. Stimpson?" and Peter would frequently say, "Yes," not wanting to debate a worthy opponent.

He entered the school at precisely 7:30 a.m., the exact time he arrived every day. The scene never changed. Mr. Wang, the security guard, was drunk, and on this particular day he could barely find the buzzer to open the main door for Peter. Just like every other day, as Peter entered the main lobby Mr. Wang jumped to attention. It seemed that he had trained himself to immediately rise from a deep, alcohol-induced sleep.

"Hello, thank you very much," he slurred, incomprehensible when sober, and just a bunch of sounds emanating from a Chinese man's mouth when drunk.

"Good morning, Mr. Wang," Peter replied.

At 8:00 a.m., Mr. Wang finished his shift and the young, overanxious guard who Peter had encountered the first day took over. Wang usually hung around, Peter guessed either to give the young guard a hard time or maybe because he had nowhere else to go. Peter entered his office and prepared his materials for the day's lesson: *Slang in America*.

He started each class the same as every other, by reviewing the previous lessons and placing special emphasis on his earliest lectures. He peppered the students with questions, speaking quickly and entertaining the class with different accents. 'Hey, where's the six train?,' Peter would ask using a thick Brooklyn accent and the students were expected to ad lib an answer based on the question. At the end of the drill, the students would ask Peter to clarify words they had not understood. The depth of the students' knowledge and well-trained ears constantly amazed Peter. He used a southern drawl, a Boston southie accent, and even attempted an Irish brogue and a cockney accent that he had tried to pick up during a semester abroad in London. The students didn't always understand every word, but they made astute guesses to comprehend the meaning and invariably answered correctly.

The previous day, Peter gave each student a list of one hundred slang expressions frequently used by teenagers and young adults. After reviewing certain meanings and word usages, he quizzed the students on their comprehension of each word or phrase. After he was satisfied that they had all prepared the lesson—and after six weeks he had yet to detect even one student who was not completely prepared—he had groups of two role play different scenes.

"Okay, Billy and Fred, stand up. I want the two of you to have a conversation incorporating as many slang terms as possible. You will be judged on creativity, correct usage of terms, and how similar your conversation is to kids in America who are the same age. You may begin."

"Hey dude, what's up?"

"Dude, check it out. I just bought this new leather basketball at the sports store, isn't it cool?"

"No way, it's phat. Let me check it out."

"Sure, dude."

"Wow, this thing is totally cool. Let's head to the park and shoot some hoops—try it out, man."

"Can't, dude, I'm actually meeting Susie and a couple of her friends at the mall in about an hour. You wanna come hang out?"

"For real? Is Jenna gonna be there? She's da bomb, she's like so hot."

"Yeah, dude. She'll be there. Like, are you in or what?"

"Dude, I'm all over that. Sounds sweet, let's go."

As Billy and Fred sat down, Peter and the rest of the class gave them a well-earned round of applause. Peter was floored; these kids were more American than he was at twelve. He just couldn't imagine how in the hell they could so easily remember all the slang words that he had given them the night before and use them so well in context. How could their English be so good?

"Okay, I think we will end class on that note. You have your assignments for tomorrow. Please make sure to give Alex the homework assignment and tell him to feel better, seems like quite a few of you have been sick recently."

After Peter was finished with his classes, he would spend time in his office preparing his lessons for the next day. It took about three weeks before Mr. Shue even allowed him to have an office. He was still technically required to leave the building at 5:00 with the rest of the employees, but Peter had impressed Shue to such a degree that he was given some leeway and on many nights would stay until 7:30 or 8:00. His office was so small and musty that Peter assumed it had once been a closet for janitorial supplies. The room had no windows and the fluorescent lighting provided barely enough light for Peter to see the words that he wrote on his yellow legal pad. Peter was still happy to have it since he found it difficult, outside of the school building, to concentrate on anything but Song May.

Peter was totally consumed with Song May and only through sheer willpower and complete concentration was he able to stay focused at work. He simply could not stop thinking about her. He had planned to meet her after work, but at the last second she cancelled saying she would stop by his place later. Knowing that sitting at home waiting would drive him crazy, Peter decided to try to get ahead and prepare for his next few classes.

Peter still had not decided how he would attack the topic: *Relationships: Sibling-to-Sibling, Child-to-Parents, and Classmate-to-Classmate*. Peter spent a solid two hours preparing the outline and he was exhausted. Shue was nowhere to be seen so Peter left his office and began walking around the building. The school building was small with four offices, three classrooms, and a conference room. From the outside of the building, you could not even tell it was a school. It had no name on the outside and was located on a street with similar-sized buildings, most of which housed small businesses. The students lived on the premises in a dorm.

Shue had given Peter a quick tour during his first week of work. The facilities were basic, but nice: very similar to what you'd find in a college dorm, except kids slept ten to a room, with five bunk beds lining the walls. As he walked up and down the halls stretching his legs, he checked the doors to the offices to see if they were locked; each one was. He couldn't understand why anyone would bother locking their doors, the offices looked mostly barren and anything important could be locked in a drawer.

The classroom doors were open. At the back of one of the classrooms was an emergency exit. It was not connected to an alarm so he tried to open it, but it was locked. "Hope we don't have an emergency," he thought. The door had an "Exit" sign on it, but he now realized it did not lead to the main street from where he entered the building every morning. His curiosity was piqued, but he had no way of opening the door. Different than every other door in the building besides the main entrance, which was keypad-protected and security-guard-controlled, this door looked fortified. It was thicker with multiple locks. He wondered where it led. It looked so out of place compared to the rest of the school. As he tried looking through the keyhole, his heart jumped when he heard footsteps from the other side of the door. He was not doing anything wrong, but he felt guilty for some reason as if he had been caught in the cookie jar like a little kid. He quickly ran to the front of the room and feigned practicing his lesson for the next day, pacing between the rows of desks as if he were in front of his class. A moment later, the door opened and Mr. Shue stood silently in the doorway with a pile of yellow folders in his hand. He eyed Peter with an intense anger.

"Mr. Stimpson, you were granted special privileges, but if you are in the building after hours, you are not to leave your office. I thought I made that very clear. Do you not understand instructions? Did you learn nothing from your million-dollar Harvard education?" Mr. Shue was visibly peeved and he addressed Peter in a serious military tone. Peter was shaken and scared of the possible repercussions.

"What were you doing here?" Mr. Shue continued.

"I … I was just practicing my lessons for tomorrow," Peter answered.

"This is a government building and foreigners are not to be roaming the halls without a chaperone. I allowed you a bit of freedom, but you have acted like a typical arrogant American and expected more."

"I'm sorry Mr. Shue." He wanted to explain, but was too shaken to speak.

"You are to leave this building immediately and in the future shall not stay past 6:00 p.m. Do I make myself clear, young man?" Mr. Shue had approached Peter and was now standing two inches from him and yelling in his face.

"Now get the hell out of my face before I'm tempted to demonstrate punishments for rule breakers."

"Ye-, ye-, yes sir." Peter mumbled and ran out of the building.

After Peter left the building, Shue walked to the emergency exit and opened the door. He was tempted to call General Wang, but thought better of it. Security had been breached and it was Shue's fault. He would keep this incident to himself. He proceeded down the steps to the basement, opened the door to the right, and began his nightly review.

Chapter 15

Tommy Anderson had been working on the Chinese economic espionage case for nine months and had almost no solid leads. Since the Chinese had embraced capitalism thirty years ago, information was more expensive, and as China opened its doors to the west, underpaid Chinese bureaucrats became clearly aware of the riches in the United States. In the past, information was shared on principal and ideology. Turncoats tended to want revenge on the Communist Party for family members who had been purged or imprisoned, or, in some cases, they personally had been burned by the Party. They hated the Communist Party and wanted to see its demise. Money, though important, was rarely the overriding reason for sharing communist party secrets.

In today's China, government employees didn't even bother to pretend they were loyal to the Communists; they knew enough about American politics to understand its flaws. That was not to say that an American passport and some greenbacks did not still open the mouths of the relatively higher ranking, normally tight-lipped officials, but idealism was dead. In this particular instance, however, even offering all of the gold in the U.S. Mint would probably still not pry open the lips of any of Tommy's most reliable resources. Any lead Tommy did get cost him more than usual and always led nowhere. Nobody had any information to share or if one did, he or she was unwilling to share it.
So, it was with pessimism that Tommy agreed to meet with a Chinese official from Jiangsu Province located in the middle of the country. Tommy had chased down so many dead leads all around the country that he had probably logged a quarter million miles in the last month alone, speaking with informers at meetings that were set up by local CIA operatives.

In China, information gathering was easier to camouflage than in most countries. Money, even among Chinese, was commonly exchanged in order to collect information or to arrange an introduction of a decision maker within the Party. Another advantage of working in China was that, despite outward appearances, the Communist Party and the military had links to all of the most successful businesses in China. The private sector as it existed in America was probably another generation away in China.

In some cases, the CEO of a company was simply a puppet figure with major decisions on corporate policy coming from top Party officials. In most cases, this made Tommy's job easier, all information could be construed as business-related. It also didn't hurt that 99% of Party officials were as corrupt as the most crooked cop in America.

He knew the Party was intricately involved with all five technology companies that had so suddenly become front-page news in the Wall Street Journal and daily fodder for the anchors on CNBC. The dearth of information actually proved how important this espionage case was since it showed how few Party members knew about it. Party officials were notorious for having loose lips. These thoughts almost led Tommy to cancel the meeting.

Mr. Chin Ei Gan of Jiangsu Province, a mid-ranking provincial official, was in charge of attracting U.S. high-tech companies to a newly established Special Economic Zone (SEZ). Mr. Chin had volunteered for his job eagerly, with dreams of emulating the successes of Shenzen and Xiamen, once sleepy farming villages that had been transformed into economic powerhouses. After one year of promotion, his initial enthusiasm waned, as he realized how many SEZs had been set up around China, each competing for the ears of the same U.S. companies. Getting U.S. businessmen to come to Jiangsu was difficult when more attractive places existed in the rest of China, so any chance to wine and dine a potential investor was never wasted. He looked forward to meeting Tommy and explaining the virtues of setting up a factory in Jiangsu.

Tommy met Mr. Chin at a small restaurant that catered to the still small but growing group of affluent businessmen of Jiangsu. A couple other white male faces were enjoying dinner with Chinese female companions, so Tommy didn't completely stick out. Nevertheless he still attracted his share of stares and glances. Over the past year he had gotten used to it. The two men sat down, were served hot tea, and ordered a round of Ching Dow beers.

"Mr. Andersen, it so nice have you visit our city and lovely province. I hope see you often," Mr. Chin, or Charlie, as he liked to be called by his western friends, spoke choppy English with a heavy accent. His pronunciation was poor, but Charlie was aware of it. To compensate, he spoke slowly, enunciating each word and opening his mouth as wide as possible as if by doing this he could make the words come out more clearly. He referred to himself in the third person.

"It's wonderful to be here, Mr. Chin."

"You call me Charlie," he demanded, oblivious to the nuances of the English language.

"Charlie, you've done a great job of building the infrastructure of Jiangsu. The last time I was here there was barely a road in the whole town and cell phones worked only from the main hotel."

"Oh, thank you," it sounded like 'sank you.' No matter how far Charlie stuck out his tongue, it seemed he would never be able to generate the 'th' sound. "What you do, what your job? You friend tell me, but Charlie forget."

"I'm a technology consultant. I work for U.S. technology companies that are trying to form joint ventures with Chinese high-tech startups and open up factories that will produce anything from cell phones to silicon chips for the domestic market and initially for export." Tommy knew he was serving up ample bait, and could already see Charlie's mouth watering at the potential investment. Tommy had committed a small sum of money to Charlie under the guise that he wanted to conduct a feasibility study and this seemed to please Charlie to no end. He had had such little success attracting capital to his backwater province that even the potential for investment excited him. Tomorrow would be the first time in months that he would be able to report positive news to his superiors.

"As I already mention, Jiangsu is wonderful place to invest. Our infrastructure is improving and the cost to set up a factory is cheaper than anywhere else in the country." The words came from

Charlie's mouth more fluently than anything he had uttered before. This speech was his pitch to American investors and he had spent a year perfecting his sell.

"Yes, we may be interested in further discussions after our initial feasibility study is complete. Most of the companies I work for are very interested in forming joint ventures with one of the high-tech companies based in Beijing's Hai Dian district. A few have recently introduced cutting-edge technology and listed their shares on the Hong Kong Stock Exchange. I think quite a few of my clients would be interested in a very sizable investment, if they were able to partner with the right company." If Tommy were in Beijing he would never lay it on so thick, mentioning investment in every other sentence, but in Jiangsu the bureaucrats were much less sophisticated and they were neophytes in the area of negotiation when compared to their savvy brethren in Beijing, Shanghai, and Guangzhou.

"That sound very interesting, if you like Charlie can give you tour of our facilities tomorrow and show you the advantage of locating a factory in Jiangsu's Special Economic Zone."

"That would be wonderful. Tomorrow is no good, but maybe it would be better for the U.S. companies I work for to tour your facilities as well. Two or three CEOs are planning a trip to China in the coming months and perhaps we could fit a trip to Jinagsu into their schedule."

"Yes, yes, that would be very good, you tell me when and Charlie set up everything."

"Before I do that though, I am having a small problem that perhaps you can help me with. I'm having trouble making contact with the right people in the five companies that have been the talk of the high-tech community throughout China. The CEOs have been unwilling to set up meetings, saying they are not ready to form any joint ventures or that they do not need to partner with the Americans."

Tommy was interrupted before he could finish his thought. "Yes, Charlie see. Yes, yes, Charlie know all those companies, they in all newspapers and they raise own capital on stock exchange, maybe they no need America. Charlie can recommend many company that look for joint venture partner." Charlie was genuinely eager to please.

"Thank you very much Charlie, that is very kind of you, but my clients have heard so much about these companies and they are not so willing to take a risk with an unknown entity. Is there anyone you know that I might talk to as a way to start negotiating a joint venture with one of these companies? My clients are very eager to invest, but they are scared. They need the right partner. You understand?"

"Yes, yes, yes! Charlie understand. Charlie don't know if can help, but maybe Charlie can help you find right person to talk to. Two months ago, I go Beijing with other government officials from Jiangsu. We meet many Beijing Communist Party officials. One man take us to visit many companies in the Hai Dian area, where many technology companies located and we also visit companies you telling me about. Charlie think the man who guide us help you, but not know. He very important man, Charlie think. His name is Shue Gao Shan. Sorry, but Charlie not know how find him. Maybe he help you make introductions to mangers of companies."

"Okay, thank you, Charlie. I'll try."

During the rest of dinner Charlie continued to speak about the advantages of locating a joint venture in the lovely province of Jiangsu. He was determined to make a lasting impression on Tommy and hoped to negotiate a Letter of Intent for an investment in the economic zone in the next couple of months. Tommy nodded and smiled a lot, but he barely heard what Charlie was saying. He was already wondering about the accuracy of Charlie's information and plotting his next step.

Chapter 16

Song May woke early, kissed Peter on the forehead, and left quietly so as not to wake him. She returned home, showered quickly, and walked the three miles to her office. She enjoyed walking to work in the morning; it was her favorite time of day. As she passed her usual breakfast stand at the corner, the boss's wife waved to her and invited her to sit down. "The dumplings are fresh and straight from the wok," she yelled as Song May passed. Song May graciously explained that she was late for a meeting. The wife barely heard her as she gave her attention to the next passerby, again extolling the virtues of her delicious dumplings.

Song May weaved across streets, between hoards of bicyclists and pedestrians. She deftly avoided a taxi, which seemed to barely notice her, and continued toward the Ministry of Information where she had her 2nd floor office. The building was empty save for a sleeping guard who barely opened his eyes as Song May passed and walked the one flight of steps to her floor. On most days Song May spent the majority of her time contacting the fifty-eight young agents scattered across America who were still in school and had not yet joined the workforce. This position was her day job and something she still enjoyed immensely. It kept her very connected to the primary focus of the operation and it was absolutely essential to future successes. The students needed to understand that they were being monitored, needed to be kept in fear and encouraged or consoled when necessary. Much was invested and the Party was committed to realizing a sizeable return. Song May was supremely skilled at intimidating and manipulating the young agents without alienating them. Most of the kids knew they were the very elite so keeping them in line required constant vigilance.

Song May worked very closely with U.S.-based agents to ensure the students always realized that big brother was watching. After an agent began work, he or she would go completely incommunicado, maintaining no contact with Beijing. A sleeper cell until it was time to supply company secrets.

All agents flew solo so that no proven links could be established with China and the Communist Party. Once the agents started working, contact wasn't necessary. They were aware of their responsibilities and at that point it was not a high risk that they would discontinue their mission.

The period where agents were most impressionable was when they first arrived in America and were forced to immerse into U.S. culture. Song May constantly checked on the families, tried to troubleshoot any problems, and alerted the agents of any possible pitfalls to avoid. The allure of an easy American life was strong. All of the children picked for this assignment were screened relentlessly, and trained and indoctrinated for twelve to fourteen years. In 99% of the cases, they followed through with their mission, but a rare few became so immersed that they refused to continue in the program, hoping to instead live the life of a true, red-blooded American.

The young agents spent an inordinate amount of time preparing for their missions such that by the time they arrived in America, they were so adept at their roles that they would sooner face death by firing squad than give up. Since the launch of the program, only two cases led to agents becoming weak and refusing to continue. In these cases, the kids were shipped back to Beijing and immediately executed. Any evidence that they had ever lived in America disappeared. Any leak by a trained operative would be disastrous for the whole program. It was no coincidence that over the past five years, since Song May had been in charge, no agents had been brought back to Beijing.

The first three months were generally the toughest for all new agents. Their assignment upon arrival was to immerse themselves completely into their new surroundings, becoming a normal American teenager with the same idiosyncrasies and insecurities. The problem all inevitably faced was a lack of supervision. The acting parents had very little control of the young stars of the Chinese Secret Service and merely provided the façade of a family. The kids' high intelligence, combined with their physical abilities and mental toughness, gave them great confidence. These powers, if not checked, were used to curry favor among classmates, especially the opposite sex, and in almost all cases the newly-minted Americans became leaders of their classes. Song May constantly reminded them of their purpose, cajoled them to excel academically since all agents found the workload in America laughable, and made each agent aware that he or she was always being evaluated. The threat of big brother acted as the most potent weapon. In her quarterly report to General Wang, she optimistically concluded that no abnormalities were present and every aspect of the mission continued to proceed as planned.

She stuffed the report into her pocketbook and left her office at 1:45. It was a ten-minute walk to General Wang's office located at the Communist Party headquarters across the street from Tiananmen Square.

Mr. Shue Gao Shan also woke early, having much to do to prepare for his meeting with the general. The prospect of being upstaged by Song May always served as an ample motivator to propel Shue out of bed. Meticulous with his clothes, Shue took his time getting dressed. He called for his driver to pick him up at 7:00 a.m. outside his apartment and walked to the corner kiosk where he bought a pack of Camel Lights. Shue enjoyed the morning's first cigarette more than any other. He smelled it as one would a cigar and carefully placed it between his lips. He found his lighter in his inside coat pocket, lit the smoke, and deeply inhaled his first drag of the day. As he exhaled and watched the smoke drift toward the polluted Beijing sky, Shue noticed a red Volkswagen turn onto his street. His driver was on time despite the traffic. Shue had no tolerance for tardiness.

When compared to Song May, Shue had a more glorious job. In addition to overseeing every aspect of educating the agents in training, he was also the Chief Party Liaison to the technology companies that benefited, or were set to benefit, from the information passed from the agents in the field. He met with the CEOs of these companies about every six weeks to discuss strategy, public relations, and the steps taken by each company to ensure sustained profitability. The military, and particularly the secret service division, had sizeable stakes in all of the companies that it fed information. All of the companies were legitimate concerns with bright, young staff coming from Beijing and Qinghua Universities, two of the top institutions of higher learning in the country. Each company was carefully selected and the CEO was screened, both to ensure that he was capable of running a highly-visible public company and to gauge how well he was willing, if necessary, to take orders from Communist Party bureaucrats.

The selection process was a very delicate balance and every criterion had to be met. First, the company had to be a cutting-edge, high-tech startup with its own solid prospects apart from the information it would receive. Initially, each member of upper management had to be a loyal member of the Communist Party with an almost spotless record, which lowered the pool of potential companies dramatically. The term "entrepreneurial Communist" was an oxymoron. Anyone under 35 could not care less about the Communists, and the most intelligent ones who were spearheading the high-tech boom in Beijing were the least likely to have any desire to tow the party line. After the first go-around, the selection committee could not identify even one appropriate company, so a compromise was needed. It was decided that the younger the management group the better. Anyone under twenty-five remembered very little of the Tiananmen Square massacre, did not care that much about democracy, and had no ill will towards the Communists. They grew up more affluently than people just five years older than them and were much more optimistic about the future of the country. That is not to say that they were all volunteering to join the Communist Youth League, but they were willing to focus on economics and not politics in exchange for the tacit acknowledgement that the government would allow free market reforms to persist.

Companies with a younger management team, although at times as stubborn and headstrong as any twenty-something, high-tech CEO from Silicon Valley, were proportionally easier to influence when necessary. They were also easily intoxicated by the allure of immediate riches. Consumerism was rampant and these young fast-trackers had no patience to work their way up. They wanted the Mercedes, beautiful wife, and new downtown apartment immediately. Dangling dollars proved to be one of two effective weapons. The other was an old staple: the threat of imprisonment. Imprisonment was an "if all else failed" decision since it ruined a company and halted the flow of money that was fattening the Communists' wallets. The Party was still all-powerful and even the young, tech-savvy rich kids feared challenging the supremacy of the Party. Shue was responsible for striking just the right balance of encouraging management to be creative and entrepreneurial, but also instilling the importance, if necessary, of taking orders. His job, while more exciting than Song May's, was definitely also more difficult.

The problem he had encountered most often over the last year was apathy. After the announcements of new technologies and subsequent IPOs, he sometimes found that the once passionate, feisty entrepreneurs had lost much of their enthusiasm. Money was no longer an issue and the technologies they had spent years developing no longer mattered. Shue was responsible for keeping these Red Stars of China motivated and engaged. To take this gift of information and use it to their advantage, to go beyond what they thought originally possible and create something completely revolutionary. He was not only responsible for letting each company understand that the Party, and specifically the military, was a major shareholder in the company, but he also played an equally important role in keeping his colleagues at bay so that each company could avoid feeling the stifling weight of the Communist Party. He spent the morning putting the finishing touches on his monthly report for General Wang and spent the hour before lunch at the school, observing Peter's English class. At 1:55 he walked up the two flights of stairs to the general's office.

The general arrived 10 minutes late. It seemed two hours was still not enough time for lunch. He greeted Song May and Shue in his reception area.

"Comrades, good day. Have you eaten?"

"Yes," they answered in unison. Song May hadn't eaten a thing all day and though her stomach was noticeably growling, the general's comment was meant more as a greeting than any real interest in their eating habits.

"Please come in and sit. I have just met with some of the members of the Standing Committee; they are extremely pleased with the results of our program. Never in their wildest dreams did they imagine that Mao's most preposterous of schemes would thirty years later become China's greatest triumph. I am sorry for not meeting with you two more often, but the Standing Committee is preparing its new ten year developmental plan and has asked for my assessment as to how we can upgrade our military and bring it into the 21st century. The task has been quite daunting."

"I have been reading your thorough reports and everything seems to be progressing smoothly. Is there anything the two of you would like to discuss?" Before Shue or Song May could respond, the general continued. "Ah yes, I'd like to know how that new English instructor is working out. I mention this only because I was surprised to hear that many of the President's top aides, and some say even the President himself, attribute the success of the mission to the uncanny ease with which the agents have assimilated to American life. They feel that the dual process of indoctrination, combined with rigorous study of English and American culture, has made the agents completely undetectable and above all suspicion. I tend to agree, it really is uncanny. They are American in every sense, from standard American accent, to marriage, to social interaction. Comrade Chen, according to your report, every one of our adult agents has married a Caucasian woman, most have kids, belong to the local clubs, and live in the suburbs, yet they are the most loyal and capable agents this country has ever had. From the information we have received, it is evident that they are highly regarded within their respective companies and have the highest-level access to information. How is the new teacher working out?" The general seemed tired from his unusually long speech.

Shue answered first. "Peter is working out better than expected. He is the first teacher with extensive teaching experience in the States and he is by far the most intelligent teacher we've had. His lesson plans are creative and demanding and his grasp of American culture is beyond all previous teachers. He seems to have taken the students' intelligence as a challenge, constantly trying to outsmart them and take them to new levels of competence. I am very impressed."

"Do you think he is too smart, does he suspect anything? Does he wonder at the students' genius and mastery of the English language?"

"No, I don't think so, General. I have been watching him quite closely and he doesn't seem to be questioning the students too much. He has asked me questions regarding their English abilities, but at this juncture he still seems to believe my explanation that we are training future leaders and that it is imperative to give them the proper skill set to succeed in a world controlled by America. I will continue to monitor the situation closely."

"Very good. Comrade Chen, what do you think?"

"General, I agree with Comrade Shue. Peter is extremely intelligent and from my contact with him, he seems to spend a tremendous amount of time preparing his lessons and takes his job very seriously. I must disagree as to the danger he poses to the project. He mentions to me almost daily how smart his students are and how puzzled he is at their proficiency in English. He's too smart and it's only a matter of time before he learns too much. He should be sent home immediately." Song May knew her opinion would be discarded, but she was curious to see their reactions.

"Comrade Chen, your opinion is valued, but don't you think you are overreacting a bit? It seems as if we have the necessary safeguards in place and to replace our instructor now would delay our scheduled exchanges."

"Comrade, that's exactly what we said when we had a similar conversation regarding Matthew. What would we do if another one of the students decided to let his teacher know that he was training spies instead of government officials, kill him too?"

"We have corrected that situation by instituting weekly evaluations, psychological testing, and additional indoctrination. That problem is solved, but yes, we will kill if we have to; it has worked out quite well thus far. Any American teacher who has contact with this program is better off dead; it's safer. Media scrutiny is too intense now that we have successfully started to receive high-level information, and we cannot risk any loose cannons. This one will be eliminated like the three before. It is too dangerous to operate any other way."

"We've killed three already. Two of them didn't know a thing, yet I dutifully carried out orders, and the third began piecing things together and was hours away from escaping. Why take an unnecessary risk when we do not need to follow a specific timeline? Is there anything wrong with slowing things down a bit and letting the media hype in the States disappear? Peter has the ability to piece it together, especially with the U.S. media's focus on suspected Chinese economic espionage. Let's not risk it; let's deport him and be done with it."

"Perhaps Comrade Chen has a point," the general said. "Comrade Shue, your thoughts."

"General Wang, as I mentioned to you last week, I did find Peter working late a few nights this week, but I don't think it is anything more than diligence. Finding qualified teachers is getting increasingly difficult and a story of another murdered teacher may cause the U.S. State Department to issue an official warning. We need to get as much as we can from this one before we dispose of him."

With this Song May jumped back in, "Why increase the scrutiny with another murder? He knows nothing now. We deport him, change locations of our academy, as is standard procedure, and look for a new instructor. Let's be sensible." She was certainly not preaching to the choir, but for some odd sense of loyalty to Peter, she felt obligated to at least give her all to spare his life.

Shue continued to push back, "Peter suspects nothing, we needn't act rash. The downside of ruffling some feathers at the U.S. State Department for another American's death seems minimal compared to the costs of delaying our planned exchange and losing the services of the best English teacher the school has ever had."

The general spoke up, "Comrade Chen, I tend to agree with Comrade Shue under these circumstances. Decisions are almost at the point of being out of our hands. The Standing Committee is very eager to play a more prominent role in the program. I'm afraid that unless the situation turns dire, we will continue as planned."

"He has mentioned 'the door' to me." Song May had not wanted to bring this up since she was unsure of how Wang and Shue would react. She anticipated one of three reactions: his execution could be ordered summarily, it could get brushed off as nothing, or they could decide to deport him as an easy way out. Bringing up the door was her last hope of saving him.

"So what?" Shue had lost his cool. "The door is connected to one of the classrooms, of course at some point he would notice it, but what does it matter? It's impossible to get through that door. It has about five locks and you, me, and Comrade Chu have the only keys. Has anyone ever gotten through that door without our permission? Why would you bring up something so inconsequential?"

"Someone is going to get through that door at some point," Song May countered. "At the very least we should add a camera or keypad to protect it, some additional security. Better yet, the facility should be separated from the dorms and classroom instruction altogether."

"That would surely bring attention to it," Shue argued. "Now it is simply a locked exit, something that can be explained away quite easily. How would we explain such additional security? And removing the rooms from the school grounds is ludicrous. You know as well as I that it's an essential part of the training—and what about all the updates we need to make to their files? General, why am I wasting time with this conversation?"

The general started to respond, "Comrades, I think this meeting has gone on—"

"Perhaps we need to rethink our methods," Song May interrupted. She wasn't ready to give in. "The chamber has served its purpose and is no longer necessary. It's ineffective and more modern and more humane methods should be instituted—and isn't it time we started using a computer to update and store our records? We have entered the 21st Century." Song May guessed that this was her last chance to influence policy. She had not had an opportunity to raise these concerns in the past six months and bringing up the door, surprisingly, had provided the perfect segue. She cared little about interrupting the general.

Shue scoffed, "Okay, I see, this is not about security or our teacher. It's about your own mission to 'beautify' the Program. Our methods have been effective for 30 years and are an integral part of the Program's success. What has worked for 30 years should not be changed! Why raise objections after so much success? And why must we discuss the issue of computers again? This discussion is a waste of all of our time. How easy would it be for someone to steal boxes and boxes of files? Where would they go, how would they be transported, how many men would it take to sort through the files, and how easy would it be to detect someone trying to steal them? Contrast that with a computer. Every bit of information we have could fit on a disk, slipped into a pocket, and 30 years of data would be gone in an instant. We do not have the encryption technology to stop a trained CIA operative from breaking any code we would put forth. That is risky. Having files locked in a room is not. General, must we continue to listen to this nonsense?" Shue, who grudgingly had so much respect for Song May, was almost amazed at her insubordination and lack of forethought. She was always so measured, and he would have been inclined to question her motives had he not been so aggravated and distracted with her outbursts.

"Comrade Chen, perhaps we should talk in private in the coming weeks. I'm quite concerned with your performance as of late as well as your attitude," the general admonished.

Yeah whatever. "Yes, General," Song May acquiesced.

"Okay, let's continue to monitor the American, but it's imperative that his instruction continue. Thank you both for coming. That will be all."

All three stood and shook hands. Song May left quickly. As she left Wang's office, she daydreamed how enjoyable it would be to kill him.

Chapter 17

At 11:30 on a Friday night Scott lay in bed trying to think of ways he could delay walking the two flights to the basement where he kept a small office with the only computer in the house not connected to the Internet. His wife lay next to him buck-naked with a sheet covering her legs and only part of her ass. She was breathing deeply and had fallen asleep immediately after sex, as she always did. Scott was confined to only a sliver of their king-sized bed with Jane's spread-eagled body occupying most of the rest. Every five minutes Scott glanced at the clock and promised himself that in five more minutes he would get up, prepare a pot of green tea, and descend the stairs to the half-finished basement for another all-nighter. He had already made the promise seven times. At 11:55, he dragged himself out of bed, threw on a pair of boxer shorts and a tee shirt, and left his oblivious sleeping wife. He opened the doors of his children's rooms as he did every night, listened to their breathing for a moment, and then made his way downstairs.

As he put the kettle on the stove, Scott began wondering what would become of him. He was a member of the very first group of agents to come to America for economic espionage purposes. As his childhood friends over the past year began successfully exposing company secrets and the U.S. press began publishing exposés on the potential of Chinese economic espionage, Scott knew his window of opportunity was shrinking precipitously. He didn't know what would happen. Would the Chinese Secret Service allow the agents to end their careers and live the rest of their lives as normal Americans? Would he be required to return to China and serve the remaining years as a pencil pusher for the Service, training new agents on economic espionage? Or, would he be treated to a vacation in China and then executed?

In recent months, regardless of how hard he tried to focus, in the back of his mind was a scene of the FBI breaking down his front door. Jane is frantic asking what the fuck the agents are doing and the children are crying. They find Scott in the basement and handcuff him. As he is led away Jane is yelling at him for an explanation, but Scott ignores her, head down. His thoughts were interrupted by the annoying whistle of the kettle. He turned off the water, prepared his tea, and went to the basement.

It was already 12:30 before Scott began transcribing the final documents. He sat at the computer sipping tea and typing non-stop. After tonight, his mission would be complete. In the morning he would take the report to Kinkos, make one copy, and then send it to Beijing. He had no choice but to finish tonight. He felt his world collapsing around him and was certain that he had little time before he would be discovered. His feelings were more paranoia than premonition, but whatever the case he wanted closure and an end to a project that had lasted for more than twenty years.

He thought again how patient he was; a distinctly Chinese trait that very few Americans could understand. He could not remember how many scenarios he had come up with to end his association with the Chinese government and simply disappear, but it had always seemed so messy. Too many questions would arise and he was unwilling to think of answers. What he would tell his wife was the ultimate dream killer. But also smaller problems that he did not have the energy to solve. Where would he go? Would the Chinese Secret Service come after him? What would he tell his boss and now good friend Biddleberry? What would he do for the rest of his life? Yes, he was a spy and that still defined him, but essentially he was a normal American husband and father. As long as he had maintained his daily routine, he could avoid the inevitable. All that changed with the first announcement of a new technological breakthrough by a Chinese company and the subsequent media frenzy surrounding the possibility of the Chinese Communist Party infiltrating some of the greatest American companies. Now he couldn't stop thinking about potential escapes. He was driven by fear, afraid for his children's and wife's lives, frightened of being discovered and the subsequent ramifications. These thoughts drove him to think of every possible scenario and to plan every possible detail.

He started rehearsing in his mind what he would say to his wife. He began researching countries that did not have extradition laws with the U.S., and he began miserly saving his money. In any case, no matter what the result, he had no choice but to finish what he had been trained to do. Since the day he had landed on U.S. shores, his mission fundamentally guided his every action.

There was no turning back and no running away, no matter how many times he dreamed about it. He could not abandon his mission. It had been ingrained in his head almost since the time he could walk. The Communists had successfully indoctrinated him and at this stage it was impossible to abandon his life's work. But, when he was finished, he would be free. He could wash his hands of everything and begin anew. The shackles that had bound him to the Communists for so long would no longer be able to constrain him. At least, this is what he hoped.

Chapter 18

Peter opened his eyes slowly, adjusting them to his room, which was lit only by the setting sun. He focused on Song May, who was sleeping soundly. She looked adorable when she was sleeping, not much different than when she was awake, but Peter liked to stare at her while she slept, when he found her to be most vulnerable. He rarely got this chance since she was gone most mornings before he woke, so as he watched her, he stayed as still as possible so as not to disturb her. She had arrived unexpectedly about two hours earlier and what began as a kiss hello soon turned into a session of passionate lovemaking.

They had been together for almost four months and he had no doubt that he was madly in love. Everything about Song May was perfect and he knew almost immediately that he would marry her. She was the one and Peter felt old enough and wise enough to know for certain. He had been in love before, but nothing he had ever experienced compared to the intensity of the feelings he felt for Song May. He tried to objectively analyze how he felt, but really could not be bothered. He was sure. What started out as a mutually-lustful attraction had grown in to a loving relationship. They spent almost every day together, sharing their lives and talking about their dreams for the future. Peter hadn't told Song May how he felt, hadn't even told her he loved her, but as he lay in bed staring at her, he promised himself that tonight he would bare all. He thought she loved him as well, but he really couldn't be certain. During the last two weeks he had gone through hell wondering if she felt the same.

Song May woke from a terrible nightmare, almost jumping out of bed and looking around as if confused about where she was. As with all of her nightmares, she remembered every detail, like a curse. This one was one in a series of three recurring dreams that had started about three months ago, soon after Peter arrived. A night rarely passed that she did not wake drenched in sweat. She looked over at Peter and stared at him with a puzzling look, wondering if she were still dreaming and fearing that the figure lying next to her was a silhouette of the man she had just fucked, his spirit returning to haunt her. The thought of executing Peter, a feeling she was able to suppress in her conscious thought, was ever-present in her dream state.

"Song May, you all right? What's the matter, did you have a bad dream?"

Song May hesitated before answering, wiping the wisps of hair from her cheeks. "I'm fine, I think I had a nightmare. I was falling or something, I can't remember." She wanted to run as even looking at Peter gave her a terrible feeling of foreboding that she was unable to deal with at the moment.

"What is that strange look on your face?" Peter asked her.

"What look?"

"I don't know if I can even describe it. When you looked over at me, it looked like you had seen a ghost or something."

"I think that nightmare really scared me. I don't know. Listen, Peter, I'm sorry but I think I have to go. I just remembered that my grandparents need help around the house early in the morning. I gotta get going." Song May started getting out of bed, she could barely even look at Peter; the intensity of her nightmare was so powerful, that she still felt spooked. Peter grabbed her hand.

"Wait, can't you leave from here in the morning? It's starting to get late, why don't you stay the night? Song May look at me, there's something I want to talk to you—uh, I mean, there's something I want to tell you." Peter heard the pleading in his voice and felt disgusted with himself. He had revealed nothing to Song May, but he felt vulnerable.

"Talk, talk, talk!!" Song May exploded back. "I'm sick of it. Why do you Americans always want to talk? There's nothing to discuss. I said I need to go home and that's what I'm gonna do. There's nothing we need to talk about."

"Whoa! What's the matter with you? I want you to stay the night; you never seemed to mind before." Song May's response was from left field. Peter wasn't expecting it at all. Song May never backed down from an argument, she was not the stereotypical subservient Chinese woman, but her reaction really threw Peter for a loop. He reacted defensively.

"What do you mean by that?" Song May responded. "What the fuck do you mean by that?" She was now shaking and holding back tears. She couldn't understand her reaction herself, but she was beyond maintaining control.

"Noth… nothing. I mean, what's the matter? I just want you to stay. I want to be with you. I'm sorry. I don't know what I did to make you so angry. Don't go."

Song May didn't say another word. She had put on her clothes and was practically out the door before Peter even finished his sentence. When she got outside, she allowed the tears to start streaming down her face. She felt cold and was shaking in the uncharacteristically cool September night. The tears continued to roll down her face until she arrived home. She was becoming a mess and did not know why. She would have to think about this, to come to grips with all the feelings she had been suppressing for longer than she dared think about, but she was too exhausted to think. She went into the medicine cabinet and found the bottle of tranquilizers. She took two and crawled into bed. The warmth of her sheets and blankets comforted and relaxed her. As she calmed down and rational thought returned, she felt a pang of guilt well up and form a knot in the pit of her stomach. The feeling was foreign to her; she had not felt this guilty about anything in years.

Peter was left distraught in his apartment. The thought had crossed his mind to go after her, but she seemed so resolute to leave and her outburst had been so perplexing that he decided against it. He unfortunately had no sleeping aids and was instead left in his tiny apartment to play back every moment of the last half hour in his mind. After two hours he had come to no conclusions and continued wondering what he had done to lead Song May over the edge. The night had started with so much promise.

Chapter 19

"Tommy, you always seem to show up at the most opportune times," Bill O'Malley said as Tommy sat down on the bar stool to his left, the only empty one in the place. The Chinese Dragon was the new hot bar in Hong Kong for the expatriate crowd. Tommy hadn't been in touch with O'Malley for a few weeks but was confident he'd find his friend at the Dragon for Friday night happy hour.

"Just having a drink after a tough day at the office, like any working stiff," Tommy answered back.

"You got the Fortune 500 paying you to find information and all you end up doing is looking for me, peppering me with questions, and then writing up reports for these corporate bozos who don't know the first thing about technology in Asia. That's about the extent of your due diligence and I bet you're getting paid handsomely for it. When can I expect the kickback?" O'Malley was speaking to Tommy only half in jest.

The sixth Chinese company had announced a groundbreaking technology in Nanotubes just two days prior and Bill had made a bet with himself that Tommy would show up within three days.

"Well now that you mentioned it, I've noticed that the rest of the media elite in the States and Asia have been focusing on the inexplicable events that have taken place over the last year, but you have remained enigmatically silent. The last O'Malley column I read in *The Examiner* was dealing with the semiconductor slowdown and how it's affecting the OEM manufacturers in Taiwan: a story about as interesting and current as Microsoft's Antitrust verdict. What the hell are you working on?"

"All right, enough with your crap. I like you and since I've kinda taken you under my wing, I'm gonna let you buy drinks and pay for dinner tonight and we'll be square. Fair?"

"It's no secret that I could go to the other end of the bar right now and start chatting up Lindsay Stevens working for the New York

Times; check it out, she's looking over at us right now." O'Malley and Tommy lifted their glasses and smiled in unison at Lindsay and then looked away quickly, not wanting to give her any idea that they were inviting her over. "She's a bit of a pain in the ass, but I'm sure she'd be happy to provide me with any information I want."

"Hey, go ahead, I don't give a shit. I think the trade-off though would cost you more in aggravation than drinks and dinner." O'Malley knew Tommy was not going anywhere and he had already decided he would order a nice steak with shrimp cocktail as an appetizer and maybe dessert. He'd let Tommy pick his brain, though he had very little knowledge outside of what everyone else knew. The reason why he hadn't been focusing on the recent technology announcements in China was that nothing new could be said. Everyone was clear that corporate espionage was happening, but nobody could figure out why no one had been arrested or why the FBI or CIA hadn't broken such an important case. He was tempted to write an exposé, as his editors were demanding, but he was sick of reading all the same crap that every other news organization was spewing out and didn't want to add to the hype. In just the last week, Bill could recall at least five special reports and three features on Chinagate.

"Okay, O'Malley, let's start with a couple more drinks. All this back and forth bickering with you has made me thirsty."

Tommy and Bill avoided talking technology until after dinner.

"Ok Tommy, let's try to unpack a little and get to the root of what has occurred over the last eight months and why neither the FBI or CIA has been able to crack this case. It has been about a year since Linksound announced that it suspected the Chinese of stealing its technology and since then five other companies' technology have been cherry picked one-by-one without, from what we currently know, even one clue. I just can't make heads or tails of the situation. Stealing corporate secrets these days is like swiping the Queen's jewels in broad daylight, or breaking into the Louvre and stealing the Mona Lisa. The paranoia is so pervasive and the security measures taken are so thorough that I just cannot

109

conceivably imagine a scenario in which after a year not one Chinese spy would get caught with his hand in the cookie jar."

It was after midnight and many of the Dragon's patrons were beginning to slowly file out of the main and rear entrances. The bar remained full with mostly middle-aged white men, the regulars who usually closed the bar down at around 4:00 a.m. O'Malley looked around and noticed Lindsay Stevens getting up and leaving with a colleague from *The New York Times*. She had spent the last two hours trying to make eye contact with Tommy with little success. Before turning toward the door, she waved goodbye. They both admired her nicely-shaped ass and long, athletic legs as she walked out the door and, as if she felt the heat from the penetrating stares on her butt, she suddenly turned around, smiled coquettishly at Tommy, and mouthed the words, "Call me." Nobody ever faulted her for a lack of persistence.

"Oh yeah, Tommy. This is gonna sound like some investigative reporter bullshit to you, but the last few times we met it has seemed like I've been dishing out a lot more information than you have regarding the impact Chinagate has had on the future of technology, on relations between the Chinese and U.S. governments, and the random eruptions of racism against Chinese-Americans in the U.S. And most importantly on what I think is happening and why. Now I don't mind doing this, I know I can trust you and throwing around ideas clarifies my own thoughts, but I'm trained to ask questions and I know the connections that you have around China and throughout the boardrooms of corporate America. I've felt for some time that you're not sharing any information you've gathered and unless we start playing quid pro quo, I'm walking." O'Malley said this in an even-keeled, serious tone, very different from his normally animated and explicative peppered soliloquies.

Tommy remained quiet for a couple of minutes and then said, "Okay, Bill, I know I haven't been as forthcoming with information as you so astutely stated. I do come across certain information that may be helpful to you and under the strictest confidence I may be able to send you a sound bite here and there. Of course, you know I get paid for finding things that no one else knows and my clients wouldn't be pleased if confidential information I supplied to them later wound up on the cover of *The San Francisco Examiner*. Understood?"

"Understood." And that was the last the two ever mentioned this conversation.

O'Malley took a deep breath and began, "Okay, let's assume that the six companies have done all they can and are working with both the FBI and CIA to try to uncover the culprits, how in the hell can it be that not one person has been identified? I mean, shit, the information stolen from each company was complex code that's been compiled from various research departments working in offices all around the world. How can one man, and let's assume each infiltration was committed by a lone operative, accomplish such a daunting task and not at least raise suspicions? There must've been mistakes made, nobody can perform under immense pressure and strain for an extended period of time and not slip up at least once; it is utterly impossible. Oh, and that's the other point I wanted to make. It must've taken years to compile the data. The Chinese companies don't just have documents that will lead them in the right direction; they have a finished product that they are preparing to sell to the public within months. And the Chinese on the inside must've had such high-level access that they knew exactly when the project would be complete because in all cases news came from China of groundbreaking technology just days before each U.S. company was to announce a new product. I'm completely perplexed, how come nobody has been arrested or even questioned?"

O'Malley took a large swig from his pint and motioned for the barkeep to bring another round.

"Unfortunately, what I think is happening is a classic case of sacrificing the lamb to catch the fox," Tommy suggested. "The first three companies have seen sales drop precipitously as well as their stock prices. Linksound and Loudenscape are in danger of being delisted from the NASDAQ. The other four have also started to suffer as sales dry up and partners refuse to work with them because they just can't trust them with anything proprietary. And,

111

adding salt to an already gangrenous wound, just heard this piece of news: two of the six Chinese companies who have inherited this technology from an uncle they barely knew, will be announcing tomorrow that they will form equity-swapping partnerships with Linksound and Loudenscape's chief competitors to bring their newly-acquired technology to market."

O'Malley hadn't heard this piece of news and almost spit out the mouthful of Guinness he was about to swallow. He was tempted to whip out his cell phone and make a quick call to his editor, but decided to wait until he was alone.

When O'Malley recovered his composure, Tommy continued. "The point I'm making is that all six of these companies and perhaps others will be sacrificed in order to break this espionage ring wide open. Every tech company in the country is scared, each believing that it will be next and admittedly clueless as to what precautions to take. If the Feds have anything solid, which at this point I doubt they do, they will most likely keep it silent until they can break the case wide open. Nobody knows how many companies have been infiltrated; it could be hundreds. Whoever's behind this has contracted a fatal case of hubris and it seems that now that the volcano has erupted, the lava can't be stopped.

"Six companies in about a year. From any logical point of view it just doesn't make sense. Why announce all within such a short period of time? Think about it, if the Chinese had been more patient, this could have gone undetected for years and a connection between each company would have been more difficult to prove. But now, the Chinese government is acting like a serial killer, leaving choreographed clues for the police; they honestly believe they're invincible. So that's why I think the CIA and FBI are taking things slowly. They know that they are not simply dealing with a rogue spy who's out to make a quick buck. The people who have infiltrated these companies are professionals and have spent enough time at each individual company to gain access to the most sensitive technology. They're completely trusted. So what I think is going on is that the Feds are laying low. If they make any arrests or even bring anyone in for questioning, the agents working at other companies across the country will simply disappear, ride out

112

the storm and wait until the hurricane has passed. A band-aid will be applied and the bloodletting will stop, but the cancer will continue to fester undetected. It's unfortunate, but the six companies will ultimately be dissolved so that this case can be solved." Tommy gave nothing groundbreaking away, but seemed to have appeased O'Malley for the moment.

O'Malley chimed in. "I've been throwing different scenarios around for the last month and you're right. If they don't crack this case at its source, it could go on for years. This is the perfect opportunity. Any inkling that arrests are imminent would send every Chinese agent into hiding. What still perplexes me is how they did it. How did the Communists recruit the spies, why have the agents remained so loyal when certainly they are not being paid that much money, and how is it that each spy managed to thwart the rigorous security efforts made by each individual company and gain access to the most highly-protected technology secrets?" O'Malley asked the question almost to himself.

It was now 3:45 a.m. and both men were tired and drunk. Tommy motioned for the check. The two left the empty bar and each flagged down a taxi.

"Ya gonna be around next week, Tommy?"

"Should be. I'll track ya down, and by the way, you're welcome for that little tip about tomorrow's press conference. I'm guessing you'll be on the phone to your editor before the cab door closes." Tommy closed the door and the driver drove off. O'Malley already had his cell in hand and speed dialed his editor's number. It was about one in the afternoon in San Francisco, his editor would just be getting back from lunch.

On the same day that Tommy met O'Malley for beers, Tommy's sometimes partner, Winston Chang, was following Mr. Shue. He had been on Shue's tail for close to a week and had not discovered anything unusual. Shue maintained a very strict routine and varied from it little during the day. He worked long hours, beginning his day promptly at 7:00 a.m. and ending sometime around 9:00 in the evening. At that time he usually met friends, or various women that he was dating, at the more fashionable Beijing watering holes and karaoke bars. He obviously had a lot more money than his government employee salary supplied, which made him no different than any other corrupt Party member, but Shue seemed to spend more ostentatiously than even New York's nouveau riche.

Once they had Shue's name, it was easy to put a face to the name. In exchange for a small fee by western standards, but quadruple the bureaucrat's annual salary, one of a number of paid Chinese informers gladly supplied a picture of Shue and gave the address of the building where he worked. Besides Shue's main office at Party headquarters, he also frequently visited various Chinese companies in Zhongguancun, and toward the end of each day he could be found at the same location, a compound of three small, non-descript buildings in a section of Beijing with very few government offices. At the front of the buildings was a courtyard with benches and potted plants at each corner, and to the side of the courtyard was a parking area for cars and bicycles. The entire complex was surrounded by a fence and at the entrance stood a guard. Chang didn't think any of this was peculiar; many institutions throughout China were enclosed with fences. It was a way to control access to government and educational institutions or other areas that at various times throughout China's history would be gathering places to incite protests or riots against the government.

Surprisingly, not one of his informants knew what the building was used for or had any idea why a high-level Party member would need to travel to such a place on an almost daily basis. At first, Winston wasn't sure if some of his usual contacts were withholding information in hopes of a bigger payout, but after peppering them with questions tangentially related to the information he was really after, he quickly came to the realization that they were genuinely unaware of this complex and its function. In present-day China, many of these compounds had been converted to office space, factories, or warehouses, but all still had guards posted outside for security purposes. Nothing about the building gave any clue as to what was going on inside. Winston couldn't see any postings of company names or government departments. Since Shue usually came to the complex quite late, other activity was absent and his was the only car that came or went. The building looked empty.

Winston was contemplating putting a man on 24-hour surveillance, but in the end decided against it. The complex was located on a dead end street and was surrounded by drab, cookie-cutter apartment blocks; one had no reason to come down the street unless you lived there or were visiting. The entire block boasted only one restaurant, where, if Winston sat at the corner table by the window, he could just barely get a full view of the building's entrance. The eatery was located a hundred feet north and across the street from the compound. Winston felt that he had spent too much time chain smoking, drinking Beijing beer, and eating barely edible meals at the restaurant, and having another stranger start coming to the same place would most certainly arouse suspicion. As his face became more familiar, the proprietor had started asking him questions about his background, what part of China he was from, and if he worked in the area; all of a very innocuous nature, but Winston started getting paranoid that he would be discovered or that somehow the owner of the establishment had a connection with the enigmatic complex that Shue entered each night.

He had almost decided he could learn nothing else from following Shue when suddenly he spotted, quite unexpectedly, a young man walking through the gates and heading north. He threw some money on the table, waved goodbye to the restaurant owner, and made his way north. He smiled uncontrollably and found it impossible to contain his pleasure from this fortuitous discovery.

Chapter 20

At midnight, Comrade Chu Young Fang walked quietly through the empty school and entered the classroom located in the northwest wing of the building. He walked methodically, unrushed and purposeful. In the back corner of the classroom, he stopped, pulled keys from his pocket, and began opening the set of locks to the door leading to the basement. As he entered, he closed the door behind him and dead bolted it from the inside.

He walked down the set of stairs and reached the basement floor, two closed doors were in front of him. The one on the right was a room that Song May and Shue used often, it contained the files of every single agent who had ever matriculated to the school. The files were constantly updated and analyzed by Song May and Shue looking for trends and characteristics that the top-performing students shared, identifying what parts of the country seemed to have an inordinate amount of quality agents, and determining which agents were approaching readiness for an exchange.

Comrade Chu unlocked the second door slowly and walked in; it had been forty-eight hours since his last visit. The room was very well-insulated, resembling a soundproof recording studio. In the room were two cells. Each cell was half the size of a standard American prison cell. Only one cell was occupied.

Inside the cell stood a boy of about seven, wearing only a pair of briefs. A light shined brightly from above, illuminating the entire cell and would almost blind the boy if he dared look up. Revolutionary songs blared from four speakers hanging from the ceiling in each corner. The boy had not slept since the last time he had seen Chu and he was on the verge of delirium. The cell had a small toilet and sink as well as a thin mattress on the floor. The cell had no blankets and the boy was shivering. Chu turned down the music and as he approached the cell, the boy reflexively flinched. Comrade Chu did not look intimidating, he appeared almost friendly and jovial, and that deception was his most potent weapon. Though his appearance would remind you of a favorite uncle, his tongue had the power of an expertly crafted Samurai Sword.

"Hello little Comrade, are you now ready to tell me why you have been put in this cell?" Throughout his conversations, he varied his tone from honey to vinegar; he started with honey tonight.

"I'm hungry. Why have you left me in this cell with nothing to eat? I've done nothing wrong," the boy whined.

"I see, and why would I put you in this cell if you had done nothing wrong?"

"I don't know. I'm sorry for whatever you think I've done, but I didn't do it."

"Are you saying that I am making things up, that I am falsely accusing you?"

"No, no, I mean there is a mistake, there is a mistake."

"So perhaps it was someone else and I have made a mistake. Would you like me to bring one of your comrades down for re-education? Would you like to tell me who is at fault?"

"No, no one has done anything wrong. Maybe someone thought I did something wrong, but I didn't."

"Oh? Comrade, we know you've done something wrong, but I can see you are unaware. I think I will provide you with another forty-eight hours to find an answer," Chu rose from the seat located outside the cell and began to leave.

"No, no, no. I'm sorry. I am ready to tell you. I will be better." The boy knew he could not survive another night in the cell.

"Okay, my son." Chu unlocked the cell door and entered. He handed the boy a t-shirt to wear and put his arm around him.

"I have not been loyal to the Communist Party or my fellow comrades. I have acted selfishly and brought shame to this school and my country."

Before the boy could finish, Chu slapped him so hard across the face that had the walls not been insulated, the entire school would've heard it. The boy was knocked to the ground and a cut on his lip that had started to heal was reopened. Blood started flowing down his chin.

"Your insincerity will cause you great harm! Do you understand me? I have no problem throwing away this key and making you live the rest of your days in this cell. You are a disgrace to Country and Party. The next lie I hear from you, I will bring both of your parents here and chop their heads off right in front of you."

"No, NO, I will improve. Please don't hurt my parents, I will be better, please." The boy was lying on the floor crying, begging Chu for forgiveness, and kissing his shoes.

"Master Chu, forgive me. I have been weak. I have lost understanding of my mission and have begged to see my parents. I have not embraced the opportunities you have given me. I will be the best student in the class and make Party and Country proud. Please, Master, give me one more chance." As the boy tried to stand up, Chu kicked him in the stomach. He fell over in agony.

"Your words are hollow. You mean nothing to this program and can easily be replaced. Your classmates will not miss you; you have proven yourself unworthy." Chu removed a 9-millimeter pistol from his pocket, commanded the boy to get to his knees, and brought the pistol to within inches of the boy's forehead. Your actions deserve the ultimate punishment." The boy was weeping uncontrollably and as Chu pulled the trigger, a stench of an uncontrolled bowel movement rose from the floor. The boy fell over, but was not dead. The gun was not loaded. Chu remained silent for quite some time as the boy lay on the cold, musty floor curled up in ball, balling. Chu waited for the boy to calm himself.

"Stand up, my son," Chu said in a soothing voice. "We will provide you with one more chance; will you begin to perform to your abilities?"

"Yes, Master. I will love the Party and serve my country until my last breath." The boy stood and Chu rubbed the boy's shoulder.

"Very good, my boy. We all care about you very much and wish nothing more than for you to succeed. You are one of our favorites. Now let's run upstairs and get you cleaned up and prepare a nice meal. How does that sound?"

"Thank you, Master, thank you."

Chapter 21

Peter walked quickly to school, stopping only to get an egg sandwich from the same vendor that he'd been going to since the beginning of his stay in Beijing. He thanked the vendor in Chinese and continued along, avoiding bicyclists and passing taxis as he comfortably weaved through the mountain of pedestrians on their way to work. He was a bit disgusted with himself; he'd been in China for four months and he could count on one hand the Chinese words that he had learned. Every morning he was reminded of that fact when he bought his egg sandwich from his regular vendor. He wanted to make small talk, to ask about her weekend, to find out if she had any children or a little about her history, and to answer the questions that she must have about him. In the beginning, she had tried, asking him something or commenting on the weather, but now she simply smiled, handed over the sandwich, and said, "Thank you." She smiled at Peter embarrassingly. They should be friendly, but Peter had not kept up with his end of the bargain. He had not adapted to his temporary home and felt guilty about this. Peter's lack of even an attempt to master basic conversation over the past few months was, in his opinion, a slap in the face to every Chinese with whom he had come into contact.

It had been three days since he'd seen Song May, but it felt like two months, and Peter was an absolute wreck. He could not sleep at night, ate little, found it difficult to concentrate on his lesson plans, and was often caught by his students daydreaming or zoning out, a word the class had recently learned and enjoyed putting to use. His life was made even more miserable by the circumstances of their relationship. He realized that he knew so little about her, and in this foreign land he had no way of tracking her down. Simple tasks like looking for a number and address in the phone book were impossible. Peter had waited outside her building asking every person who left if they knew Song May. His students taught him how to say "you know" in Chinese and laughed so gleefully at his pronunciation that he wasn't even sure whether they had taught him the correct word. He couldn't figure out if the people he asked didn't know who she was or if they didn't understand what he was saying. Most didn't even bother stopping, and the ones who were kind enough to help, simply listened to him, said "No" in English, and continued walking.

Peter had also camped out at night waiting for Song May to return, but had yet to see her. He had started questioning whether she really lived there or if she had lied in order to avoid him encountering her parents.

"Had she lied about other things as well?" he wondered as he crossed Nanking street and headed west toward the school. He had no way of contacting her. Beijing had an information service that was meant to help expatriates find out anything they needed to know in the city and Peter tried to find Song May's number and address through that service, but when he had given her name, they asked for the spelling and he didn't know. He made an attempt to sound out the spelling of her name phonetically and found that at least 100 people in the city had the name Wang Song May. He never knew the name was so common, how could he?

The only certain way he could reach her was through her cell phone number. He'd already left twenty-two messages in three days, pleading with her over the phone to contact him so they could work things out. He had given up playing it cool. He knew no other way of expressing his love for her than to tell her as plainly as possible, even if he was only talking to voicemail. She had yet to call him back. As he walked into his office, he replayed the events of three nights ago in his head for the 100th time, but still could not figure out what had sparked her inexplicable outburst. He checked his watch and realized class was set to start in one minute.

Song May had continued to follow Peter as her assignment required: wearing wigs, dressing conservatively, and most upsetting to her, not wearing any makeup. She had stayed pretty far away, blending into the crowd, but she'd had a couple of close calls. Peter had looked directly at her a couple of times, but she had managed to turn away or hide her face before Peter had the opportunity to recognize her. In any case, she had become so adept at disguising her looks that on occasion she even fooled her parents. So, she was not worried about being identified. The greater torture was following him around and not being able to talk to him or wrap her arms around his shoulders and bury her head in his chest. She missed him and staying away had been a great test of her willpower.

Peter was an easy mark to follow. He rarely strayed from his normal schedule, though the last two nights, instead of staying in his apartment and working on his lesson plan for class, he had started frequenting a famous expatriate hangout located close to his apartment. Song May would wait patiently in her car until he came out and then follow him as he stumbled home, surprising her when he never lost his way and didn't die in a traffic accident. Fortunately, she had been able to hide her current conduct from Shue and General Wang. If they knew she wasn't spending almost every waking minute analyzing every thought of their golden boy, she would probably be executed.

The Standing Committee had been on edge lately as the U.S. media continued to focus on China's alleged corporate espionage. She laughed, again baffled by the stupidity of her superiors and their limited understanding of the U.S. media machine. They thought that after no arrests were made, the story would go away. Party members were even sharing rumors that the Navy had begun to harass U.S. spy planes flying in international airspace in order to divert attention away from Chinagate. The ploy had failed dramatically as the ratings of Chinagate stories on the major networks and cable channels had soared to heights not seen since the OJ trial.

Song May had started coming to grips with her emotions about Peter and facing the fact that she had fallen in love with one of her potential victims. She really couldn't say how it had happened. In part she blamed it on the fact that she had not been in a normal relationship for the last two years. Her assignments had completely dominated her life, leaving her little time for recreation or even a bit of relaxation. Unlike the others, whom she simply looked at as jobs to get done and the sex as pleasure for herself, Peter had proven, unbelievably, to be her soul mate. She couldn't wait to be with him. She loved spending afternoons in the park exchanging stories of their disparate childhoods and distinct yet converging lives. Conversation never waned and the excitement of seeing Peter and making love to him never diminished. Staying away from him for this long was torturous and listening to his messages painful, yet she longed for the next message and waited anxiously for her cell phone to ring just so she could hear his voice. She compared the feeling to when she was a child and would push against a tooth that was close to falling out. It hurt as the tooth stretched from the gums, but she always wanted to see how much pain she could endure by pushing the tooth with her tongue or forefinger just a little bit farther each time. She was invariably disappointed when the tooth finally fell out.

She loved Peter, and although staying away from him for the last few days had caused her unbearable heartache at times, it also allowed her to think more rationally and detach herself from her emotions.

Song May's love for Peter would remain foremost in her mind when she met with General Wang and Shue later in the week to discuss his future. More than any other teacher in the past, Song May would continue to insist that Peter be deported and argue that whatever he already knew or would soon discover was merely hearsay. She was sure that he did not have any hard evidence, at least none that he was hiding in his apartment, and questioned whether he knew anything at all. But she was certain that would change at some point in the near future.

Wang and Shue were unresponsive when she requested a special meeting in between their bi-monthly scheduled sessions, but she persisted until both reluctantly agreed. If she had attempted extracting an extra minute on General Wang's time even two weeks ago with trivialities, as he referred to most matters important to Song May, she would have been politely but firmly rebuked. They had a firm belief that the sacrifice of human life for the ultimate success of a greater cause was justified, and in the case of an American life, was not even debatable. The "cause" in this instance, Song May thought cynically, was the career advancements of Wang and Shue. She was concerned that they would order his death immediately and bring in another teacher within the month. Regardless of how well Peter had performed, any and every American, in their minds, was undeniably expendable. This very real fact frightened her. She would have to carefully craft a strategy convincing both of them that he knew nothing, but was close enough to be deemed dangerous.

Song May had recently begun thinking about the prospect of having to kill Peter. It wasn't that she wondered if she could do it, she was certain she could, notwithstanding her affections. Rather, her thoughts involved calculating the pros and cons of killing him. Was it worth it to kill him?

Song May, an emotional and sometimes hysterical woman in the eyes of her superiors, considered all decisions with reason and logic. She analyzed every potential scenario in her head and only came to a conclusion after every angle had been considered and the most reasonable choice was evident. Decisions affecting her love life were similarly analyzed, her affair with Peter being the surprising exception. In calculating her next move, she wouldn't have the luxury of frivolity because too much was at stake. If she disobeyed an order to kill Peter, she would not only be risking her own wellbeing, but also her family's safety. If she chose to spare Peter and help him escape, she would betray her country. The prospect of such betrayal and ultimately having to flee the country that she would always love was devastating.

While these were all significant considerations, they paled in comparison to the loyalty and devotion that she felt to her deceased grandfather. If she betrayed her country, she did not think she could ever deal with the guilt that she would feel for destroying the Chen family name and causing the posthumous loss of face of her grandfather. She felt his presence constantly and he remained her absolute rock of certainty through the constant turmoil she had endured since the beginning of this current assignment. With all this in mind, the decision was clear if it needed to be made, but she was sure she'd spend sleepless nights questioning her judgment.

Chapter 22

Scott knocked on the CEO's door and entered without listening for a 'come in.' He had known David for 10 years, and happily for both of them, their working relationship only enhanced their friendship. That was until the last few weeks.

Scott entered with his usual easy air of confidence and nonchalance, but felt a bit of trepidation as he crossed the threshold to David's office. Scott had felt the general stress level within the company increase when Chinese companies had begun announcing new technologies, but the overwhelming consensus was that it could never happen to them. It was somewhat akin to a proactive neglect of reality. Since the IPO announcement of Chinasea Technologies, which three days ago had leaked to the media that they had developed groundbreaking technology involving Nanotubes, the mood around the offices had been depressing. During the last 48 hours, Sageware's stock had fallen from a high of $68 per share to its current price of $2.30, and the only thing keeping it above $2.00 was a massive purchasing scheme by Sageware to stem the Tsunami-like devastation.

With pre-announcements of groundbreaking, totally disruptive technology, Sageware had risen meteorically over the last year and very few had exercised their stock options, thinking that the rise would continue in perpetuity. Every employee, from the receptionist to the CEO, who had all counted their riches and only two weeks ago were racing to the office and gladly putting in 18-hour days, now had trouble crawling out of bed and even making it to the office before 9:00. No impassioned speeches or company parties at the trendiest bars could boost morale. Top programmers were already starting to leave, and for the top software engineers, base salaries had to be increased substantially to retain them to work on projects that had already made it to market. The company was collapsing.

Scott felt horrible about the entire situation. Regardless of the concerted effort to distance himself, the crisis that had ensued since the completion of his mission had thrown his life into complete disarray. He now wondered why he hadn't foreseen the aftermath of his mission and realized that he must've blocked the repercussions of his espionage out of his conscious thought. He no longer felt any loyalty to the Chinese Communist regime, and despite his attempts to continue life as usual, he felt unmotivated at work and distant at home. It was suddenly clear to him that it could not be any other way. Returning to normalcy was not an option. For the first time in his life he was at a loss of what to do next. He was hoping to delay his meeting with David Biddleberry, the man who had built the company from his dorm room as an undergraduate at Stanford and hired Scott as the company's fifth employee. He had betrayed his closest friend and confidant and was wondering if it had been worth it. He had been so driven to succeed in his mission, but now in the aftermath, he suddenly had clarity and felt his mission had been pointless. Thirty years of brainwashing had played its course and had now lost its efficacy. He was serving a country where he no longer belonged. He caught David's eyes immediately as he sat down and saw a look that he had never witnessed before: defeat.

"Scott, thanks for stopping by. If you're like the rest of the company, you haven't been able to get much work done recently. I'd like to get an update on some of the projects you've been working on besides the Nanotubes research, but that can wait for another day." As David spoke he stood and motioned for Scott to take a seat in the comfortable chairs located in the far corner of his office. They both sat and said nothing for a few seconds.

"How you holding up, Dave?" Scott finally broke the silence with an innocuous question.

"Jesus, I have no idea where the fuck to begin. I had thought of a thousand scenarios of how this company could fail and I made sure that we took precautions to prevent them from ever happening. We had the best researchers in the industry, a work environment cited in Forbes as one of the top 100 companies to work for in America, a loyal staff with a low rate of attrition, and we're involved in today's hottest area of technology. Shit, we have the most advanced security systems and checks and balances in the industry, designed to prevent a catastrophe from occurring. Never would I have guessed that we could have been sabotaged by the Chinese, and regardless of the fact that I had concocted at least a hundred possible scenarios of how this could have happened, I'm still utterly perplexed. It's an absolute fuckin' nightmare."

Again, silence. Scott didn't know what to say, but he could tell David was setting him up for a surreptitious interrogation. Scott greatly respected David's intelligence and his capacity to manipulate and gather information from his adversaries, but he had been trained to identify and calmly deflect techniques used to obtain knowledge. He put his game face back on and realized that this meeting could completely ruin him. He empathized with David, but this was business.

"Let me know what needs to be done, what strategy you plan to use to take on the Chinese." Scott wanted the company to remain solvent and ultimately succeed. His loyalties to David and Sageware outweighed most everything else, besides his self-preservation.

"I just don't know, Scott. I've been unable to think about anything besides doomsday scenarios. I can't focus on anything except the break-up value of the company. I'm in salvage mode right now, I just don't think there's a way to save us."

"David, there's so much more to the company than just Nanotechnology. What about the inroads we've made with our software applications that will allow more secure internal corporate communications? That's a growing field. It's also groundbreaking and we're currently the market leaders. Once 5G is introduced by the major telecoms, our stock, as well as company morale, will be flying again." Scott was making an excellent point, the company was close to profitability and revenues were increasing 35% year-over-year. Sageware's future would no doubt have been the Nanotube project, but even without it, other projects were still viable.

"Scott, I wrapped our future around Nanotubes. As a percentage of revenues, we've invested an inordinate amount of cash flow on research and development. We're leveraged to the hilt. I'm meeting with bankers this very afternoon to restructure our debt, and if we don't hammer out an agreement, Sageware will be liquidated within 60 days." David was speaking vehemently and Scott didn't know if his anger was directed at him or at the situation in general. He felt that David was blaming him for the current predicament.

"Shit, I had no idea we were so leveraged. What about a potential suitor or white knight who could swoop in and bail us out? I know we had talks with Middleqwest and Andotech, have any of those discussions resulted in anything?" Scott was grabbing for anything he could think of.

"Do you seriously think anyone would continue to have interest in us after last week's news? Are you fuckin' mad? Scott, I don't even want to fuckin' discuss this anymore. I've gone over every possible scenario and the only solution that will keep us solvent in the short-term is a reprieve from the banks. Yes, many companies were interested and a deal could have been struck in days if we were the same company that we were last month. Nobody is interested in our software, what attracted them was our R&D department and our groundbreaking discoveries. This reality is obvious to every one of our senior executives, except you. Why is that Scott?" Scott took the position that the question was rhetorical, though it was obvious David was looking for an answer. The pre-dance warm-up was over and the waltz was about to begin.

"I'm just trying to look for a solution. That's what I was hired to do. There has to be a way out of this. I'm as devastated as you are, but now is the time to take definitive action and map out a step-by-step plan to bring this company back to life. We cannot continue to dwell on the negative. David, I've never seen you like this." David nodded but said nothing. They both sat there for a minute, looking at each other, trying to read each other's most inner thoughts, but both were as tough to read as any executive in the Valley.

"Scott, how long have we've known each other? Ten, fifteen years it must be by now. You're a trusted friend and my most loyal confidant inside the company. We've accomplished great things together and I hope in the future we'll continue to collaborate. I need to ask you, I just have to hear it from your mouth," David hesitated, but continued before Scott had a chance to speak. "Are you involved in any way with the stealing of company secrets and transferring them to the Chinese government?" David spoke slowly and enunciated each word for full effect.

Only two other executives within the company had the same level of access as Scott, but neither of the other two was capable enough to organize the information in such a manner that would be useful to anyone who had not been involved in the research from the beginning. Scott was the only one. Of course, David thought, he employed executives of Indian descent, African Americans, Hispanics, and Caucasians, but he had ruled each one out as the Judas with the primary reason that each was too cowardly to commit such an act. Also, he thought, the Chinese couldn't provide the kind of money that would entice a top executive of his company, or any successful technology company, to sell secrets. They were all already rich enough. There had to be a greater cause, one of Nationalism. The trader had to want to help China improve itself and compete with America on a level playing field. In some areas the Chinese were twenty years behind and from what David ascertained, they wanted to leap frog into the information age, skipping all of the grunt work that the rest of the developed world had endured for a generation. It was with these thoughts that David admittedly hastily concluded that Scott was involved in the espionage.

"No," Scott said, adding nothing more, knowing that David would continue his assault.

"Scott, I think you are involved. I know you came to America when you were three and have about as much of a link with China as I do, but your parents were from China as well as your ancestry. Regardless of how Americanized you are, it's obvious there's a link. I'm sure you wouldn't deny that. And this link is what led you to want to help your brethren across the Pacific. It's obviously not the money; none of us need any. Yes, the stock has tanked, but even so, every member of the executive team is a millionaire many times over. And Scott, no one else, including the other Chinese members of the executive staff, has the intelligence to pull this off. Why the fuck did you do this to me?" David was methodical as he

129

was with all matters concerning the company. He spoke with equanimity, neither raising his voice nor showing any emotion. Even his last question was almost deadpan.

"David, your normal level of paranoia has ballooned to unhealthy proportions. I'm insulted and deeply disturbed by your accusations. I had nothing to do with any form of corporate espionage. My stake in this company is almost as great as yours and my research has helped the company thrive and reach a position atop the tech world. This company would not be nearly as successful without me. And as you point out, I have no ties or loyalties to China. I arrived in this country as a baby and spent my life as an American. You're attempting to persecute me unjustly. I can say unequivocally and to your face, I had nothing to do with the transfer of information from Sageware to the Chinese. I regret what has happened as much as you do and would like to find a solution so we can move forward and achieve some of the goals that we've been dreaming about for ten years." Scott knew that this would be the last conversation he would ever have with David.

"I'm sorry," David softened. "I shouldn't accuse you. This whole Chinagate incident has put the entire technology industry on alert and pushed this company over the edge. Nobody knows who's going to be hit next. I've heard that companies throughout the Valley, Seattle, and Austin are refusing to hire new employees with even a hint of Chinese ancestry and at the same time laying off an inordinate amount of Chinese workers to avoid the problem in the future. Class action discrimination lawsuits have already been filed against at least ten companies, but the CEOs I've spoken with don't seem to care; they're in survival mode. It is all anyone is talking about nowadays. I'm sure you can sympathize with my position." David hadn't finished grilling Scott, but wanted to see if he could induce some sympathy and get him to relax a little and perhaps open up.

"What have you heard from the FBI?" Scott asked. "Do they have any leads? Surely they must be working with you and the other CEOs whose companies are affected. What have they come up with?" Scott was selfishly curious to know, but doubted if Biddleberry would give any specifics. Though it was improbable

130

that David knew anything that had not already been reported by the press.

"Yes, I've been working with them and have actually been on their asses since the story broke. They're probably getting sick of me, but fuck 'em. Chinagate has been going on for a year with seemingly no progress. It's an outrage. Just yesterday one of the supposed higher-ups in the CIA told me the investigation was moving forward. When I grilled him for specifics, he balked, but I believe the CIA does have a cadre of people combing the streets of Beijing for clues."

David was hoping for a change of expression in Scott's demeanor, a slight twitch, a drop of perspiration, a sweat ring around his pits: anything that would indicate nerves. But he saw nothing. Scott was the calmest and most confident person under pressure that he'd ever met. He was so completely sure of himself in every situation, whether at work or a social situation. When they were younger and around women, or in a physically dangerous situation, Scott always knew what to do and never overreacted, to the point of being abnormal. David's instincts were excellent as well and he was positive Scott was guilty, but he knew this conversation was going nowhere.

"Let me know how I can help, I hope our friendship and the company can move beyond this," Scott offered.

"Scott, did you have any involvement in this? The writing is on the wall for all to see, I just need your confirmation."

"Fuck, David, you don't need anyone's confirmation. Evidently your mind has already been made up and nothing I say or do to express my loyalty to you and the company will make a difference. Your trust in me has eroded; perhaps it would be best if I moved on. This is fucking unbelievable." Scott was on the edge of his seat. He felt the life that he had spent fifteen years building disintegrating before his eyes.

"No, Scott! What has happened to this company is what's totally fuckin' unfathomable." As he spoke, David walked back to his desk and opened the middle drawer. "You're guilty and I couldn't give a shit how cool you are under pressure, you are fucking involved in this and I want to know why. Come on, Scott. I'm not wearing a wire, the damage has been done, it's just you and me. Tell me why you did this and stop being a pussy."

"David, what the hell are you talking about? I helped build this company and I refuse to watch you just give up. We've surmounted …"

"I am sick of your fucking bullshit. Only one person could've done this, only one person smart enough, confident enough, and with the access to pull it off." David was yelling now and both had stood up and were facing each other across David's desk. "That person is you, Scott. But, I want to hear you say it. I want you to fuckin' admit it and I want to see you burn in fuckin' hell." As he said this, David reached into the drawer and pulled out a 9-millimeter Smith and Wesson, calmly lifted his arm, and pointed the pistol at Scott's heart.

"Now, tell me." Both men remained silent, both waiting for the other to flinch.

"Drop the gun, David," Scott almost whispered. "This is not China and I am not a Chinese National. I will not be coerced to confess to a crime that I did not perpetrate. Put that gun down and I will walk out of here and never return."

"I have nothing to lose, Scott. You've taken the only sure thing in my life from me. You're guilty and I will get my confession with whatever method that works. The gun is loaded and I will use it. Tell me who you are working for and why you've done it. I have to know." David stood motionless, with his outstretched arm less than three feet from Scott's heart.

"David, you've lost it! Your dream is gone and all you have left is what's standing before me—a pathetic, insecure failure. If you choose to shoot me, so be it. I'm ready to die. What I've endured throughout my life is something you can never even begin to fathom. Go ahead and pull the fuckin' trigger, come play in my world. Come on, go ahead." They were both silent. "You don't have the fuckin' balls to fire that gun. Now, I'm gonna walk out that door and never return and I'll pray that you pull that trigger and join me in hell."

Scott turned his back and walked out the door. Although David refused to lower the gun, he stood there wishing he had the courage to shoot. Scott Chen deserved nothing less.

Scott left Sageware shortly after 3:00 p.m. He had been played for a pawn, brainwashed and indoctrinated by a malevolent government. He wondered if he had any possible options for making things better, anything at all.

He thought about how easy life was when he first came to America. He fit right in as if he had lived his whole life in the States. Every aspect of his first thirteen years of life had prepared him well for the very individualistic America. The culture shock and fear of fitting in never materialized. Scott's English also proved to be undecipherable from anyone else's. Except for the occasional slang expression, he was always able to understand everything anyone said. He found it almost amazing, he reflected as he drove home, how he could learn English in the confines of a classroom in China and come to America and be considered a native. All of the studying and exhaustive repetition had paid off. It was the first time in his life that he had experienced true freedom. His previous life was extremely regimented and accounted for down to every minute of every day. His pseudo parents didn't need to care for him, and besides the occasional PTA meetings and showing up perfunctorily at his soccer matches, they mostly stayed out of his life.

His previous life contained intense competition with people of similar abilities. Going to America and competing with normal, everyday kids seemed easy. In a country that admires confidence, individuality, and accomplishment, Scott could do no wrong. He was an instant hit among his new classmates, and became a class leader, academic award winner, and a star in soccer as well as the high jump. His success in America threatened to go to his head on many occasions, but his thirteen years of training in China kept him focused on his mission and the constant watch from big brother in China also left him vigilant, knowing he had no escape. The fear the Communists had instilled in him as a child reverberated through his subconscious and kept him focused, though the allure of having a normal, carefree American life was ever-present. He enjoyed his childhood and longed for those innocent days.

He pulled into his driveway and the recurring thought again entered his mind—why hadn't he escaped when he knew he could? He had planned down to the very last detail how he could disappear and take his family with him. They would never have found him and yet he still couldn't come up with a plausible explanation of why he had stayed, concluding that the constant training, intimidation, and fear that his masters instilled in him for thirteen years was the obvious answer. Would he ever escape them? Maybe he still had time to disappear and right his wrongs … maybe.

Chapter 23

Tommy met Winston Chang at their offices in downtown Beijing. They both avoided going to the office of their consulting company because it always reminded them of how much work they were not doing to maintain the legally legitimate reason for both of them being in China. The receptionist had about ten messages for each of them from Chinese companies that had been promised meetings with U.S. importers and led to believe that signed contracts were imminent. Every time they entered the 13th floor office, they both instantly realized how difficult it was to run a successful consulting company and also how much they both hated it. Facades needed to be maintained, but more importantly, salaries needed to be paid to the Chinese receptionist and administrative assistants who ended up doing most of the work.

Tommy quickly checked his messages and heard the familiar voice of Charlie Wang, the man from Jiangsu Province who had given him Shue's name about a month ago, and was now, in exchange, looking for what he assumed would be a sizable investment in his city. Something was going to have to be done about this guy. He was becoming a nuisance and didn't seem to understand that he was being blown off. Budgets were so tight at the CIA that Tommy had very little wiggle room when it came to throwing cash around. He had done a couple of favors for a small time importer from Reston, Virginia who was looking for a good supplier in China a couple of years back. Through that connection the importer had become one of the top distributors in the U.S. of #2 pencils and other back-to-school products. This guy (Tommy couldn't remember his name) owed him and perhaps could be persuaded to make a purchase from one of the small factories located in Charlie's city. Tommy quickly put that on his two-page-long to-do list, grabbed a cup of freshly made coffee, and went in to the conference room to meet Winston, who had already been waiting for ten minutes.

"I'd thought you'd be running in here to hear what I have to say, what the hell were you doing in your office for so long?" Winston asked.

"I'm trying to run a business and if it weren't for frequent cash infusions from headquarters we'd have been bankrupt long ago. This pencil pushing stuff is not exactly my forte."

"I've noticed."

Tommy sat down and placed the cup of coffee on the mahogany conference table, spilling some in the process and burning his hand. Any meeting of a confidential nature always took place in the conference room on the 13th floor. The room was checked nightly with the same equipment that the embassies used to check for bugs and any other high-tech listening devices. It was completely secure.

One of Tommy's responsibilities was to make initial contacts and put out feelers with government officials or well-connected businessmen who might have information they were willing to share. Tommy met a lot of people. He had the type of personality that left people at ease and instilled confidence in them, a very rare gift that the CIA valued greatly. After assessing the trustworthiness of a person, Tommy would introduce the people he found most promising to an intermediate CIA operative, who in turn would look for any information that could be ascertained from a particular Chinese bureaucrat or businessman. These people never knew they were dealing with the CIA until they made contact with Winston.

Initial contacts were made among many people, either at U.S. trade shows or gatherings of businessmen. The potential suppliers of information would never have been able to guess the connection among Tommy, the intermediate operative, and Winston.

Winston knew Beijing better than anyone in the agency, and though the CIA had many agents of Chinese ancestry, Winston was one of the few who could completely pass as Chinese: down to his standard Beijing accent and vernacular, the way he carried himself, and his understanding of the adversary's thought process. He was one of the agency's most trusted agents. Tommy had worked with him on numerous occasions and been surprised at his phenomenal success rate. He wondered what Winston had for him today.

"Okay, Winston, you've piqued my interest. I'm sorry we didn't catch up with each other sooner. I'm anxious to hear how the surveillance has been going with Shue and what leads you've come up with. You mentioned that you have something that will floor me. I find it hard to believe. This case has consumed me for the last year and at this point I doubt anything you say will garner more than a raised eyebrow; please prove me wrong." Over the last two weeks Tommy had become a bit exasperated with the case. Every lead went nowhere and the pressure from headquarters, as well the White House, had recently grown dramatically.

"I'd usually prefer announcing I had nothing and have you pleasantly surprised. I learned long ago that high expectations tend to disappoint, but in this instance my recent surveillance has led to a monumental case-breaking discovery. I spent the last ten days following Shue's every move. It was really quite easy once I picked up the trail. His schedule changes very little, though his workaholic routine combined with his penchant for partying and beautiful women did wear me down to the point that I'm still recovering. As you suspected, he is inextricably involved in the day-to-day operations of the six companies that recently announced breakthroughs of the stolen technologies. He has also recently visited three other companies in the High Dian district, probably to prep them for their own announcements. The espionage seems never-ending. I listed the names of these companies and the officers in the brief report that I've prepared."

"Is there any way to get information on the type of software these companies are currently developing to see if there is a match with an American company?" Tommy asked. "It would be great if we could warn a few future victims of the imminent threat of losing their Intellectual Property."

"The problem with these companies is that they are all small, government-backed startups. As best as I can guess, there is a very precarious relationship between the Communists and the executive teams of the start-ups. In exchange for funding and preferential treatment, each company allows the Party to be involved in the daily running of the business. The Party, in exchange for quasi-obedience from the best tech minds in the country, voluntarily limits its prying and gives these companies free access to all top-secret military technology that could assist in developing IP for their nascent high-tech sector. Notwithstanding a recent surge in Nationalism, these kids are the brightest minds in China and without such perks would not waste their time essentially working for the government. They could command ten times the salary working for a U.S. tech giant, not to mention more prestige. To answer your question, the government protects these companies as if they are the most confidential state secrets. It's very difficult to obtain any information or even attempt to find informants; the risk is just too great. Recent media coverage in the U.S. and China has also put these companies on even higher alert, so the prospect of gaining entrance is close to nil. That said, I have put out preliminary feelers and will let you know if I find anything."

"Greatly appreciated," Tommy said. "So Shue seems to be the Communist Party representative and liaison to these companies. From your preliminary report on Shue, he is the perfect candidate. Modern, a very atypical Party member who can relate to a younger more carefree and independent generation, yet he spent twenty years in the military and Chinese Secret Service and served as a diplomat in America on two different occasions. He's from an old communist family with connections at every level, but he was most deserving of all his promotions on merit alone, refusing to rely on his family's position. A rare communist indeed. If need be, we may have to set up a meeting with Shue, presenting ourselves as representatives of U.S. companies who wish to do business with the newly-minted Chinese software giants, but I fear the negative press if they publicly announce that they were pursuing such a partnership.

"A meeting with Shue would be difficult under any circumstances," Winston stated, "but nearly impossible at this time. The situation is too precarious, and from recent intelligence reports, the Party is extremely worried about all of the negative press emanating from the U.S. One report hinted that the entire Standing Committee is glued to the TV watching live broadcasts of CNN's comprehensive coverage of Chinagate. They are worried and ready to tighten their reigns. I feel our window of opportunity is closing rapidly."

"Yes, you may be right. In any case, I think I'll make a discreet attempt to organize a meeting with Shue or one of the CEOs of the six Chinese companies. It's unlikely that we'll discover anything new, but even the slightest bit of information may lead to a domino effect. I feel we are teetering on the brink of discovery and the right lead could vault us over the fence. Before you move on, was there anything else about Shue's routine or the people he made contact with that put up any red flags? You said he spent his downtime partying, who was he with? Party officials, business executives, any Caucasians in the mix?"

"At least two or three times, I did notice a fairly prominent government official in his party and a few known business executives, but generally he liked to spend time with the beautiful people—movie stars, models, and TV personalities. I never saw him with anyone besides his own countrymen."

"What else?"

"At the end of every day, he visits a non-descript building in a rundown but gentrifying area of Beijing. I didn't even attempt to enter the place for fear that I would draw attention to myself, deciding instead to watch Shue from the outside. Very few people came in or out during the day. I'm still unsure about what goes on inside the concrete walls of that building, but I think we'll be able to find out shortly. Shue would spend about an hour there every night and then go home and change into his evening attire. On the second to last night of my surveillance an unexpected surprise appeared from the building," Winston hesitated before he continued.

"What is this—a goddamn mystery novel? What the hell are you getting at? Come on, Winston, out with it. What do you want me to do, admit that I'm intrigued?"

"I was sitting in the café across the street from the compound, drinking watered-down green tea, when a white male about twenty-eight, twenty-nine years old walked quickly through the front gate and up the street toward the main road leading to downtown. He looked American by dress and appearance, an all-American boy type. He was wearing khakis and a blue-striped, oxford, button-down shirt: very preppy and unmistakably American. I abandoned my watch on Shue and followed him to a building where he must be renting a room. It was an old building, no doubt set for destruction. A light in an eighth floor window went on a few minutes after he entered the building; he remained there for about 30 minutes. I waited across the street reading the paper, and at about 9:00 p.m. he left the building heading north towards Beijing University. He turned down one of the side streets and entered a crowded bar. I followed him in and sat alone drinking while he mingled easily with both Chinese and other Americans. Though he was talking with an extremely attractive Chinese woman, he left alone and returned to his apartment at around 2:00 in the morning."

"Holy shit, what a stroke of luck." The wheels were moving, Tommy was instantly thinking of every possible scenario of how this American could be involved. A smile arose from the frown he had been sporting for the better part of two weeks.

Tommy continued with excitement, "This may be the link we've been looking for. I'm baffled as to what connection Shue and this American have, if any. Were you able to find out anything about him? Did you approach him at the bar or overhear any of his conversations?"

"No, nothing. He really didn't do anything out of the ordinary. Had a few drinks, spoke with some friends, and left. I wasn't clear on how to proceed and assumed that you'd be taking over the investigation from here. After leaving Shue's trail last night, I checked back in at the bar where the American went the other night. I believe it's called the Cowboy Bar; he was there again."

"I'm probably overly optimistic, every lead has led nowhere up to this point, but I think our luck is a changing. What did our American friend look like? I think I'll pay him a visit at the OK Corral tonight."

"Handsome, blond hair, parted to the side, about 6'0'', medium build with a fair complexion. You can't miss 'im."

"Okay, thanks, Winston, this may make our careers."

"Keep me in the loop," Winston said. "I'm off to the airport soon. I need to catch a flight to Shanghai tonight." The two men shook hands and exited the conference room together. Winston returned to his office and Tommy headed for his apartment to relax and form a strategy for tonight. He only had one chance to get this right; he had to prepare for every possible outcome. He had no idea what if anything he was going to say to his new best friend.

Chapter 24

Song May arrived early to the bi-monthly meeting with Shue and General Wang. Unsurprisingly, the impromptu meeting she had tried to schedule had been cancelled at the last second. Song May didn't find out until she reached the General's office and found him gone for the day. No explanation was given nor was a belated apology bestowed as Song May walked into his office and took a seat. Shue followed almost immediately and the meeting started more tensely than any previously had.

"Comrades, thank you for joining me today. There is much to discuss and I don't wish to bore you with the details of the five-day retreat with the Standing Committee of the Communist Party from which I have just returned. As both of you can imagine, the central topic of discussion was the events that have recently surfaced regarding the corporate espionage case. It seems that in the rush of success we might have gotten a bit ahead of ourselves."

Song May frowned at his use of words that were obviously avoiding the gravity of the matter.

Noticing her change of expression the General, uncharacteristically defensive, addressed Song May. "Comrade Chen, do you wish to add something to the discussion or shall I proceed?" He was sick of her. Her time was coming to an end; he would see to it.

"My apologies, I meant no disrespect." Song May could almost feel the General's blood pressure rising; she had overstepped her boundaries with a simple frown. It was a poor start to an already tense meeting.

"The media circus over the last couple of months has caused the leadership to reevaluate our project. They're extremely disturbed that we have failed to maintain control of the actions of our agents in the field. The goal was to have a slow, methodical transfer of key U.S. technologies with an aim of developing commercially viable products in China and once and for all leap-frogging the technical superiority of the West and gaining the respect we so aptly deserve. We were to see Mao Ze Dong's vision of

142

reestablishing the Middle Kingdom as the most powerful nation on Earth to its fruition. Comrades, what has gone wrong?" The question was asked almost rhetorically and in a pleading voice, but it was clear that the General was visibly upset. He had taken a grilling from the Standing Committee over the events of the last month and this was the first time since his return that he had the chance to vent and transfer blame to his subordinates.

"General Wang," Shue began deferentially, "our fundamental success of the entire corporate espionage program has been based on our agents going completely native. After they graduate college and enter the workforce, we completely cut off all contact with them. The agents who had acted as the parents are relieved of their commission and given new assignments within the U.S. This carefully calculated strategy initially laid out by Mao himself leads to agents that are beyond suspicion and thus able to gain the trust of the executives of the companies they infiltrate and gain access to the most sensitive documents. It has been the key to our success. Unfortunately, one of the repercussions of cutting off all contact is that we no longer have total control of their actions. The training and indoctrination we provide to the agents as children almost ensures that they remain loyal, but I can only guess that once the first so-called transfer was made, the pressure for the others to follow suit became too much for even the most disciplined agents to handle. Admittedly, the flurry of information in such rapid succession was unintended, but the benefits to the six companies that inherited this technology are immeasurable. And with all due respect, General, just weeks ago you and your colleagues didn't seem to have a problem with the pace." Shue delivered the last line in the most deferential way possible, but he couldn't resist calling Wang out on his sudden hypocrisy. Shue suddenly felt vulnerable and worried he would have to take the fall for the General.

"Mr. Shue, I understand how the operation works, what I fail to grasp is why the two of you did not establish a proper procedure. If the agents had resisted the temptation and bided their time for a few extra months, our operation could have gone on indefinitely. Weren't they trained to withstand intense pressure? I need answers and I need solutions. How could the two of you have fucked up so badly?"

Song May chose her words carefully so as not to further upset the already irate general. "General Wang, there are also extenuating circumstances that we wouldn't be able to control even if we had maintained contact. Our agents have been gathering information over a long stretch of time and if the technology is being prepared for release in America, in many cases, they have no choice but to finish their mission and send what they have."

"Understood, Comrade, perhaps they should have waited for the next new discovery once they saw how the media had pounced on this story. There was an obvious lapse of planning by the both of you."

Song May responded, "General, some of our agents have been undercover for ten plus years. Even the most patient agents are stretched to their limits after such a long period of time. The pressure is unbearable. We ask them to become American in every respect, but they must hide their real identities. Imagine having a spouse who assumes she knows you, but in fact hasn't the slightest idea who you really are; it must be maddening. I suspect a domino effect: once the first announcement was made, every one of our people wanted to complete the assignment before the scrutiny became intolerable. Having been in America for so long, they understand the media better than we do, they must've expected a frenzy would ensue and wanted to be out of the line of fire. Their missions complete, they assumed they would now be able to begin lives as true Americans, something I imagine they long for after such an extended period of time undercover. I might add, General, that it was ultimately the Standing Committee's decision to release the specific technology to our companies. They could have sat on the information until the media got bored or used the material to develop new, more advanced technologies to be released at a later date. News of the information did not have to be released to the public; it could have remained top-secret and used as a springboard to launch our own Silicon Valley in the years to come. General, my apologies for my insubordination, but it's quite obvious the Standing Committee and the other rulers of the Communist Party became intoxicated with all of the money that was being made on the Hong Kong Stock Exchange and it was greed that clouded their judgments and influenced their decisions to proceed down this catastrophic path. The agents acted honorably."

"Comrade Chen," the General began mockingly. "So experienced, so knowledgeable, comprehending all aspects of all situations," the General continued condescendingly. "Always quick with an answer and solution, able to fix any problem. I assume you understand the extent of your accusations? Men have been beheaded for far less. Your value is diminishing and incompetence increasing. I shall repeat this for the very last time," his voice rising with each sentence, "your opinion is unwelcome. I want only facts; cease second-guessing the Standing Committee. You do so at your peril. Our project is not yet in jeopardy of being relegated to the chopping block. The Committee unanimously agrees that the long-term survival of this project is primary to national security and development, but all agents currently in the field are to go into stealth mode, scaling back all espionage activities until tensions have eased. We must proceed with caution and patience. Comrade Chen, I want these agents contacted and made aware of the gravity of the situation, making it clear that this order is coming straight from the President. Deploy the predetermined emergency procedure. The President has been under intense strain trying to deal with an unforeseen crisis. He has spoken with his counterpart in the U.S. every day for the last two weeks and the Secretary of State is planning an unscheduled visit to China next week. They are recommending a joint U.S.-Sino taskforce to stem the growing tide of corporate espionage. We have balked at such a proposal, insisting that no problem exists and that China has simply caught up in the high-tech arena. The U.S. is threatening to block imports of our goods if we do not cooperate. The resulting economic turmoil would be catastrophic.

"We will of course threaten with retaliatory measures, but it's quite clear that we would feel the major brunt of any such sanctions. Due to the very precarious grip on power the Party maintains and the increasing unrest among the peasants in the countryside, any unnecessary instability must be avoided.

"I admit that many inside the Party have gotten rich through the recent IPOs of the six chosen companies, and in hindsight perhaps we should have proceeded more cautiously, but that is water under the bridge. We must now focus on the steps needed to guarantee the future success of our project," the General finished.

Both Shue and Song May were surprised at the General's admissions. They had never before heard him even hint at the possibility of impropriety of a member of the Standing Committee. They were both suspicious of his candidness.

"Now, comrades, I'm quite certain that at this very moment the CIA is tracking down every plausible lead both here and in the U.S. We need to troubleshoot, plug the leaks, and return to the fundamentals that led to our initial successes. What must be done?" As the General spoke, his mind wandered to the Standing Committee. He started to think that he would eventually take the fall for their current predicament. He knew his prospects of being invited to serve on the most elite boys club in the world were now nearly impossible, but he also feared that his corner office in the politburo and his command atop the secret service, as well as the numerous perks that accompany such power, were also in jeopardy. He wondered if Comrades Shue and Chen could see the fear on his face. He hoped he had done well to conceal it.

Song May piped up, "General, I have already contacted our agents scattered across the United States who are still in school and they are aware that nothing has changed and they are to continue their assignments as given. As for the agents currently working for U.S. companies, we must assume they have already taken the necessary precautions. Besides the demise of the mission, their very survival and life in America is in jeopardy. They are the smartest we have and we must assume they will act appropriately. If need be, I can use the emergency contact procedure, but it is a last resort. "

"Shue, what steps are being taken on your end?" the general asked.

"General, we have ceased all discussions with potential U.S. and European partners. We will put together a viable organization and increase our research and development teams in all six companies to ensure that the information gathered will lead to successful product and software development. We are carefully screening all new employees and debriefing current ones, putting them on alert that classified information is only to be shared with trusted colleagues. The executives are all aware of the gravity of the situation. I still believe the best course of action is to eventually partner with powerful companies in the West to bring these products to market expeditiously, but we have put all discussions on the backburner until media scrutiny subsides."

The General nodded, "Very good. Ah, yes, Comrade Shue, beginning immediately you are to remove yourself from the limelight and tone down your, how should I put it, hectic lifestyle. Your ubiquitous presence at news conferences, your capacity to always be in front of the camera at the most opportune times, and your impeccable wardrobe has not been favorably received by a few of the Party hardliners. We are not mafia dons and you'd be advised to curb your flamboyancy. The government openly admits to having stakes in some of the top technology companies, but we insist, regardless of the truth, that it is investment alone and we maintain no influence over the day-to-day operations of the company. Having our top liaison so visibly present sends the wrong signal and questions have been raised as to your exact role with these six companies. Please display some tact."

"Understood, General Wang. The six companies continue to perform well on the Hong Kong Stock Exchange. All six companies remain well above their IPO prices and have held up despite all of the negative publicity. I'm sure this pleases the Standing Committee." Shue couldn't control his desire to openly air that the greatest beneficiaries of the entire project were the higher-ups in the Communist Party. He assumed Wang was now worth millions. Though, Shue thought, he shouldn't be a hypocrite. The IPOs had added millions to his own offshore bank accounts. Wang ignored the comment, but stored it away for possible later use.

Wanting to end on a positive note and convince Shue and Song May that they were safe from retribution, he moved the conversation back to the current project and focused on the issues of the day. "Okay, as for our current situation, how are our new recruits progressing? If I'm not mistaken, we have three or four who are ready to make the trip across the Pacific."

"Our latest crop of recruits is our best ever and should lay the foundation for future success stories. They have all performed admirably in physical training and academics, and are the most mentally strong group I've seen since our very first class. I might also add that they are all as American as apple pie. They have perfect English and an outstanding grasp of U.S. culture, history, and the complexities of the relationships that will affect them upon entry. Their progress had been remarkable."

"Thank you for the update, Comrade Shue. On a positive note, the Standing Committee and all of the prominent Party officials that attended the retreat were quite amused at the ineptness of the U.S. authorities in the investigation of our corporate espionage. They have made no arrests and seem to have very few leads. With all of the media attention and the length of time that has passed since the first secrets were made public, it is most astounding that not one of our agents has been detained. This is a great leap forward and quite different from all previous attempts to infiltrate U.S. companies for either economic or military reasons. In previous efforts our agents stuck out like weeds in a perfectly groomed field, but now, even though all evidence points to Chinese involvement, our people remain safe. The Standing Committee is genuinely impressed and almost baffled at the success of our training methods. I do not need to repeat myself, but they once again emphasized how easily our agents have blended into mainstream America and attribute much of the success to rigorous training in the English language and U.S. culture."

"Yes, General," Shue agreed, "and I think our language and culture program has taken us to a new level of excellence, but recently I'm starting to think that bringing in outsiders may be more risky than it's worth. I'm beginning to suspect our current teacher has discovered something. He seems distracted. Comrade Chen, have you any explanation for the recent change in his demeanor?"

All four eyes shifted to Song May and she hesitated before responding to their very innocent inquiry.

"Yes, he has been acting strange and a bit distant," Song May was almost 100% positive she wasn't being followed. Wang had tried once before and within 24 hours she discovered the tail and sent a message back to the General, along with two broken legs, to never do that again. He never did.

Song May continued, "I've questioned him, but he seems reluctant to share his thoughts. This is quite odd because he has been extremely open with me thus far. I really don't know what to make of it, but I will reemphasize that he is extremely intelligent and I would not be surprised if he started wondering about the geniuses that he is training and their real future careers. He has served us well and should be deported as I previously suggested. It is the only way to confidently close up a potential leak and not arouse additional suspicions from the U.S. government. I would recommend hiring a new teacher and sending this one home immediately."

"In the current environment I would tend to agree with you, Comrade Chen. But wouldn't it be best to just kill him? What if he has made a discovery?"

"Although that is possible, he is not acting overly nervous. I think any ideas he has are merely guesses. I don't believe he has anything concrete. In this environment, I don't think we want any more American blood on our hands. We send him home immediately, case closed. Another death would create another problem that we just don't have time to deal with now." Song May was making a logical case; it served her interests and was best for the project. She again thought of the personal trauma she would have to deal with after killing Peter. It was not a thought she enjoyed dwelling on.

"Comrade Shue, what do you think?" the General asked.

"The students respect him and have learned a great deal over the last few months, but under current circumstances I would have to defer to Comrade Chen's opinion and terminate his contract. We can ill afford any leaks at this juncture, but I would favor a deportation over execution."

"Yes, yes, we don't want to kill indiscriminately. If we can achieve the same results by sending the American home, then perhaps that is the best route to take. But if we send him home and he does alert authorities to whatever he thinks he knows, that could cause irreparable damage to our already precarious position. An American 10-feet under would be safer, no? Of course, another death wouldn't do much to smooth already strained U.S.-Sino relations." Wang hesitated, wiped his forehead with a handkerchief, and breathed laboriously. "I do apologize; it has been a long day. Let me sleep on it. Comrade Chen, I'll let you know of my decision for the fate of the American over the next day or two."

"Yes, General. Will that be all?" Song May asked.

"Yes, thank you both for coming. Please keep me informed of any unforeseen developments." The three of them stood and exited the building together. Shue and General Wang's chauffeurs were waiting at the curb and Song May headed east on foot through Tiananmen Square. It was an ideal night to walk the five kilometers home, cool with no breeze, a perfect, early autumn evening. She was still unsure of what would happen to Peter and the General had done little to assuage her worst fears.

Chapter 25

As Scott weaved his way through the tree-lined suburban streets on his way home, he tried to think of a way to reveal his true identity to Jane. Scott had thought of 100 different ways to break the news, but each ended in disaster. He finally settled on silence. At some point the truth would be known and Scott feared the end of his charade was drawing near. He had called to tell Jane that he would be home from work early and when he entered the front door, he found the kids gone and Jane sitting at the kitchen table crying.

"What happened? What happened? Why are you crying? Where are the kids, did something happen to them? What happened to the kids? Jane, Stop crying and talk to me." Scott took his wife by the hands and waited patiently for her to calm down.

"The kids are fine, I sent them down the street to Karen and Bill's house for the afternoon, they'll be back for dinner." She removed two tissues from the box, blew her nose, and wiped the dripping mascara from her face.

"What's the matter then, honey? What's wrong?" In retrospect Scott should have known the reason for his wife's tears, but over the last month he hadn't even thought about how his moods were affecting her. He was completely perplexed.

"You're having an affair." And with that she burst into hysterics, crying uncontrollably.

"What, what are you talking about? What, are you crazy? Jane, Jane! How could you ever come to such a conclusion? I would never have an affair." He tried to console her. "Jane, honey, stop crying and look at me. You're the love of my life. I adore you as much now as I did on our wedding day. I knew at once when I saw you in the library at MIT that you were the one. I knew instantly and I still know. There will never be anyone else. Where did you get such a thought?"

Jane wiped the tears from her eyes with the back of her hand and let out a small laugh of embarrassment. She thought of what she must've looked like to Scott as he walked in the house. She tried to regain her composure.

"Scott, what am I supposed to think? We haven't had sex in a month and you've been so distant. You've been spending almost every waking minute either at work or in your self-prescribed Siberia in the basement. I wake in the middle of the night expecting to find a warm body to hold and the only thing I get is a handful of cold sheets. About the only time you resemble yourself is with the kids, but they have even started asking what's wrong with you. You've lost ten pounds, you barely touch your food at dinner, and you don't participate in dinner conversation. You're off in space somewhere while your family remains on Earth attempting to maintain some semblance of a normal life. I don't know, I just can't go on like this. What's wrong?" Tears started rolling down Jane's face once again, but her eyes were intense and focused on Scott who had taken a seat next to her at the table.

"I'm sorry." Scott didn't know how to start and Jane barely gave him a chance to gather his thoughts.

"I need more than that, Scott. I've been giving you the benefit of the doubt for the last month, attributing your silence to some nascent Chinese cultural response to conflict. I need to know what's going on in your head. If you don't start communicating with me, our marriage is doomed. Scott, baby, tell me what's wrong."

"The pressure at work has been overwhelming. This whole Chinagate fiasco has the entire company wondering if I sold company secrets to the Chinese. The entire company is in disarray, the best software engineers have left, nobody trusts anyone anymore, and every Chinese employee has been ostracized. Scuffles have broken out three times in the halls and arguments among the rank and file are a daily occurrence. It's absolute mayhem. Everyone had been counting their millions for so long that the thought of becoming like every other white-collar zombie living from paycheck-to-paycheck sickens them. Each second feels like a minute, each minute an hour, and each day a month. Even David has thrown in the towel." By simply opening up just a little about what he had been going through over the last month, Scott's blood pressure seemed to decrease dramatically. He wondered why he hadn't at least somewhat confided in his wife before now.

"David's ready to give up? I can't believe it. Sageware is a diverse company with a wide product mix, can't you weather the storm?"

"David is handling the entire situation worse than I could have ever expected. The day he saw the news conference on CNBC of the Chinese company introducing groundbreaking technology on Nanotubes that resembled our own research to a tee, he had a fit, running around the office accusing every Asian employee in the company. He filed about ten lawsuits and injunctions that day and swore he would not rest until he found the "Chinc" who had stolen his baby. He's fuckin' gone off the deep end. Not that I can completely blame him; we spent years and 90% of our R&D budget developing a viable, marketable product based on Nanotechnology and I was the lead on most of it. I feel horrible as well, but if we don't regroup, the company will be bankrupt in 60 days. Shit, I have as much to lose as him, I invested my whole life into that place, but you don't see me accusing him of anything."

"He's accusing you, what did he say? Did he fire you? Scott, our mortgage, the kid's college fund. What are we going to do?"

"Relax, honey, relax. Everything's going to be okay. We'll get through this. David brought me into his office today and pointblank accused me of being the mastermind behind the corporate espionage. In his mind, I'm the mole; I'm guilty of sabotaging the company. He said he worked it out logically in his head and that I am the only person capable of pulling off such a scheme as well as the only person with the motive. I don't know. I don't really want to discuss it. I tried to focus on the positives and strategize for the future, but he didn't want to hear it. I don't know, like I said I can't blame him for being upset, but ... something in the case will have to break soon." Scott looked at his wife and waited for her next question. It was only a matter of time until she would ask and Scott preferred to get it out of the way.

"Scott, did you—did you have anything to do with it?" She looked at him intently and grabbed his hand as she waited for his response.

"No, no! I knew that you were going to ask me that question at some point and it's okay. I had nothing to do with the selling of Sageware's technology to the Chinese." Scott hated to be splitting hairs. He felt like Clinton must've felt when he was asked if he had ever had sexual relations with Monica Lewinsky. Technically Scott did not 'sell' anything to the Chinese. It was a rather feeble attempt to avoid the issue, but he wasn't prepared to tell her just yet. He certainly knew that at some point he would have to tell her, but he didn't know just how to do it and when. He felt most comfortable procrastinating as long as possible.

"I love you, Scott."

"I love you too, Janie, I love you too."

That night Scott and Jane had the best sex they had had in years. All the stress of recent months seemed to manifest into passionate lovemaking. Jane slept soundly for the first time in weeks and felt confident that the man next to her was the same man she had fallen in love with fifteen years ago. Scott, just as tired, was unable to rest his racing mind. He was still unsure what to do, but the realization that he probably had less than forty-eight hours to hatch a plan of action as well as a contingency plan was ever present. His survival was in jeopardy, but he thought very little of his own wellbeing, instead focusing on shielding his family from a possible devastating, unrecoverable upheaval of their lives. He whispered softly in Jane's ear, asking her continuously if she were awake until she woke up.

"What is it? Are the kids okay?" She was groggy and a bit disoriented. Scott could tell she was in a deep sleep, but this couldn't wait.

"The kids are fine. Jane I need to tell you something very important so please listen to every word I have to say." Jane leaned herself against the headboard, her eyes suddenly alert and focused on Scott. "Jane you remember where we always used to meet, when we first started dating."

"Of course I do, I could never forget. You would walk over to my study carrel and surprise me with a small gift. Do you know I still have every one of those gifts stored away in the closet? Remember the time after we had just gotten engaged and you gave me a drawing of the two of us in our wedding outfits getting married on a white beach on a small island in the Pacific. I still cry when I think of that picture."

"I remember. I drew that picture two days after we met and would look at it every night before I went bed. I dreamed of the day when that picture would be a reality."

"I would wait expectantly for my small treasure each day. And you always knew how to find me because I always sat in the same exact place each day. That was my spot. We would talk for hours in that small little cubicle."

"Janie, if anything should ever happen to me—and please don't get upset—if anything at all should happen to me, I want you to go to that desk and look underneath it. In the back left hand corner there'll be something for you." Jane looked at him and was hesitant to say anything.

"Why will something happen?"

"This whole Chinagate thing scares me; there's a lot of animosity within Sageware against the Asian workers and I don't know; I'm just getting a bad feeling. I don't want you to worry; I just want you to be prepared in case."

"Scott, nothing will happen. We're going to get through this. I'm here if you need me. I can only begin to imagine what you must be going through. This will pass and everything will be back to normal." Jane moved closer to Scott, grabbed both his hands, and laid her head on his chest.

"I love you, Janie."

"I love you." They lay there in silence, both aware that neither one was sleeping, but neither had the courage to say anything more. It took Jane almost two hours to fall back asleep. When Scott heard her breaths grow deeper, he whispered in her ear that he was going downstairs to work. She awoke momentarily, mumbling something about not wanting to be left alone, and then rolled over and fell soundly asleep once again. Scott opened the doors of his children's rooms and listened to their methodical breathing. How devastating they would be if their father disappeared, Scott grudgingly thought. The possibility was real and Scott forced himself to focus on the gravity of the situation. He went to the kitchen, brewed a cup of tea, and went to the basement. He sat in front of the computer for a long time staring at a white Microsoft Word screen. Finally, he lifted his hands to the keyboard and began typing.

Chapter 26

Peter walked into the Cowboy Bar, took a seat, and motioned to the bartender. A moment later the small Chinese man working the taps, who everyone referred to as Hank, laid a coaster down and placed on it a fresh brew from the Ching Tao tap. After two weeks of nightly visits, Hank recognized Peter and knew his drink of choice. "This is new keg, I just change myself. Very cold and fresh."

"Ya know, you can't get this stuff out of the tap in America, only out of the bottle." Peter pointed to the pint glass to emphasize what he was talking about.

"Bottle no good, too many chemicals. You drink, stay happy, don't think about Chinese girl, they make you crazy. Cheers." Hank walked away to serve the next foreign ghost.

On a quiet Monday night two weeks ago, the first time Peter entered the bar, Hank had become Peter's confidant and advisor on how to treat Chinese women. Peter poured his heart out to Hank, wondering all the time what Hank understood. Regardless of what Peter said, Hank always nodded and said, "Yes I understand, I understand." His generic advice about how to treat a Chinese woman was both laughable and occasionally wise. "You treat Chinese women like chicken, keep it warm and nice bed to sleep and it give you eggs, but never let chicken know warmer inside the house, only let it guess it warmer." Peter interpreted this to mean, always keep a women guessing. "You no marry Chinese girl, marry Japanese, they better," Hank once said. When Peter asked why, he simply said, "You listen me," and walked away. On this day two weeks later, Peter's daydreaming was interrupted by a fellow American asking if the seat next to his was free. It was the only one left in the bar. After a swig of beer, Tommy Anderson turned to Peter. "Hey, how ya doin?"

"Doing okay, I'll be better once I drain a couple more Ching Taos." Peter lifted his glass and chugged the remnants of his first beer. Barely before the glass hit the bar, Hank was there with a fresh refill. The Communists have learned service, Peter thought.

He turned to his new neighbor, "Haven't seen you in here before. You here on business or are you living in Beijing?"

"I've been here a few months," Tommy answered. "I work as a consultant for the Fortune 500. Basically my company serves as corporate marines, first one in, canvas the territory, search for opportunity, and call in the cavalry once all of the land mines have been detonated. You know the drill, I'm sure. My name's Tom." Tommy stretched out a hand to Peter.

"Nice to meet ya, I'm Peter. Cheers." The two men lifted their glasses and drank.

"So what brings you to Beijing, Peter, business or pleasure?"

"I guess a bit of both," Peter responded. "I'm pretty much like most of the Americans you see on the streets of Beijing. Over here on a one-year contract teaching English. I was loving life up till a couple of weeks ago when my Chinese girlfriend dumped me with no explanation. The fucked up thing about it is that I have no way to get in touch with her, don't know where she lives, don't know the spelling of her name, nothing. The only thing I have is her cell phone number and she never ever answers her phone. Hey, I'm sorry, my bad. I don't even know you and I'm laying all of my troubles on your lap. If it's any consolation I've been confiding in anyone I can."

"Hey, it's cool, I get it," Tommy smiled. "When I first moved to China, I was seeing a girl that I thought I would marry and it turned out she was just after American citizenship. When I told her I wasn't planning on returning to America for a few years and wasn't prepared in the near term for marriage, she just walked. She was pretty much the only person I associated with in Beijing, so when she left I was devastated."

"So you can empathize," Peter said. "I hate to harp on it, but I've just never been in a situation where I had no way of contacting someone. She can find me, but I can't find her."

"Well, it's never too soon to get back on the horse," Tommy suggested. "Take a look behind you. I think those two girls are checking us out, pretty hot."

Peter shook his head. "Man, this one's not going to be easy, it'll take a while. Would love to be your wing man, but it ain't happenin' tonight."

"No worries," Tommy said. "So what's next? You heading back home or you gonna keep teaching? What language school are you at?"

"I teach at a language center for future diplomats and government officials, kids that are supposedly going to run the country someday. The guy running the school said the kids were selected at a very young age based on their intelligence and physical attributes. It's been good, a real challenge to teach such intelligent kids. Never in my life have I seen any group of kids so disciplined, innately intelligent, and interested in the subject matter. Every single one of these kids speaks English as well as, if not better, than any normal American student growing up in the States. It blows me away sometimes. The last few weeks have been tough; I'm just not into it anymore, but I think I'll stick it out. I did make a commitment and I think they're counting on me to honor the contract."

"Sounds interesting," Tommy responded. "I've never heard of such a program. It seems strange that the government would invest so much time and money to make these kids fluent to the point where they speak as well as American kids. Do they speak with a Chinese accent?"

"No, they all have a standard American accent. The head of the school stressed that in the future China will join America as the only two superpowers in the world and it is important for the future leaders of China to be able to understand and easily converse with their American counterparts. He looks at it as politically, militarily, and commercially advantageous."

"Do any of these kids study in America or do they essentially experience America in the isolation of a classroom in Beijing?" Tommy asked. "It seems that they wouldn't be able to grasp very much of the culture besides very superficial aspects."

"That's what I thought initially as well, but these kids are phenomenal. The questions they ask show just how deeply they comprehend the cultural nuances and idiosyncrasies that differentiate two diverse lands. When discussing the history of immigration in America, one student asked why second and third-generation Americans were generally against liberal immigration policies when their families had benefited and probably thrived from relaxed restrictions just a short time before. He said it was hypocritical. The perceptive comment led to a discussion on racism and the double standard between the favoring of European over Asian immigration. A precocious topic for thirteen year olds, no doubt, but these kids loved it. They have an insatiable desire to learn everything they can about America; it was something I never expected."

"That's incredible!" Tommy gaped. "Never would I have ever imagined that such a school exists. It seems more like they're training spies than diplomats."

"It's funny, I've thought about that as well. Security is pretty tight, doors are locked, and some rooms are completely off-limits. One night, I was working late and I saw the head of the school enter a classroom from the only fortified door in the place. He was carrying a bunch of files in his hand and was not expecting to see me. He's an intimidating guy, but generally affable. When he saw me, his demeanor changed on a dime. He gave me a dressing down like I've never experienced. I almost pissed my pants. I thought he was about to take me to a torture chamber. He pretty much insinuated that if he ever saw me in the building again after hours that I'd live to regret it. Pretty fuckin' scary. It seemed to be a complete overreaction. Unless of course there's something they're trying to hide."

"Bizarre."

"I don't know ... once, I asked the director if the students would ever have the opportunity to travel to America, but he said they would not be assigned to America until they finished graduate work in the People's Republic of China. He said that the government feared if they let the students leave the country at too young of an age, they could be easily impressed by life in America and potentially tempted to defect. He said for all the time and resources invested to train the children, it wasn't worth the risk to let them visit America until they were assigned as diplomats. It made sense to me, but it's pretty crazy. Who the fuck knows."

They both checked their watches almost simultaneously and realized it was almost 1:00 a.m. "Shit I didn't realize it was so late," Peter said. "I better hit the road. Hey, it was great meeting you, haven't met too many quality people thus far. Would you be up for grabbing some dinner some time?" Tommy wanted to continue the conversation, but knew it was too late to do so now.

"Great meeting you as well, yeah sure."

"How 'bout we meet at the Hard Rock on Thursday at about 8:00?"

"Sounds good. 8:00 at the Hard Rock. See you then."

Chapter 27

Regardless of the intense pressure Tommy was feeling to solve the Chinagate espionage case, he refrained from revealing too much to Peter. He was tempted, but after the initial conversation, Tommy realized that the matter needed to be handled a bit more delicately than he had originally envisioned. Peter's breakup had left him emotionally unstable and Tommy didn't want to risk Peter rebelling and possibly walking right out of the place. He had struck gold—English teacher, genius kids, and a beautiful woman. The pattern fit perfectly with the three previous murdered teachers. Over dinner, Tommy thought, they could speak more intimately with fewer ears around. He also didn't want to reveal his motive for his chance meeting while Peter was drinking. Many expatriates in China would be incensed if they knew they were being followed. He wasn't certain how Peter would react. Tommy arrived at the Hard Rock early and requested a table towards the back of the restaurant, away from the band that usually started playing around 9:00. Peter arrived shortly after 8:00.

"How goes it?" Tommy asked him.

"Pretty much same ole, same ole," Peter answered. "On Wednesday morning I was surprisingly hung over. Could barely get through my classes. Didn't think I was that drunk."

"I know what ya mean, I slept right through my alarm clock. Any word from your girl?"

"Shit, you trying to ruin my evening before the waitress even has a chance to bring my first drink? At least let me have a couple shots of Novocain before you start drilling." They both laughed.

"Peter, I'm afraid I have some other news that may do more than just ruin your evening and it wouldn't be fair of me to keep it from you any longer." Tommy hesitated and studied Peter's features. He wondered if Peter had any idea of what he was going to say next. From the curious and slightly annoyed look on his face, Tommy doubted it.

"I don't know what you're getting at, but out with it," Peter insisted. "I've had enough bad news recently, so I don't think anything you say will make me feel any worse." Peter thought for a second. "Is this about Song May? Do you know her?" Peter was suddenly anxious to hear Tommy's news and resented his silence.

"No, this is not about your girlfriend. Have you been following the Chinagate story?" Tommy asked.

"Yeah," Peter said. "Not closely, but I know what's going on. Pretty unbelievable that no one's been caught. What are you getting at?"

"I was just home," Tommy explained. "In the States it's as big as any story in the last five years. Six companies have been infiltrated and not one person has been arrested; it's unheard of. Never has a corporate espionage case been so widespread and successful."

"What's your point?"

"Peter, I'm a private investigator. I was hired by a consortium of the six technology companies that have had proprietary company information stolen by the Chinese. They spent a few months working with the FBI and CIA to no avail, and have decided to take things into their own hands. I was hired a few months back to see what I could find and you're my first solid lead. You are training spies." The two remained silent as the waitress brought their drinks.

As soon as the waitress walked away, Peter turned to Tommy. "This is fuckin' crazy! What the hell do I have to do with Chinagate? How the hell am I involved with any of this crap? How the hell did you find me?" Peter somehow felt violated. He wanted to bolt from the Hard Rock at that very moment.

Could this be true?

"We've been following you the last two weeks," Tommy explained. "We received a lead and began following your boss; I believe his name is Mr. Shue. During a routine surveillance we saw you coming out of a building that we now think is a training facility for spies."

"We? What, do you have a whole operation here? Who the hell are you working for? How'd you get a visa to remain in the country so long?"

"I have one partner, a former Chinese national who does most of the fieldwork. My day job is as a consultant. I speak fluent Chinese, was army intelligence for five years, and am a retired marine. Peter, unfortunately we don't have time for this banter. I'm getting paid a ton of money and I will find out what happened, but I need your help."

"Help with what? How? You know, I don't think I want to be involved with any of this shit." Peter got up to leave, but hesitated. He wondered how he might be involved. He was scared.

"Peter, give me five minutes." Tommy was relieved when Peter sat back down.

"We believe that the supposed language school where you teach has been and continues to be the main training facility for spies being sent to the United States. The spies are trained to obtain secrets from U.S. high-technology corporations. We think this facility has produced the very agents that have infiltrated six U.S. companies in the past year. We are working to determine how many other agents are still in the States stealing secrets for the Chinese government." Tommy continued, laying out almost every speck of evidence he had, but stopped before asking Peter for help. He wanted him to at least start absorbing the gravity of the situation. Both men sat silently nursing their beers.

"This is all a big joke right?" Peter finally breathed out. "I don't know what the fuck you're talking about and I don't particularly like being tailed. You're drawing 101 different conclusions from what seems to be very circumstantial evidence and I don't want any part of it. You're an asshole. I'm outta here." He stood to leave.

"Peter, I found you and felt it worthwhile to approach you, risking an operation that I've spent countless hours investigating. You are inextricably involved. There is no running away from me or from the Chinese. You're in danger and I may be the only guy who can help you." Tommy stood as well and looked at Peter.

"My knight in shining fuckin' armor," Peter said sarcastically.

"I'm the only friend you got left," Tommy answered.

"Friend? If I can help, you'll keep me around; when you're done, the Chinese can have me. Completely expendable." The two men sat back down. Peter had no choice but to listen, but as Tommy spoke Peter began crafting his own plan of escape. He was still in shock, but in thinking about thirty different small things that he'd observed over the last few months, he reluctantly admitted to himself that Tommy was no scam artist. He couldn't be trusted, but Peter's pragmatic side took over and he came to the realization that he needed Tommy as much as Tommy needed him.

"I'm going to give you information that I shouldn't give you and would lose my job if the CEOs back in Silicon Valley knew, so I'll request that this conversation remain confidential, but ultimately I can't control who you choose to share this information with."

"Unless you kill me."

Tommy thought about it but chose to ignore Peter's childishness. Tommy could only take so much, and if need be he would have no remorse breaking Peter in two, but restraint was called for and Tommy continued unabated.

"We've been working on this case for over a year. During the last eight months the Chinese spies have become increasingly audacious. Their espionage, stealing secrets of advanced technology on the verge of entering the market, has forced CEOs to take the story public and demand action from the government to solve the case. The companies have had little influence with the CIA or FBI, which is why they have hired me and my team. Smaller cases have been surfacing for at least two years. In each

165

case the Chinese were very careful, they controlled the release of the information in China and would not allow any mention of it in the State-controlled media."

"Then how did you guys find out about it?"

"It was only in the last month that we were able to piece everything together. Now it suddenly all makes sense."

"Then why do you need my help?" Peter flippantly questioned.

"Listen Peter, enough with the fucking childish antics. You are a last resort for us. We still have no idea how many companies have been infiltrated nor do we have even one lead on a possible suspect. This is the most successful infiltration the Chinese have ever had, so although we've gotten some scraps here and there, only the highest ranking Chinese officials have been privy to this information. You're involved now and I'm sorry. We have come to you because we believe you have or could obtain information crucial to our investigation. Please just hear me out and then you can objectively decide if you can help. If not, at least you're now aware what you're involved with and you can make arrangements to leave the country as quickly as possible." Tommy was searching for a way to connect with Peter on a more personal level. He needed Peter's confidence and trust.

"All right, Tommy, I'm listening, but I will make no guarantees to help."

"Fair enough. I was personally hired as a consultant by The Ultralight Corporation as soon as the news of a new product launch by a Chinese startup hit the international wires. Ultralight had developed some sort of face recognition technology that blew everything else on the market off the map. This technology was something that the U.S. Government had planned to use to combat State-side terrorism, so suddenly the case took on more immediate significance."

"The Chinese government, we came to find out, was greedy. The Technology Index on the Hong Kong Stock Exchange had been shooting up, so they figured this was a good way to secure an immediate monetary return on their espionage. The Communists invested in or took over Chinese startups that were doing research similar to that of the infiltrated U.S. companies. These Chinese companies had major international news conferences announcing groundbreaking technologies and floated shares on the Heng Seng. They took careful steps to ensure that the companies were legitimate high-tech startups in order to appease the investment banking community. As of today, six companies have had IPOs and each one finished the first day of trading with a market cap in the billions. Are you following me so far? Do you have any questions yet?" Tommy asked Peter.

"Go on," was all Peter said.

"Okay, the entire project has been an astounding success for the Communists, but recently it seems that greed and arrogance have caused some missteps. For starters, it looks like the chiefs in Beijing can no longer control their agents. After the first big announcement, company after company in the U.S. brought claims that Chinese companies were stealing their intellectual property. The spies have either decided to finish their mission and wash their hands of the case or the comrades in Beijing think they're invincible and have ordered an opening of the floodgate. The reality is probably a combination of both." Tommy stopped talking, finished his beer in a gulp, and ordered another. He looked around and realized the place had filled. Young Chinese executives as well as a crowd of expatriates were crowding the dance floor and letting off steam. Peter also took a look around. He had become mesmerized with Tommy's account and hadn't noticed how packed the Hard Rock had become.

"So where do I come in?" Peter asked.

"Well, it seems as though your boss is some sort of liaison between the Standing Committee and the Chinese companies profiting off of the espionage. The young executives of these companies, though Communists, are not keen on having Big Brother oversee their every move and pocket most of the money from the IPO, even though the executives get to keep and develop the technology and make millions in the process. The Party officials for their part don't want some punk kids calling the shots and controlling the future of technologies that the government has worked so hard to steal from the Americans. Your Mr. Shue maintains the calm between these factions, deftly explaining the positions of both sides. He should be an invisible advisor, but he has become seduced with the media coverage and has let himself be photographed and interviewed on several occasions. We have been following him for a month and one day spotted you coming out of the same building Shue had just walked into. It was our first real lead."

As Tommy spoke these last words, he wondered if he should have revealed so much to Peter. He had considered prevaricating or withholding certain information, but he knew Peter was smart and decided he would be able to recognize the truth and appreciate it. Tommy hated relying on only one lead, but he had no choice.

"So let's cut to the chase. What do you want from me?" Peter asked.

"It's very simple. If you have seen anything strange during your time at the school, please let me know. If you see anyone that you recognize as a top government official, let me know, and keep your eyes open for anything suspicious. This very basic information will assist us greatly. Is there any information about the kids or the school that you can tell me besides what we've already discussed?" Tommy asked.

"No, not really. Listen, I don't know what I'm getting myself into, but I'll start keeping my eyes peeled. I really don't know what you expect me to do."

Tommy knew Peter was lying. He'd interrogated a ton of hardened criminals who lied so well they could fool a polygraph. Peter, in contrast, though confident enough to fool the untrained observer, was not so skilled to outwit a professional. Tommy needed the information Peter was hiding, but decided to wait and consider how best to get it. He would get what he wanted and would use any means necessary.

Tommy personally abhorred some of the tactics the CIA used to extract information, but this case was too important. Although he hoped to avoid the extreme, he looked at Peter and guessed he had a very low tolerance for pain.

"Listen, Peter, unfortunately you are intricately involved in a very serious case of espionage and could probably be convicted of aiding and abetting the enemy, with a maximum penalty of life in prison."

"Tom, I've had enough of this shit. I need to get the hell outta here."

The check came and Tommy grabbed it, laid the money for the beers on the table, and followed Peter, who had already begun working his way through the now completely packed bar. When he got outside, Tommy saw Peter was already halfway down the street.

"Peter!" Tommy shouted. He had one other piece of information that he needed to tell Peter, but as Peter turned around, he decided it would have to wait. It was something he could use as a bargaining chip later if needed. "Keep in touch!" Tommy yelled as Peter quickly turned the corner.

Chapter 28

It was late November and the Beijing nights were starting to get frigid. Peter was tempted to take a taxi home, but he had too much to think about and the prospect of sitting in his poorly heated studio was unbearable at the moment. He thought for a second how nice it would be to be back in Seattle, even if the rainy season had already begun, snuggled up in his down comforter and blasting the heater. It was the very first time since he'd been in Beijing that he had had such a thought. Recent events, from his inability to track down Song May to Tommy's revelations, had worn him down to a point that he wondered if he'd ever be himself again.

He believed Tommy—every word—and he now realized that he had been suppressing similar thoughts, convincing himself that he was letting his imagination, or more appropriately his paranoia, get the best of him. Now he knew that all of his suspicions were true. His thoughts centered on Song May. She was the one; he knew it from the first time they met. This was the woman he wanted to marry. But after listening to Tommy, he knew instantly that she was also involved; a self-created block was suddenly lifted with his words. Meeting her was just too much of a coincidence. His head was spinning with scenarios. What was she planning for him, why had she left? Was it all planned to cut any ties between the two of them? It was all so hard to believe. Just a few short weeks ago, he was so certain she felt the same about him as he felt about her.

With difficulty, he forced his thoughts back to Tommy and for the first time all night, he was able to think rationally. The walk through the brisk November air was having its desired effect. Beijing is laid out similarly to Los Angeles. Its suburbs stretch 100 miles in every direction, creating an expansive urban sprawl that Mexico City would be hard-pressed to match. Though he had been walking for well over an hour, he was still at least two miles from his apartment.

For the first time he noticed his surroundings and wondered if he was being followed. It was another foolish thought. As he turned his head east and west and behind him, he noticed 100 suspicious faces. He felt his fate slip out of his hands and with great effort focused on how he should respond to Tommy. He needed to make a decision before he reached his apartment. He had heard very little about the corporate espionage case even though it was the biggest story of the year and suddenly felt the full weight of his isolation. Now close to home and well past midnight, Peter stopped at the first open pay phone, found Tommy Anderson's card, and dialed the number.

"Hello, Anderson here."

"Tommy, it's Peter."

Chapter 29

Shue walked out of his apartment perfectly groomed and went to the corner kiosk to buy his cigarettes. He had given his driver the day off. General Wang had called last night and informed him that the Communist Party Secretary, Cheng Gao She, wanted to discuss the recent insubordination of the executives of the 'chosen' technology companies.

From what General Wang relayed, reports indicated that the CEO of Yong Gan Tech was constantly making derogatory remarks about the Party to a Comrade Cheng, who Shue was told was a first cousin of the Party Secretary. Bullshit, thought Shue. What the hell did the Party Secretary think would happen? He places a relative at a company to serve as a representative of the Party, a person who doesn't know the first thing about technology or even what the company produces—then the representative is given a ton of stock and does jack shit. Of course the executives are going to react with animosity. Shue had been asked by a coalition of the executives to request that these 'party representatives' stay at home. It was one thing to have to pay them to do nothing, but to have them there day after day meddling in company affairs and giving suggestions on issues they knew nothing about was degrading and more than the company executives could take. The majority of the senior executives at the 'chosen' companies were under thirty; they had grown up in an era where initiative was rewarded and success was market-driven. Shue agreed with them, but had to toe the party line: it was pure self-preservation. In any case, Shue knew that he could do nothing to change the situation. Very few in the People's Republic would dare defy the Party Secretary. *The classless society.*

Ironically, as Shue continued wondering about the inequities of modern Chinese society, a limo pulled up and a driver rushed out to open the door for Shue. As the limo weaved through Beijing morning traffic exacerbated by never-ending construction, Shue began to get a very bad feeling about his meeting with Cheng. They pulled up to the Great Hall of the People and as Shue climbed the steps leading to the Hall's entrance, he was met by the Party Secretary's secretary.

"Comrade."

"Comrade."

"Right this way. Comrade Cheng will be with you in a minute." As the secretary departed, Shue took a seat in the standard, red-upholstered, high-back chair.

"Ah, Comrade so good you could make it. I saw you so infrequently this summer and fall, besides on the cover of the People's Daily that is; you've been well?" The Party Secretary was gracious, Shue thought, a very bad sign.

"Thank you for your concern, Party Secretary Cheng. Yes, everything is wonderful."

"Can I offer you a hot cup of Wu Long Tea? The winds from the Gobi have started to invade our humble city and I'm afraid I've caught a bit of a cold." Without waiting for a response General Cheng poured two cups of tea from a teapot that was sitting at the edge of his desk. Shue rose quickly to receive the cup that the Party Secretary handed to him.

"Thank you, Party Secretary, please don't go to any extra effort on my behalf." Shue spoke a very deferential classic style of Mandarin that he found usually ingratiated himself to the top cadres.

"Comrade, the reason I've called you hear today is, for a lack of a better way to express myself, to tie up loose ends. It seems that as of late our little mission has been unable to surmount various obstacles that have been preventing its smooth progress. In order to guarantee continued viability, we have to make some drastic changes to our operations." The Party Secretary took a sip of tea and examined Shue for a moment, giving him an opportunity to interject.

"Yes, Party Secretary Cheng. I have already spoken with the executives of all of the 'chosen' companies admonishing the CEO of Yong Gan Tech in particular. They are all aware that they are to include the party representatives in the decision-making process and provide weekly reports in writing to the Standing Committee. I emphasized that none of them would have a job if not for the brilliant work of the Party's finest international agents. I don't foresee any additional problems." Shue had expressed himself well and felt comfortable enough to lean back in his chair and wait for the Party Secretary's response.

"Yes, yes. Very good, comrade. These kids need to recognize who feeds them. They would be begging in the street if not for the Party. Truly ungrateful, this generation, they have no idea what sacrifice for country and Party means."

"You are quite right, Party Secretary." Shue felt he was winning Cheng over.

"Comrade, as I was saying, we have become sloppy with success and have distractedly let down our guard. We have confirmed reports of considerable CIA activity in and around the city. There's fear among the top Party brass that our project is in jeopardy and we believe your desire for the limelight may be to blame." The Party Secretary slowly refilled his cup of tea, ignoring Shue's empty cup, and awaited a response. The Party Secretary noted to himself that Shue looked like a deer in headlights, a stark contrast to his haughty expression of a moment ago.

"Party Secretary, General Wang has briefed me on my minor indiscretions and I have taken the necessary steps to avoid all public appearances. I felt it was necessary to have a more public presence at the beginning in order to clearly establish that the Party was watching vigilantly and in ultimate control of every company. Party Secretary Cheng, I assure you I had the best of intentions." Shue realized the futility of his argument, but he refused to go down without voicing his objections.

"Comrade Shue, you've basked in the glory of the market economy and a media that, to my chagrin, is gaining power every day. From the recent acts of insubordination among the top executives of the chosen companies, it is evident that you have failed in your goal of establishing Party dominance within these organizations. What you have done is clearly establish a link between these companies and the Party. If you've forgotten, these companies obtained their technology illegally and to have the Party linked publicly in any way to them greatly threatens our credibility in the international community. Comrade, we have learned from very reputable sources that the CIA has identified you as a possible link to the corporate espionage taking place so triumphantly in America." He paused to take a sip of tea. Shue, whose mouth was dry, needed the tea more than Cheng.

"Party Secretary, my actions are inexcusable and I take full blame, but please take note that I was simply following orders."

"Comrade, I don't quite understand, you take full blame, but you were simply following orders? Are you prepared to implicate one of your superiors?"

"No, no, Party Secretary."

The Party Secretary took a deep breath and continued. "Comrade, I have seen you on the cover of the People's Daily at least ten times over the past year and you've been on the evening news so frequently that I am starting to mistake you for a movie star. You are spending money as if you personally earned it. Comrade, you are not an entrepreneur. You were granted privilege and you have abused it. Your Armani suits and million-dollar smile will be purged. The intoxication of money and power has plagued our Party for too long. You are far from the first and will not be the last, but you will be made an example of." The Party Secretary paused for a moment and then went on.

"Comrade you have served our country admirably for over thirty years and I knew and served with your father. Your life will be spared and you will remain a Party member for now. But, your recent ineptness will cost us dearly. I am relieving you of your post and reassigning you to the Xinjinag Autonomous Region where you will report to the Board of Agricultural Oversight. That will be all." The Party Secretary rose indicating that it was time for Shue to leave.

"Party Secretary, please be reasonable. I'd almost rather be in Russian Siberia. Please reconsider." Shue pleaded in desperation on deaf ears.

At the same time that Shue was getting his new assignment, General Wang was calling Song May with instructions.

"Hello," Song May answered her phone.

"Comrade Chen, this is General Wang. I've been thinking about our next move regarding the boy."

"Yes, General. I'm listening."

Chapter 30

Comrade Chu both immensely liked and thoroughly disliked his trips around the country to find new recruits. He was very surprised to receive a call from General Wang that he should prepare for another trip. He had assumed the entire operation was on hiatus. The General assured him that the operation would continue indefinitely. Chu never traveled alone on these trips, emotions ran too high with the birth parents of potential recruits. Two career military men accompanied Chu and exerted force where necessary. Their presence was usually enough to avoid confrontation. Chu called it the "intimidation factor."

Hospitals around the country reported monthly to the Ministry of Health on many matters. Peculiar outbreaks of diseases, women having more than one child, the number of abortions performed each month, among others. The only statistic Chu was interested in was the number of identical twins that were born each month. It was a statistic that the Ministry only began recording with the start of the espionage program. Every single set of identical twins was tracked from the time they were born to the time they were two years old. At that point, doctors were able to determine superior intelligence and agility. Doctors received a large bonus from the government if they identified extraordinary children who were later admitted to the program. Monetary enticement is what has made the program such a success.

In the early days, fear was the Party's only weapon and results were mixed. As China grew economically, the lure of financial security for doctors who are paid as public servants proved to be an extremely successful motivator. Money also helped ease the pain of the families who lost their children, especially if they were boys.

During his most recent trip, Chu made stops in villages in Sichuan and Jejiang Provinces. His first stop was to a small farming community in Sichuan named Tan Village. The parents were not aware of Chu's visit until the morning of his arrival when they were notified by the Party representative. Keeping the parents uninformed until necessary prevented escape or an attempt to hide the children. The parents were told that the children had been identified as exceptional and invited into an elite educational program in Beijing; it was an honor. Most parents readily accepted, not realizing that they would never see their children again. All were compensated.

As Chu's driver navigated the "Made-in-China" Buick through the potholed, dusty dirt road, Chu reviewed in his head the standard remarks that he had been making since his first family visit. He expected the same concerns and questions and had prepared standard answers. In the past, most villagers Chu encountered had feared him and thus put up very little resistance, but as communication with the larger cities improved and villages began entering the mindset of the 21st century, his job had gotten a little more difficult.

As they pulled up to a two-room shack, the driver deftly avoided chickens darting in front of the car. The Chief Party Representative of the village opened the door and greeted Chu, the father of the two boys stood next to the party chief.

"Comrades."

"Comrade." The three men shook hands and entered the house. The mother and the two boys were sitting at the kitchen table. Snacks had been prepared and tea water was boiling on the wood-fired stove.

"So nice to see you, Mrs. Tai."

"Please have a seat, my apologies for not preparing a proper lunch; we were not given any advance notice of your arrival. I only had time to prepare a few snacks."

"Mrs. Tai, you should not have gone through any trouble on my behalf. The snacks look delicious and I'm sure will taste just as good." The snacks were actually more than a meal and the very best the Tais had to offer. In the finest of Chinese traditions, a woman of the house would never receive a guest without preparation of some type of meal. Mrs. Tai was being modest as custom called for. After hearing the news that a guest was visiting from Beijing, she had spent every second preparing for the visit, and was confident Mr. Chu would find the foods she had whipped up to his liking.

"And these must be your little ones. Hello, boys." The two nodded and greeted the stranger in unison.

"You must be so proud of them," Chu smiled.

"Yes," Mr. Tai answered. The four adults made customary small talk until Mr. Tai broached the subject of Chu's visit.

"Comrade Chu, may I ask you to explain the reason you have journeyed so far from Beijing to visit our very modest home"

"Mr. and Mrs. Tai, thank you so much for receiving me into your fine home. As you may know, the Communist Party is always looking for gifted children to attend special, highly competitive schools in order to train the next generation of leaders." Chu paused for a second, but the Tai's remained silent. "We search the country for the best and brightest and invite less than a handful to Beijing to be taught by the preeminent teachers in the land. Students who are invited pay for nothing. Everything is provided by the Party.

"We have been informed that your boys are of above-average intelligence and have the potential, with proper training, to lead the Motherland to greatness in the 21st century. I would like to be the first to congratulate the two of you that your two sons have been chosen among millions of candidates to join the Elite People's Academy in Beijing. This is truly a great day."

"Thank you, Comrade Chu," Mr. Tai responded. "This is quite an honor. When will my boys be starting this school? They are now only just over two years old. Isn't it a bit soon to be having such a discussion?" Mr. Tai was honored, but could not conceive of what Chu was about to do.

"Mr. Tai, your boys have already been identified as truly gifted. Your doctor lists these two youngsters in the top 100th of 1% in intelligence and motor skills. They are already advanced well beyond their years. They need stimulus that unfortunately Tan Village is unable to provide. The early years are the most important." Chu hoped the Tais were getting the hint.

"Comrade Chu," Mr. Tai bristled. "I have not received a formal education in my life, but I've learned a thing or two over the years. I don't like what I'm hearing. Do you mind if I cut to the chase?" Chu nodded his acquiescence.

"Are you telling us that you would like to take our babies today?"

"That's exactly what I'm saying," Chu conceded. "To receive the proper training, we must start educating these fine young lads from an early age." Mrs. Tai let out a loud scream and brought both boys closer to her. She dare not speak, it wasn't her place, but would let her actions speak for themselves.

"And if we refuse this opportunity?" Mr. Tai challenged.

"Comrade Tai, this is not about accepting or refusing. The Party is simply trying to work with you to provide the ideal learning environment for your children. We have to think about what is best for them."

"Comrade Chu, with all due respect, I have been blessed with two healthy boys and education is all well and good, but I need these boys to work the land, tend to crops, and be there for me and my wife in our old age. This is our family." Mr. Tai spoke well for not having an education. He was obviously a smart man who'd been dealt a bum hand of cards.

"Mr. Tai, these boys will always be part of your family," Chu lied, "and with the training and opportunity we will provide, you can be guaranteed your boys will be able to provide for your future much better than if they stayed by your side tilling the land."

Mr. Tai could see the writing on the wall. He knew protest was futile; he would not win. His whole life he had tried to fight, whether it was the ever increasing taxes he had to pay to the corrupt local officials or the increasing costs for basic supplies, he had never won and he would not win today, but he would get something. He was aware of what he had and he knew Chu was no ordinary country bumpkin official. He had room to negotiate.

"With all due respect, I need to worry about how I'm going to put food on this table year in and year out. I don't have time to plan for the future. I need these boys taking on some responsibility at an early age."

"Mr. Tai, the Party wants to make sure that you have all of the support you need to work your land even without these boys." Chu played along. The dumb ones accepted what was offered, but the smart ones knew to negotiate. Chu happily provided fair compensation, it was the least he could do.

"Well, that sounds fine," Mr. Tai pushed, "but I don't think these boys should be leaving their mother's side at such a young age."

Chu cut to the chase. "Mr. Tai, in my pocket is $25,000. That is more than you can hope to earn in ten years of toiling on your land. I want you to have this money for your troubles and for your generosity and loyalty to country and Party. Please accept my inadequate offer." Chu stood up and handed Mr. Tai an envelope. "My time is short and I must be going." Chu shook Mr. Tai's hand, bowed to Mrs. Tai, left the house, and entered the back seat of the car. He could hear the mother's wails and the boys' crying. Chu sometimes encountered a strong-minded wife and that's when things got nasty. It didn't look like that would happen today. After five minutes, Mr. Tai dragged the boys to the car and said goodbye.

As the car rode off the boys were still wailing.

"Soldier, take care of these boys," Chu commanded. The soldier pulled two syringes from a bag and quickly plucked both boys with a mild anesthetic; they were asleep in minutes. The boys would never see their parents again. Mission accomplished.

"Driver, to the airport. Let's get these boys on the first flight to Beijing. Their indoctrination cannot start soon enough."

"Yes, Comrade Chu."

Chapter 31

Tommy knew that if he were this close to cracking the case, the Chinese were just as close, if not closer, to knowing their most successful U.S. corporate infiltration was about to come to an end. He did not have a minute to spare. He decided to have Peter meet him outside of a local watering hole that many English teachers frequent in the south end of downtown Beijing.

Within thirty minutes of Peter's call, Tommy and Winston Chang had picked Peter up and brought him to a CIA safe house on the outskirts of Beijing. The traditional four-corner house was in an old neighborhood in the city. It was secluded in a dark alley and the neighbors generally minded their own business. The CIA had rented the place only two months before and in another month would put it up for rent and move somewhere else. Even in modern-day China, the police still had informants and Caucasians were still forbidden to live in certain areas of the city. A trustworthy Chinese "friend" had rented this place for the agency. At one point the CIA had thought about just renting an apartment in the new, posh, expatriate section of Beijing, but decided against it after learning that the Chinese Secret Service closely monitored the actions of the executives living there. Introductions were made, but little else was said as they drove through a still bustling Beijing, even at 2:00 a.m.

After Winston prepared a pot of strong coffee, the three men sat down around a small wooden table, located in the middle of a sparsely decorated living room.

"Like what you've done with the place." Peter tried to lighten the mood a bit. He was intensely nervous.

"I'll put you in touch with our decorator," Tommy joked tersely.

Nothing else was said for a couple of minutes while Tommy gathered his thoughts. He hadn't expected Peter to contact him so soon.

"Okay, Peter. You mentioned that you believe other parts of the school may hold information about their operations. In particular, a fortified door that you discovered, but have not been able to access. I've given some thought to how we may be able to gain entrance, but why don't you tell me a little bit more about the building and the personnel."

Peter wasn't ready to start giving up information. "Before I get started, I'm curious how you plan to get me out of the country or is your helping me contingent on the quality of my information?" Peter did not distrust Tommy, but could not completely rely on him. Unfortunately, he had few other options.

"Peter, no matter what, we will get you out of the country. We'll get you a new passport with all the correct stamps. It's foolproof."

"The school is not heavily fortified. The front door is watched 24 hours a day by two guards who each work a twelve-hour shift. There is no key to the door, the guards control access and there is a keypad combination that will unlock the door. The guard who works the night shift is old and an alcoholic. I've come in early on numerous occasions and the guy is barely coherent. I am supposed to be out of the building by 5:00, but it would probably be easy enough to hide and stay after hours. Shue, as you know, comes to the building every night round 7:00 p.m. and does a walkthrough. He almost never misses this. The aforementioned door is in the corner of one of the classrooms."

"There are no other guards who work the nightshift besides the old man?" Tommy asked.

"Not that I know of," Peter said.

After their phone conversation, Tommy had hatched the beginnings of a simple plan, but he now worried that it might be too late for it to work. "Peter, I don't know what you must be thinking at this point, a few exciting months in Beijing teaching English has put you smack dab in the middle of the biggest corporate espionage ring America has ever seen. I still have no idea how they've pulled this off so efficiently, without the slightest suspicion, but I've been told the CEOs main suspects are the ones who are most American and have spent their entire lives in America. Listening to your story, I now understand they must teach their agents as children to talk, act, and think like Americans. They seem to have done this so successfully to be beyond reproach, and unfortunately you and many before you have assisted in the training. I know you're frightened and probably wish you'd stayed in Seattle, but you're here, you're intelligent, and you have inside knowledge of their operations—and now we're asking you to help us break this case open." Tommy was trying to connect with Peter; this case would not be solved without his help. The signs coming from the States were already indicating that Silicon Valley was returning to normal, the agents are obviously going into sleeper mode again. Peter was essentially the CIA's last reliable resource.

Peter responded honestly. "I don't know what the hell I'm getting myself into. You're asking me to do something I'm in no way trained to do that will certainly put my life in danger. I don't know. This is fucking insane."

"Peter, I'm not stroking your ego here," Tommy said. "We've checked your background. We know you graduated *summa cum laude* from Harvard and were captain of the Varsity basketball team your senior year. You're an extremely intelligent leader. You have a cool head and the balls to carry this out." Tommy was trying to strike a balance between praise and encouragement without coming across as too complimentary and desperate.

Peter stiffened at the clear insight into his past. "So you've already done background checks, how the hell did you gain access to my background?"

"Peter, I'm getting paid a lot of money because I know how to get information."

Peter was unfocused. He was in a situation that he dreaded and he was racking his brain to find an escape; his frustration only increased as he realized an escape didn't exist. He took a deep breath and turned to Tommy, "Okay, what is it you want me to do?"

Tommy leaned in. "In order to crack this case we need to infiltrate the school. I have no idea what's behind that door, but if this is the only door in the whole school that's fortified, it's got to have something behind it. We need you to find out what that is. Now, you mentioned that one day when you were working late you saw Shue come through that door carrying a stack of files under his arm."

"Yes," Peter nodded. "Like I told you, he was pretty pissed when he saw me in the classroom."

Tommy continued, "We need you to get onto the other side of that door. We are going to supply you with easy-to-use lock picking devices as well as a digital camera and a hand-held scanner that will instantly make perfect copies in case you find any important documents. That should be all you need. Get as much information as you can."

Peter felt a bit queasy. "I don't know if I'm up for this. I'm watched quite closely and given little time alone. What if I can't pull this off? If they find me, I'm dead."

"You'll be dead anyway." Tommy had refrained from telling Peter long enough. He paused for a moment to allow Peter to grasp the gravity of the situation. "Peter, I've recently learned that over the past two years, three teachers from America were killed. They had all been teaching at different locations, but we believe at the same training facility. The teachers who had your position prior to your arrival in Beijing were both murdered. The school, Mr. Shue, the Communist Party will not allow you to leave this country alive. The Communists have too much invested and they are not about to let a loose end fall out of their control. If you choose to help us, we can guarantee your safety." Tommy was not going to let Peter out of the room without a firm commitment.

Peter's eyes narrowed a bit. "Let me get this straight. Knowing what you know of my eventual death, if I do not choose to help, you will do nothing to help me get out of the country alive?"

"Peter, don't put me in that position. I want to help you get outta here, but one hand washes the other."

"How can you be so sure the deaths of the other teachers were related?" Peter was trying to convince himself that he wasn't involved, that he was safe, despite mounting evidence to the contrary.

"The deaths were ruled accidents by the Beijing Police. Supposedly workers from the countryside murdered these kids for their money. U.S. officials were only given the result of the investigation and not allowed to view any of the factual findings. Over the last two weeks we've done a search of all American deaths that occurred in China over the last five years. There have only been twelve, two of those being from old age. We narrowed it down to English teachers working in Beijing and we came up with three.

"All three deaths occurred in the last two years. A colleague in the States interviewed the parents of the teachers and the parents of all three were keen to discuss what had happened to their boys. The parents of the teacher most recently killed, a kid named Matthew Barley, had visited Beijing twice attempting to locate the school where he taught and the Chinese woman he was dating. Both girl and school had mysteriously disappeared. Peter, all three sets of parents told stories similar to yours. They said their sons had told them about students with extraordinary intelligence and mastery of the English language. All three sets of parents kept emphasizing how their sons had repeatedly told them how amazed they were at the students' fluency of the language and understanding of American culture. Peter, they all also mentioned that their sons had told them that they were dating a beautiful Chinese woman." Tommy stopped and allowed Peter to absorb what he had just been told.

After a long silence Peter finally dejectedly responded. "From the moment you told me who you were at the Hard Rock, I knew that Song May was involved. I tried to shake it off, but with the clarity of hindsight, it all seems too much of a coincidence. How we met, our courtship, our love affair—it was all too perfect. I still love her, can't stop thinking about her, and I'm still convinced she had genuine feelings for me. I don't know, I just don't fuckin' know." Peter sat there looking off into space, broken by the realization that he'd never be able to see Song May again—and worse still that she may have been involved in a plot to kill him.

"Peter, I'm sorry. I know you loved her. Maybe now we can try to even the score. It's almost 5:00 a.m., the sun will be up shortly and you'll be expected at class. Do you want to talk about the plan now or do you want a short catnap before we begin?"

"No, let's do this and get it over with. I want to get the hell out of the country as soon as this is over, I'm not going to fuckin' die here." With renewed focus, Peter looked to Tommy for instructions.

Chapter 32

Peter arrived home shortly after seven in the morning. He showered in his rusty tub with lukewarm water for what he hoped was the last time and hastily packed all of his belongings. He picked up his teaching materials and realized for the first time that he'd have to wing it in class. He hadn't had time to prepare anything. He cared little at this point and decided to stray from his previously assigned lecture on the differences and similarities between states and instead focus on curse words. He'd already decided the topic would be "four-letter words." He wouldn't need any preparation for this lecture.

He left the door unlocked; Winston would come by just after dusk to collect Peter's things from the apartment and then head to the school to wait on the street until 4:30 a.m., the agreed upon rendezvous time.

Peter needed to proceed through the morning in accordance with his established routine. He walked quickly to school, stopping for his daily egg sandwich that was now always waiting for him, piping hot and delicious. He nodded to the vendor, paid her, and continued to the school. As he entered the building, things appeared to be as they always were. He prayed that he'd be able to get through the day. As he got ready to begin class, the old guard entered the room, handed Peter a note, and left without saying a word. Peter was tempted to put the note in his pocket and wait until after class to read it, but his curiosity was piqued and he read it immediately.

> *Peter, meet me tonight outside the main entrance of the Friendship Hotel. I have to see you one more time before you leave Beijing. Love, Song May.*

Peter reread the note several times, ignoring childish taunts from his students that the note was from his girlfriend, studying it for any hidden clues. For an instant he thought about actually meeting her, he so badly wanted to see her one last time. He was brought back from a momentary daze by incessant badgering from his students.

"What did the note say, teacher?" The group questioned in irritating unison. "Who was it from?" Before responding Peter glanced at the note one more time and wondered how she knew he was leaving Beijing. He looked at his hands and noticed that they were soaked in perspiration.

"Okay, okay, let's begin. I have a surprise for you today. It's a topic I think you will enjoy, but you must promise me that you will not discuss today's lesson with Mr. Shue. Today's topic will focus on curse words in English."

The class unexpectedly erupted in cheers, high fives, and shouts of 'Yes!'. Peter hadn't been sure they would know what the word 'curse' meant, but their reactions once again proved that there was little that these kids didn't know. He marveled, as he tended to do on a daily basis, at how these kids had managed to master the English language in the confines of an isolated school on the outskirts of Beijing. Peter looked in the eyes of the eager class and thought that it was almost too bad that these kids would never be able to apply their incredible knowledge of the English language in America. At least not if he could help it.

Chapter 33

Shue was a bachelor. No wife, no kids, and both of his parents were dead. That made his decision to flee the country a little bit easier. The Communists were known to punish the families of high-ranking defectors, jailing and sometimes severely torturing them. Shue would've left anyway, he just had too much to lose if he stayed, but he felt a lot more comfortable knowing that he had left nothing behind; his conscience was clear.

He took one last look at his apartment and felt another wave of anger at the members of the Standing Committee for inflicting so harsh a punishment and stealing his ambition. He would have to leave everything behind: his apartment in the best section of Beijing, his antique furniture—some pieces dating back to the Ming Dynasty, his art collection valued conservatively at one million U.S. dollars, and his Tang Dynasty calligraphy sets. He had spent years collecting his treasures, calling in favors from around the country and causing just enough angst to the business elite for them to offer such princely bribes. He had worked hard to get to his position and never would he accept a face-losing post in the boondocks. Not at his age.

Shue was at the height of his career. His insatiable thirst for power, status, and money almost quenched. He closed his apartment door, got into his BMW, and started his drive south to Shanghai. It didn't matter anyway, he thought. Though his stock portfolio had been confiscated, he had amassed a small fortune through bribes, kickbacks, and an astute business sense—and when he got to Taiwan, he would make more. Thinking of his stocks brought a fresh wave of anger. "Fuckin' Wang!" he yelled above the music blaring from his CD player. It would all be okay once he got to Taiwan, he hoped. He wasn't happy about paying 50,000 U.S. dollars for a Taiwanese passport, but he needed guaranteed perfection. Getting caught in customs was not something he was even willing to think about; he would pay whatever necessary to ensure success.

Shue had considered going to America, but the risks were too great and he could blend in better in Taiwan. He initially cringed at the thought of spending the rest of his days under a government he was taught to hate, but after a moment's reflection, he gladly renounced all political loyalties and acted, as any good Communist would, in his own best interest. He drove the rest of the way to the Shanghai International Airport in a bit of a daze, struggling to keep his eyes open. He could usually make the trip in eighteen hours driving 100 miles per hour, disregarding and unencumbered by the law, but he chose to drive more cautiously with the hope of making it to Shanghai without incidence.

He entered the airport at 8:00 a.m. and parked in the long-term parking lot. He would first travel to Hong Kong on China Eastern Airlines and then connect to Taipei on Cathay Pacific. He had practiced his Taiwanese accent over the last couple of days and had developed a believable story of a business trip that he could use if asked. He checked in without trouble, but he had never been worried about the airline; it was the thought of customs that had driven his blood pressure close to cardiac arrest. He had gotten the necessary stamps copied into his passport from China, Taiwan, and Honk Kong for an additional $25,000 U.S. It would all be worth it for a successful escape. He couldn't wait to step foot in Taipei. As he inched closer to the front of the customs line, Shue felt his blood pressure rise. He confidently walked up to the agent, his countryman, and handed him his passport.

"Hello, returning to Taiwan today?" The agent didn't look up.

"Yes, yes, my business in China is done for a while." Shue replied in a flat accent, effectively curtailing his thick, Beijing accent.

"What type of business are you in?" The agent was no-nonsense, not suspicious just simply asking the standard questions.

"I have a factory outside of Shanghai where I manufacture DVD players for export to the U.S.," Shue answered confidently. The agent looked up at Shue one last time, glanced back at the line that was at least 100 people deep, and stamped Shue's Taiwan passport. He was almost home free.

The next hour before he boarded the plane felt like an eternity. He read two daily papers at the airport bar as he sipped on a Beijing beer and chain-smoked Marlboros. The cigarettes curbed his appetite, but his stomach was in such knots that food did not even enter his mind. He felt a great sense of relief when boarding started and he finally made it to his seat, 14C. The plane was only half full, with very few people sitting in the middle seats. Shue stretched his legs and closed his eyes; he had made it. Taiwan wouldn't be so bad, he thought. He could find a beautiful trophy wife, settle down, maybe start a small business exporting Taiwan-made goods to the mainland. He would let the dust clear for a while before he made any contacts with former associates. 'Who knows, maybe I'll even be able to return to China one-day,' Shue thought to himself and smiled for the first time in his long journey.

As the flight attendant was about to close the gate, she was called outside to the gangway. Shue had been watching the door from the second he sat down. When it closed and the plane pulled away from the gate, he would be home free. He wondered what was going on right outside the door of the plane. She came back in and began moving down the aisle slowly as if counting passengers. The door remained open and the person she had been talking to in the gangway remained out of sight. As she passed by Shue's row, she hesitated for only a second and looked at Shue. Shue prayed that everything would be all right. This couldn't be happening. *I'm so close, I am so close*, he continually repeated to himself.

As the flight attendant finished the count, she walked quickly toward the still open door and let inquiring passengers know that the plane would be departing shortly. She again left the aircraft, but this time only briefly, returning with three members of the military police and a fourth well-dressed man. They came directly to seat 14C and stopped.

"Mr. Shue, please come with us," said one of the young military policemen.

"Why, what seems to be the problem?" Shue asked feebly, his fate inevitable.

This time the man with the suit spoke. "Comrade Shue, you are wanted on official Party business, please come along so as not to disturb the rest of the passengers." The man spoke matter-of-factly and Shue rose obediently; he was broken. Shue reasoned that he must've been followed from his apartment, how else could anyone have identified him? "Why did you wait until I was already on the plane, why the hell did you wait until I was almost free?" Shue asked, but received no answer.

His death certificate had been written.

Chapter 34

After his classes were over, Peter went to his office and pretended to work on his lessons for the next day. At 6:00 p.m. he would go into hiding in one of the janitorial closets and wait until 8:00 p.m., when the old man went on duty. He spent his time daydreaming about Song May while he waited, wondering why she wanted to see him and whether he had made the right decision to blow her off. He also wondered about Tommy. He seemed to know more than any private investigator should, it was a story Peter found very difficult to swallow. He had doubts about Tommy's plan, but focused on thinking positively—not wanting to consider what would happen if he got caught. His stomach was tight and his throat dry. He didn't have the makeup for this type of stress. He considered walking out of the building and trying to make it on his own, but Tommy's words, 'you'll be dead anyway,' reverberated through his conscious thought. He could not back out. He looked at his watch and realized it was 5:50 p.m. The young, cocky guard whom Peter had met the first day would be making his rounds shortly.

Peter was surprised he hadn't run into Shue. Over the last few weeks Mr. Shue had been coming by the school every evening and spending an inordinate amount of time quizzing Peter on how the job was going and what he thought of the program and the students. Peter was sure Shue would show up tonight and see the anxiety and unease on Peter's face. He took Shue's absence as a particularly good omen.

Peter quietly made his way to the janitor's closet and found a place in the corner that would require anyone who happened to be looking to come all the way in, bend down, and look under the bottom cleaning supply shelf to spot Peter. Peter crouched as if a catcher ready to receive a pitch and bent his head toward his right knee to fit under the shelf. It was bearable if not awkward, but Peter knew that after a few hours it would be excruciatingly uncomfortable; nonetheless, it was the absolute best hiding place in the building.

After a short time he heard footsteps drawing closer to the janitor's closet and he knew the young security guard was making his rounds. Peter took in one last breath and concentrated on staying as steady as possible. The door to the janitorial closet swung open unexpectedly and caused the dust from the floor to blow into Peter's eyes and nose. He felt a sneeze rising quickly. He slowly moved a finger to his nostrils and held it there praying for the guard to exit as quickly as he had entered.

The guard stood at the door for what seemed like a few minutes and then he slowly began to enter the closet. It was about 15 feet from the door to the back of the closet. When the guard reached the back, he stopped and stood motionless, waiting for his eyes to adjust to the diminished lights before looking around. He peered inside the two garbage cans filled with discarded paper and lunch boxes from that day and stuck his hand in one of them, but removed it quickly when he realized that he had found someone's half-eaten egg-drop soup. He bent down and looked under the bottom shelf on the opposite side from where Peter was hiding. Peter decided that if the guard turned to look under the shelf where he was hiding, he would jump out to surprise him and knock him unconscious. Seeing nothing under the one shelf, the guard stood and stretched his back. As he bent down again, a gust of wind from an open window across the hall caused the door of the janitorial closet to slam shut. The guard, completely surprised, jumped so high his head almost hit the ceiling. He yelled at the top of his lungs and rushed for the door, and then ran into the hall panting uncontrollably and frightened as if he had just seen a ghost. Peter, too frightened to sneeze, used his right shoulder to wipe the sweat from his forehead. He was perspiring as if he had just finished a game of pickup basketball on black concrete in the middle of a hot summer day.

The next few hours were just as excruciating as Peter thought they would be. His knees were beginning to buckle and he wondered if he'd ever be able to straighten his neck again. He dare not move and prayed that the young guard wouldn't bother with another check of the closet. He waited until 10:30 before he moved, just to be safe. After listening at the door for a few minutes, Peter slowly stepped into the hallway. He was sure that the old man at the desk was already halfway through his first bottle of the Chinese equivalent of moonshine. He walked methodically through the dark hallways to the last classroom and slowly approached the door leading to the basement. He was now focused on the task at hand and curious to learn what was behind the secret door.

He had made it through the most difficult part and would not worry about the old guard until he had to leave. He had all of the tools in the inside pockets of his all-weather jacket and he slowly reached in to grab the electronic pick gun. Tommy had said it was the most advanced model and should easily pick the majority of locks. Tommy had shown Peter the technique and Peter had practiced for an hour until he had the system down. He easily opened the first three locks using the pick gun and then reached into his left side pocket and removed a set of keys known as "Auto Jigglers." They were generally used to open car doors but were also perfect for padlocks. He tried a few keys and on his fourth try he opened the padlock. He hesitated for a second wondering if the door was connected to an alarm. He saw no wiring, so he slowly opened the door. Just past the doorway was a flight of stairs leading to what appeared to be a basement.

Peter removed a small flashlight from his pocket and waited at the top of the stairs until his eyes adjusted to the darkness. He gently closed the door. At the bottom of the steps he looked around. He saw two doors. A pang of anxiety pierced his stomach and he considered an immediate retreat. On the floor he noticed two sets of footprints in the dust that had collected on the cement floor. One set of prints was fresh and distinct and of a larger shoe size than Peter's. He could make out portions of a smaller set of footprints, but they were mostly covered with a new layer of dust. Peter followed the prints with his flashlight until he reached the door on the left. That door was more fortified than the one he had just entered and the one on the right had a small lock similar to the ones used on the offices upstairs. It wasn't hard to decide which door likely led to the secrets Peter needed to uncover.

He quickly unlocked the more fortified door with his set of tools and opened it slowly. The door creaked open and he entered a large office. Inside the office was a small desk and boxes upon boxes were stacked to the ceiling along every inch of the four walls. Peter walked over to one box sitting on the floor next to the desk and opened it. Inside he found about twenty files, each in its own separate file folder. Peter opened the first folder to find what looked like a police record. In the upper-right-hand corner was a picture of a young boy wearing a white shirt, a crew cut, and a blank expression. The picture could have been any one of his current students. Along with the picture were fingerprints, basic statistics that looked to be height and weight, and a bunch of other information written in Chinese. The rest of the folder held several other documents in Chinese. Peter quickly glanced at the other folders and found they were all the same. As he reorganized the folder of the first boy, he noticed something at the bottom written in English: *San Francisco, Scott Chen*. His heart started racing uncontrollably. He knew he had struck gold.

He turned his flashlight towards the boxes on the wall, grabbed one, and placed it on the floor. He took another and placed it right next to the first. Using one of the boxes as a seat, he opened the top of the other and began removing files. He again leafed through the top file looking for any documents written in English. Stuck in the middle he found something in English that looked like an evaluation similar to the one's he was required to fill out for each student. He looked to the bottom of the document to see if a previous teacher had signed it, but found no signature. The report was straightforward, similar to what Peter had written on his own evaluations. The student excelled in English, seemed to have a better grasp of English grammar and vocabulary than American students of similar ages, and had a particular interest and fascination with America. The student was outgoing and confident. Peter quickly looked at another file and found another English evaluation almost identical to the first, and Peter guessed that the previous teacher would agree with him that these evaluations were useless. Every student was suspiciously almost perfect. He recalled a discussion with Shue months earlier, in which he'd tried to explain that the evaluations were a waste of time and bureaucratic nonsense. Shue was emphatic that the evaluations were part of the job and in the job description and therefore needed to be completed. Peter replaced the document and turned to the first page of the file. At the bottom, he again found an English name and the name of an American city. In this case it was Sam Chang and the city was Chicago. He looked at another file with the name Robert Wu and the city was Seattle. Each file he opened showed the same exact thing.

He quickly removed the mini-scanner and focused the flashlight. He only had to copy the main page listing the student's vital information, picture, and most importantly, his or her English name and the American city. By now Peter realized that each student had clearly spent time in the listed American city and connections were firing in his brain, itching to take a moment to put the pieces together. If the students in these files had anything to do with the espionage in America, Peter was sitting on a gold mine. If he got caught, he was a dead man. He pushed away the urge for more analysis and got right to work. He probably had 400 hundred files to copy. Peter had practiced using the copier at the safe house and had become rather adept at it, but even so it would take him about a minute to copy each file, return it to the proper folder, and replace it in the box. The scanner was small, so he had to go over each page twice to get a full copy. At the rate he was going, Peter would be lucky to finish by 4:00 a.m. Winston would drive to the front of the building at exactly 4:30 a.m. and take care of the guard at the entrance. He would only wait two minutes for Peter. If Peter didn't show, he was on his own. Peter figured that left him a thirty-minute cushion to get everything done. He worked quickly and paid little attention to time.

At about 1:00 a.m., he heard footsteps from the floor above. They were uneven as if the old guard were staggering and he thought he heard him singing. Poor old guy, Peter thought. He wondered what would happen to him once they figured out that Peter had stolen their most sensitive data. Peter hoped that the guard would be asleep when he had to leave. While Winston was taking care of the entrance guard, Peter had to make it past the old drunkard on his own, and he still wasn't sure how he'd handle a confrontation.

At about 4:14 Peer finished the last file in the last box; his right wrist was throbbing with pain, but he was happy to be finished with phase one of the plan. Everything had gone smoothly, but the most unpredictable part of the mission was next. Peter returned the boxes to the exact spot he had left them, put the scanner back in his pocket, and walked back up the steps of the basement with flashlight in hand. It was 4:25. He used his jacket to brush away any footprints he had left in the thick dust on the floor and before he left the basement he brushed off all of the remaining dust from his jacket and hands. He slowly opened the door and listened for a minute. The entire place was pitch black and silent. It was cold and, despite the heat being turned off hours before, the smell of coal still permeated the entire building. Peter stepped slowly toward the main entrance and listened once again outside the thick metal door that led to the reception area and front door. He heard nothing, but he also knew that no matter how drunk the old guard was, he would hear the door open and try to stop Peter. Peter decided to open the door and run, hoping that by the time the guard realized what happened, Peter would be gone.

He quickly opened the door and took off. The guard, sound asleep, was quickly aroused by the loud noise of the slamming door, but by that time Peter was almost out the door.

"Hello? Hello!" Peter heard the guard yell as he crashed through the locked glass door and ran to the main street hoping Winston Chang was waiting for him. As Peter made it to the street, as if on cue, headlights turned on and the car raced forward. Peter got in and the two were off. Out of the back window, Peter saw the old man looking in disbelief, his gun still inside its holster. Winston raced to a main street and eased the car to below the speed limit. Very few cars were on the street, but Winston noticed that a Buick was close behind them; he couldn't tell if they were being followed.

"What happened to the guard by the entrance?" Peter asked Winston.

"He should come to in a couple of hours. I knocked him pretty good over the head with a piece of concrete, but don't think I killed him. How'd it go in there?"

Peter's head was reeling. He couldn't believe what he had just done. "Went well, no major problems. I was almost discovered by the day guard, but besides that one close call everything was fine." Peter was still breathing heavily, but he was slowly beginning to calm down. He was still in shock at what he had accomplished and the exhilaration of his achievement was beginning to permeate through his entire body.

"Good, glad to hear it. Hand over the scanner, Peter." Winston asked good-naturedly enough, but Peter heard it more as an order.

"I think I'll hold onto it for a while, it makes me feel safe, like I'm still worth something. I carried out my part of the bargain and if you don't mind, until you deliver me safely to friendly soil, I think I'll just hold onto it." Peter noticed Winston's demeanor change.

"Okay, Peter, quid pro quo." Winston reached into his briefcase and pulled out a Swiss passport and $2000. "As of right now, you are a Swiss National. You entered the country three days ago on a tourist visa. All the proper stamps are inside. There's a backpack and a change of clothes in the trunk. We'll be driving north to the Chinese border with Russia. We'll be ditching this car soon to travel by truck with a Chinese National who will be going to Russia to sell Chinese-made shirts and pants in the Russian border towns. It's quite a common practice and the Chinese border guards have become very lax. The driver has made this trip many times before and is friendly with most of the guards. I will ride up front with him and you'll hide in the back under the clothes. The Chinese do much more thorough searches of the trucks returning to China, so we don't foresee a problem. Once in Russia, you'll be met by one of our associates who will make sure you get home." As Winston explained each detail of the escape, he drove through the streets of Beijing circling the city twice in an attempt to lose the Buick that he was now sure was following him. Peter, so engrossed in the details of his border crossing had ceased to notice anything.

"Okay, that makes me feel a bit better, I just hope those border guards don't check the back of the truck."

"Don't worry, if need be we'll throw a couple hundred bucks their way and all problems will be solved. We're almost home free.

201

Now Peter, please hand over that scanner. I need to have it in my hands," Winston pressed.

"Okay, take it easy. What the hell do ya think I'm gonna do with it? Here take it." Peter removed the scanner from his pocket and lightly tossed it onto Winston's lap. As he did this, a silver Buick with black, tinted windows pulled up beside the car on the driver's side and knocked into it trying to run it off the road.

"Shit, Peter, this car's been following us almost since we left the school. If I can't ditch it, we may both have to make a run for it." Sweat dripped down Winston's cheek as he maneuvered the car on the still empty 3rd Ring Road. They continued racing down the highway at 80, 90, then 100 miles an hour, but no matter what Winston did, the Buick remained on his tail. Every few seconds the Buick bumped the rear bumper, each time causing the car to almost lurch off the road. Winston did everything he could to outrun the Buick, but it continued to apply pressure, with each contact nudging Winston and Peter closer to careening off the road. He tried to lose the Buick by taking the Song San exit back to central Beijing. It was now 5:00 a.m.; the winter sun wouldn't rise for another two hours, but the city was already beginning to wake up. The Buick anticipated the move and followed closely behind. As they reached the bottom of the exit that connected to the main road, the Buick sped up and rammed the car with enough force to cause Winston to lose control. He rammed straight into some bamboo scaffolding located at the edge of a huge construction site. Both Winston and Peter staggered out of the car and began running. As they crossed a mostly empty street, a shot ripped through the quiet Beijing morning and pierced Winston's right thigh. He fell, unable to move.

"Peter, take the scanner and run. Get to the U.S. Embassy; you can get help there. Run, Peter, or you'll be dead too." Winston tossed the scanner to him and Peter took off down a side street.

He wanted to look back, but forced himself to stay focused on the road ahead. He ran straight for the Shin Dong neighborhood about a ¼ mile away. It contained more hutongs per square mile than anywhere else in China. He would lose his assailant in the alleys or he would die trying. He was about five miles from the embassy. As Peter ran, the person driving the silver Buick slowly walked up to Winston, raised a 9-millimeter pistol, shot once, and then continued running down the street toward Peter.

Chapter 35

Peter continued to run until he reached an entrance to a cluster of hutongs. Very little light filtered into the cluster, but Peter had been through this maze at least twenty times. He started walking and thinking how he would escape, relieved that he had taken the time to become familiar with these paths when he first arrived in China. He wondered if Song May was chasing him; she was as familiar with this area as he was. In fact, it was she who had originally introduced Peter to this section of Beijing. He made his way slowly through each passage, contemplating at each crossroad which path to take. As he turned left into a long, dark passage that would eventually lead him out of the maze and hopefully to safety, he heard footsteps and began to run.

Peter was an in an all-out sprint, knocking over water pails, tripping over hoses, and scaring the old men and women who were just stepping outside to begin their morning stretches. As fast as he ran, he still heard the footsteps behind him and they seemed to be getting closer. Peter decided to cut back through a different alleyway, one with more dead ends and endless tributaries. It was his only escape. He cut down one street, taking countless rights and lefts in succession and then listened for the footsteps. He heard none, but kept running. He felt his jacket to make sure the scanner was still there. It was. He made one more turn and then headed down the last hutong before the main street. As he approached the street, a man dressed in all black, like a ninja, jumped out from behind a dumpster, grabbed Peter from behind, and pointed a gun at his temple.

"You are a stupid American, no one can maneuver the hutongs better than a Chinese. You're a dead man, but perhaps I'll make a deal for the right information." The man spoke perfect English. Peter wanted to say 'Fuck you,' but remained silent, praying for a miracle and watching his life flash in front of him.

"Who are you working for? Are you CIA? How many others are there?" As they spoke, the man tightened his grip on Peter's left arm as if he were about to break it. It hurt like hell.

"Who the fuck are you?" the man repeated with more vehemence. As he asked, he punched Peter in his solar plexus with such force that Peter had to be physically held up to not keel over.

"If I don't get an answer from you in the next three seconds, you're history. One, two—" Before the man finished his count, a gun shot silenced him. Peter screamed and as the man's flaccid body dropped to the ground, Peter fell on top of him. As he looked up, a beautiful woman looked down on him. It was Song May.

They stared at each other for a moment, saying nothing.

"Come with me, I know a safe place to hide until we figure out what we're going to do. This one had followed me; there are no doubt others." Song May grabbed Peter's hand and he followed obediently wondering what would happen next.

Chapter 36

They quickly walked in silence along a side street and arrived at an old, dilapidated, soviet-style building. Very few lights were on and the hallway looked like it hadn't been cleaned in months. Two bicycles with flat tires were chained to the railing leading up to the first floor. They looked like they had been there for twenty years. Song May and Peter walked to the second floor and Song May felt above the door for a key.

They entered a clean, lived-in apartment. To the right of the front door was a folding table and chairs and to the left was a chest of drawers and a small bed. Directly in front of them was a small temple that Peter knew was used to honor and pray for a family's ancestors. It was a small studio with a tiny bathroom and kitchen: no bigger than the average walk-in closet.

"Nobody knows about this place so it should be safe for you until we figure out what to do next. My grandfather's closest friend used to live here. They served together in Mao's army and walked side-by-side in the Long March. They were best friends and were both idealists until the day they died, oblivious to what was going on around them. He died about two months ago, but I didn't have the heart to clean the place up."

Song May talked a mile a minute, avoiding the inevitable conversation and not allowing Peter to get a word in edgewise.

Song May looked at Peter as they sat in silence for a moment and then hugged, both feeling the stress and anxiety release from their bodies. They were crying. When Peter finally spoke, his practical mind returned to how they would escape.

"Song May, I want you to come back to America with me. I won't leave here without you. I don't know how we'll do it, but there must be a way out of this country. I mean thousands of illegal immigrants arrive on U.S. shores from China every year."

"I wish it were that simple, Peter. It's easy to leave if no one cares if you stay. Our situation is slightly different, but I do have a plan."

Peter had taken a seat on the bed and leaned up against the wall. Song May sat directly opposite him on a chair from the kitchen table. Her whole body looked exhausted but her eyes were alert. She looked beautiful even in her disheveled state.

"Peter, you deserve an explanation." She lifted her hand to stop Peter from speaking. "Please listen to what I have to say. I need to get this out. Peter, since we last saw each other I've been watching your every move. It was the most difficult thing I've ever had to do in my life. I followed you to the Cowboy Bar and watched you stagger home drunk. I was with you when you circled the city for two hours like a lost little puppy. I wondered if you'd ever make it home." They both laughed. "I saw you speaking with Tommy Anderson." Peter was surprised, but let her continue.

"He's CIA. I wasn't sure at first, but I also followed him and his partner until I was convinced. I don't know what he told you, but I'm positive it wasn't the truth. They are using an international consulting company as their cover."

"Song May, I don't know what the hell to believe. Tommy gained my trust, told me my life was in danger, and I came to the conclusion that he was my only way out of the country. I wondered where and how he obtained his information, but there was no way I could draw the connection that he was CIA. He did honor his end of the agreement. He provided me with a Swiss passport and would've helped me out of the country … or maybe I was being used. I'm so fuckin' naïve."

"Peter, you were in the wrong place at the wrong time. There was no way you could even begin to fathom what was involved. But, Peter, Anderson doesn't give a damn about you. I wanted to protect you. I knew you were getting yourself into a situation that you would never be able to free yourself from. I wish you knew how many times I recommended to my superiors that you be deported, but nobody would listen. I watched your every move, Peter, and saw how much you were suffering. I wanted to be with you, but I had to deprive myself of everything I desired.

"For the last thirty years I've been indoctrinated to serve and do anything for my country, to die for my country. As a child, I wanted nothing more than to be a revolutionary and as I entered the most elite military schools, my love and loyalty to China and the Party increased to an almost manic state. It was country over anything else. Every time your face appeared in my mind or I daydreamed of being with you, I thought of my grandfather and how ashamed he would be of me if I betrayed China. I sacrificed everything for my country from the time I was a child, but my country has stolen my soul and denigrated me to the point of questioning my own self-worth, something that I could've never imagined happening to me. I've committed my life to my country but it has given me nothing in return. I refuse to live my life like that anymore." Song May abruptly stopped her emotional confessions. She was so uncomfortable with sharing her feelings and expressing emotions that she returned to her pragmatic side almost in mid-sentence.

"Peter, Mr. Shue is dead."

Peter leaned further towards her, "I copied every document in the basement; I know everything." They were talking in non-sequiturs. So much needed to be said and shared. Peter was starting to realize the power of big brother and the tight grip the Communist Party held over even the most powerful citizens.

Song May continued with her confessions, "The Standing Committee is tying up all loose ends. Protecting itself by permanently silencing anyone involved. I was sent to kill you tonight, but they obviously didn't trust me to complete my task. The Communists will do anything to preserve the mission. I'm sorry you ever got involved. Peter, I've done some terrible things in my life. I've murdered, I've manipulated, I've played on the emotions of others, but over the last few weeks I've been able to think, to make peace with myself and the legacy of my grandfather. I refuse to deprive myself of the things that matter most. Peter, I love you, I always have."

Peter lunged for her and pulled her into his arms, talking into her neck, "I love you, I knew it from the first moment we met, I knew." They were standing in the middle of the room hugging, the morning Beijing sun having barely escaped the clouds and entering the room through a small window on the south side of the apartment. They were both crying and kissing uncontrollably.

"I want to be with you always," Peter whispered in her ear.

"Peter, I will never let them hurt you. I will call in every connection I have ever made to get you out of the country. I promise."

Tommy Anderson was at the safe house when he heard the news of Winston's death. The embassy called and said that he had been shot in the head at close range. The local news' leading headline was of a high-speed chase on the 3rd Ring Road. The driver of the other car, a silver Buick, was still missing and police were searching the area and questioning witnesses, the reporter said. No mention was made of Peter, but Tommy couldn't trust the Communist-controlled news to report anything accurately. He was certain someone must've seen a white male running from a car wreck and being chased. Even at such an early hour, there had to be at least one witness. Tommy figured if there were any witnesses, the police had already gotten to them and were pursuing any leads.

Tommy was in damage-control mode. Winston's death would be traced back to the faux consulting firm, and with too much scrutiny Tommy's cover would be blown. Tommy couldn't even be sure whether Peter was still alive. The police that arrived at the car accident could've carried him from the scene in order to avoid CNN or some other western news agency picking up the story. Of course, he hoped Peter was still alive, but more than that he hoped Peter had been able to uncover useful information at the school and scan evidence of the Chinese espionage. His gut instinct and what he wanted to believe contradicted one another dramatically. He needed to know the status of Peter and that scanner.

Tommy was to call his boss back in Virginia that afternoon. He dreaded the conversation and knew reassignment was inevitable. He'd be pushing papers behind some desk at headquarters for at least the next six months. He was still upset that his plan had gone so terribly wrong and angry with himself for never seriously considering that anyone would be tailing Winston. In hindsight everything was so clear. He knew it had to be Peter's girlfriend; she had been following Peter's every move and most likely every other person who came into contact with Peter. He was pissed at himself for his inattention to detail. His carelessness blew the only lead he had, cost his colleague his life and potentially Peter's, and would cost his career dearly. "I really fucked up this time," Tommy said aloud as he got up from the kitchen table and headed for the bathroom to get ready for a day he was sure he would not soon forget.

Chapter 37

Peter and Song May spoke of her plan to get them out of the country. It was late morning and both assumed the city was already swarming with undercover agents looking for both of them.

"Peter, we are going to have to leave the country separately. You first and then I will try to get out a couple of days later."

"Song May, I'm not leaving without you."

"Peter, I may never get out of this country. They want you dead simply because you may know something, but they are currently unaware of the documents you possess. Me, on the other hand, they know I have all of the information to destroy the mission. To allow me to escape would mean the end of the most successful espionage program perhaps in the history of the world. Every woman crossing the border will be scrutinized, all loads will be checked, and all border crossings will be secured. It will be next to impossible, but I have to try. It'll also be difficult for you, but I will convince them you're already dead so that they can stop looking for you. It will buy you some time. I'll have you cross in the south at a less secure border. A car will pick you up within the next hour."

Peter did not like this plan one bit. "Song May, this is crazy, let's leave together. Go for broke and if we don't make it, then we die together. Why are we splitting up?" He was getting scared.

"Peter, listen to me. You need to leave as soon as possible and I need to set the plan so you can leave. There's no time to contemplate what the ideal way would be. I may not make it out of the country alive, but I will not take you with me. You will be safe in forty-eight hours and if all goes to plan, I'll be with you."

"Where will I go? Where will we meet?"

"I'll meet you in a week at the Three Delights Guest House on Kao San Road in Bangkok, Thailand. If I'm not there in seven days, I want you to fly home. Promise you'll do that."

"I don't know if I can do that."

"Peter, do you realize the danger you're in? If the corporate espionage program is revealed, the entire nine-member Standing Committee will be impacted. These nine people control 1.3 billion people and a land mass bigger than the States. Besides the President of the United States, no one in the world is more powerful. Do you understand what I'm saying? Your life is meaningless to them. They will not let a lone American teacher impact their careers, their retirement, or their legacy—they want you dead. Can you grasp what's involved? You will do exactly as I say and if we're lucky, one of us will get out alive." Song May was yelling at Peter. The conversation was over.

Peter dropped his head and then looked back up at Song May, "What do I need to do?"

"Four things. One, wait for the driver to pick you up and do exactly what he says. Two, call your parents; it may be the last time you ever get to speak with them. Three, whatever money you have, tell your father to take it and sell the following Hong Kong Stock Exchange traded companies short." She handed him the list. "Once the information leaks, the companies that received the stolen technology will tank and there is no reason why we shouldn't benefit. Four, whatever you do, do not give any of the information you have to the CIA. I've been working against them my entire life and I'm not about to help them solve the most important case of the last hundred years. Do as we discussed." She handed Peter the phone, kissed him, and left.
Peter used the apartment phone. It was still working, though the connection was horrible.

"Dad—"

Peter's father didn't give him time to finish. "Peter? Where the hell have you been? We haven't heard from you in two weeks. We tried calling you at that school number you gave us before you left, but no one speaks a lick of English. What've you been teaching them over there, French?"

"Dad, I'm sorry. Listen I need to talk to you."

"Your mother's half out of her mind, thinking the worst. Wondering if the Commies arrested you for preaching human rights or something. She knows how passionate you are about your causes. She's already called the U.S. Embassy once, but they've been no help. Bunch of bureaucrats! Your mother's gonna be upset that she missed you, she just left to catch a movie downtown with her sister." The more Peter's father talked, the calmer he became. After not hearing from Peter last Sunday, he had spent almost every waking minute worrying.

"Dad, I'm sorry. The last two weeks have been more traumatic than any time in my life. My girlfriend left me, and—"

"You've left us in the dark over some girl? Who is this girl? Your mother is frantic, Peter. What were you thinking?" William's rational, calm demeanor, which had made Peter's father so successful in the workplace, was nowhere to be found when matters of his son were involved.

"Dad! Dad! Jesus! Enough!" Peter had to cut to the chase. "There are things I can't explain to you. I'm in trouble."

"What kinda trouble? I can barely hear you, speak up."

"Dad! Just listen. I think I'm going to be all right. One day I hope I can tell you everything that's happened to me in China, but I can't right now. I need you to trust me. Everything's going to be okay. I need a favor, but I need you to believe in me on this."

"Peter, when have I not believed in you? I don't know what you've gotten yourself into. Tell me, what do you want me to do? Should I send money? I don't know what I can do from 6,000 miles away, but tell me what's on your mind." His father had started to calm down and then suddenly remembered what had been said earlier. "What kind of trouble are you in? Did you knock some girl up?"

"Jesus Christ! NO! Just listen to me for a second." Peter decided to just blurt it out. "I want you to take the $150,000 Grandpa left for me and use it to sell a few companies short on the Hong Kong Stock Exchange."

"What—" William tried to interrupt.

"Dad, I need—" Peter started before William persisted.

"Peter! I heard you just fine. I'm just going through the process of the outlandish scenarios or the possible circumstances that would require you to make such a request, but absolutely nothing comes to mind. This is way out of left field, Peter. Selling short is extremely risky, you know how difficult it is to predict the market, but besides that fact, Grandpa worked his whole life for that savings. Remember how proud he was every time he got his monthly statement from Washington Mutual? He'd look at that thing for hours. He left every cent of it to you and he'd be turning in his grave if he knew you wanted to risk it on some speculation. Why, Peter? What has suddenly brought this on? How much trouble are you in? Have you been kidnapped, why do you need the money?" His father was listening intently on the other side of the world and feeling completely helpless.

"I'm not in any financial trouble, don't worry," Peter assured him. "This is a sure thing and if you hold your tongue, I will elaborate. I know this sounds like pure folly and I can only imagine what's going through your head right now, but I need your blind trust and if I'm wrong, I'll earn it back through hard work. But, this is guaranteed and I need you to trust me."

William could not even fathom what Peter was into. He simply could not come up with any logical reason, but he knew that he was not going to get any answers. He gave in and listened.

"Have you been following the Chinagate scandal going on in the States?" Peter felt he was starting to crack through his father's skepticism.

"Of course, it's been plastered all over the news for months; I'm tired of that damn story."

"Well, it's all true! The story is going to break within the next week. I'm involved!" Peter reflexively laughed.

"Involved with what? Peter, what kind of nonsense is this? Peter, when are you coming home? Let's continue this conversation stateside. Do you need money for a plane ticket?"

Peter was starting to panic. He only had about ten minutes before he was to meet the van. He was shocked that he had maintained his composure this long. He thought for a moment that this could be the last conversation that he would ever have with his dad and regretted making the call and discussing some money-making scheme.

"Peter, I don't know what you've gotten yourself into; are you in danger?" William sensed the desperation in Peter's voice and the tenseness. "I'm worried about you. I want you to get out of the country. I'm calling the Embassy ..."

"Dad, I love you." Peter's hand was trembling and his voice was beginning to crack. The only thing that had been keeping him level-headed was the unwavering confidence in Song May, but for the first time he seriously thought of how slim his chances were of getting out of China alive. Tears began running down his face.

"Peter, what's going on?" Peter could almost feel his father's blood pressure rising and sense the stress he was putting him through. He started to regret ever making this call. Until he was safe, his parents would be worried sick. He didn't need to put them through this, and if it was the last time they would speak, why was he bringing up money? The whole call was a bad idea. He shouldn't have listened to Song May. What the hell was her problem? It was the first time he questioned the soundness of her plan. He was now in too deep with his father and against his judgment, continued the conversation.

"Dad, I need you to believe in me, to have confidence that I can make my own decisions, just this once." Peter knew what buttons to push to get his father to listen. Anytime Peter questioned his father's confidence in him, he would subsequently get what he wanted. It was an abuse of the father-only-son relationship that Peter used infrequently, but to his advantage to get what he wanted from time to time. He invariably felt guilty after the manipulation.

"Dad, I want you to take my $150,000 and I want to borrow $100,000 from you. I promise I will pay you back every penny with interest. I don't have any more time to discuss this, please have faith in me. Place all of the money in offshore accounts and sell the following stocks short. Do you have a pen?"

"Peter, I'll set this up for you and invest your money, but will only lend you mine if I think what you say is sound. Damn it! I wish you were here so I could discuss this with you face-to-face. I hate making decisions based on pure speculation and emotion; they always end badly, but it seems I have little choice in the matter. Okay, what are the names?"

"Yong Gan Technology, FutureScope Tech, Dynasty Tech, SunMoon Tech, Chen Labs, and Coastal Technologies."

"Peter, maybe you should go straight to the Embassy?" Although phrased as a question it came off more as a plea.

"They'd never let me make it there. I'm gonna be okay. Tell Mom I love her. Dad, I love you, I'll see you soon."

"Wait, Peter, who are 'they'?" He wanted to delve deeper, but had a horrible premonition emanating from the pit of his stomach. "Peter! I'm proud of you," William hesitated for a moment, "Always have been. You're the greatest thing that's ever happened to your mom and me. You can't imagine how much you've enriched our lives. I love you, Peter. I love you more than God knows."

"Dad, I'll be home soon; I'm going to make it. I love you too." They hung up the phone simultaneously, both unable to control their tears.

Chapter 38

At exactly 2:30 p.m. Peter went downstairs. As he exited the front entrance he saw a black Chrysler minivan with tinted windows. As he approached, the passenger door opened. Peter stepped in and was face-to-face with a short, bald Chinese man sitting in the driver's seat. He looked to be about sixty, and Peter guessed he barely weighed 100 pounds. Most notably, he had what looked to be a knife wound running down his left cheek. He blinked uncontrollably. A mound of sweaters piled to the roof filled the entire van right up to the front seats.

"I Chang," he said in heavily accented English and pointed to himself. "You down," he said and pointed to the floor. Chang seemed to think it necessary to compensate for his limited English skills by yelling, thinking this would assist Peter in understanding him. It didn't.

"I stop," Chang yelled as he demonstrated pounding his foot on the brakes, "you in," and he pointed to the sweaters. Peter couldn't completely tell because he couldn't see through the sweaters, but he assumed that the seats had been removed from the minivan to fit more product. The sweaters weren't folded, wrapped in bags, or protected in any way. They were simply stuffed into the van until not one more could fit. Sweaters from floor to ceiling.

"I stop, you in!" Chang repeated even louder after he did not get a quick enough response from Peter.

"Okay," Peter said. He gathered that if the van stopped for any reason he was to hide in the pile of sweaters so as to go undetected.

"Now! I go, you down," he pointed to the floor again and Peter took a seat on the floor between the driver and passenger seats on top of a few sweaters that had fallen from the heap.

Song May had said that Chang was a trader. He bought the sweaters for cheap and then drove them into Laos where he would set up a small stand in an outdoor market and sell his wares for a tidy profit. He had a cousin in Laos who had escaped China during the Cultural Revolution who would help him bargain with the locals. She said he had been doing this for at least seven years so he knew all of the border guards. Song May was confident it wouldn't be a problem, but worried slightly that security might be tighter even in the south. Song May assured Peter that Chang could be trusted. He was a close friend of the family. He was once a loyal Communist Party official but was purged during the Cultural Revolution because he had an uncle who had fled to Taiwan during the war with the Nationalists. He was imprisoned and tortured for six years, and according to Song May, his survival is a testament to his courage and will. His antipathy toward the Communists bordered on manic. Song May also said that she chose him because he had once said to her, and demonstrated with his careless behavior, that he had not felt fear since he was released from prison. He had said, 'Nothing can be as horrific as what I went through during the Cultural Revolution.' She was confident he could easily get through every checkpoint.

As Peter headed south on his forty-eight-hour whirlwind tour of Southern China, Song May returned to the safe house after taking care of preparations. She had spoken to her parents earlier and explained to them as directly as possible that she was about to defy the Standing Committee and allow the exposure of the most successful U.S. infiltration in China's history. Song May was fortunate that she had no brothers or sisters and that her immediate relatives, but for her parents, had all fled the country years earlier. She would feel no guilt about leaving, confident that no one from her family would suffer repercussions from her decision.

Her parents realized the gravity of the situation and understood they had little choice but to follow Song May's instructions. They were actually only mildly upset at her for planning to disgrace the family name by betraying the Party. Her parents had become sedentary in recent years and Song May thought perhaps this dramatic change in their lives would benefit them. She hoped they would feel the same way. Her parents had both become dispirited as mid-level bureaucrats working in the Ministry of Information. They jointly edited newspaper articles, making sure that nothing printed disparaged the Party. They lived their lives with as much enthusiasm as a child has before going to the dentist's office. Song

May could barely remember how her parents were in their idealistic days. She was too young to see them at their best, but vividly recalled their transformation from a young couple with a bright future to lifeless souls waiting to die. The weight of the Party had crushed their dreams and ambitions. The economic reforms over the last twenty years only exacerbated the problem.

Song May's aunt, her mother's sister, lived in Taiwan, having escaped China about fifteen years ago. Song May had already called and told her aunt that her parents were coming. Song May used most of her meager savings to purchase perfectly-copied Taiwanese passports for her parents to get them across the border. Her aunt understood without needing to ask any questions. Song May didn't think her parents would be targeted until after it was confirmed that Song May had betrayed her country and fled, and by that time she planned on them being out of China.

Song May's next stop was the fashion shopping district in downtown Beijing. She bought her parents the latest fashions straight from Taiwan. Her parents no longer wore the Party-issued, blue 'Mao' jumpsuits, but their senses of fashion hadn't advanced much beyond China in the '70s. She wanted them to blend in right away, at least with their appearance. Taiwan would be an easier adjustment for her parents, especially compared to the West, Song May thought. They had family and knew the language and the culture. Despite fifty years of separation, Taiwan and the mainland still had much in common. She wasn't sure if she was just trying to rationalize her feelings of guilt for putting her parents in harm's way and burdening them with her troubles, but she hoped the move would be good for them: a new start.

Her parents had said little on the phone, simply accepting their fate—as the Chinese seem to do so well—neither rebuking Song May nor consoling their only child. Song May gave them little chance to protest as she launched into an explanation of what would happen in the next forty-eight hours; they knew they had no choice but to listen.

Song May left Liu's apartment for the last time and walked three blocks to an open-air vegetable market. She was certain that she was not being followed, but not certain whether any red flags had gone up at Party Headquarters. She was scheduled to meet the General at 3:00 p.m., fifteen minutes away. She would go to the meeting and say Peter was dead. It would give her parents and Peter the requisite time to safely flee the country without scrutiny. Eyewitnesses had probably seen Peter being chased, but she was confident that nobody had seen her take him and lead him to the safe house. Song May would attend the meeting, confirm that the mission had been accomplished, and explain everything that had transpired the previous night. This would temporarily ease General Wang's fears and give Song May valuable time to arrange for her own escape.

The market was teeming with activity; each stall was crowded with grandmothers wearing polyester pants and thick, brightly-colored sweaters haggling over price as if it were sport. Buyer and seller enjoying the process of doing business, laughing as money exchanged hands. Song May was a regular at the market. As she passed by each stall, the vendors yelled for her to come over, enticing her by holding up fresh oranges, her favorite fruit, and promising special discounts especially for her. She responded to each pitch with a smile and a promise to return later. She continued walking until she reached the end of the market, and then she turned left and walked down a store-lined side street. The street was crowded with afternoon bargain hunters searching for deals among the many daily sidewalk sales. Song May walked into a small kiosk that sold cigarettes and candy. An old woman with dyed jet-black hair tied in a bun and held up with a chopstick was sitting behind the counter looking bored as she read the China Daily.

As she noticed Song May enter, the old woman's energy was immediately restored at the surprise of seeing an old friend. "Song May, it's been so long, where have you been?"

"Hello, Auntie Liu! I was by just last week and spoke with your son; he said you've been feeling ill. How's your arthritis?" Song May grabbed both of Auntie Liu's hands as she asked. Mrs. Liu wasn't Song May's aunt by blood, but she had been a friend of the family for so long that Song May felt as close to her as she did with any relative.

Mrs. Liu brushed aside Song May's concerns. "Oh, I'm fine, don't fuss over me. The bones and joints just don't function as well in the winter. I'm brewing some Beijing Green Tea in back, why don't you stay for a while? Sit down, sit down, it's been too long. You never seem to age, look how beautiful you look." Auntie Liu admired Song May as if she hadn't seen her since she was a child. It had actually only been about a month.

Song May shook her head. "I wish I could, but I have an important appointment that I mustn't break. How about next week?"

"Fine, fine. The world seems to have taken on a new speed in the last few years but old Auntie Liu is still cruising in low gear. Okay, my dear, Auntie Liu's old and may have some marbles loose, but she knows when her little niece is on edge. How can I help you?" Auntie Liu was now looking at Song May and waiting expectantly for a response.

"I have something for Mom and Dad; can I leave it with you?" Song May reached into her jacket and pulled out the two passports, plane tickets, and 500 U.S. dollars. They were tightly wrapped and taped in brown paper, the kind used to wrap meat.

"Of course, is everything all right?" Auntie Liu knew not to ask too much. The request was unusual. She knew Song May's parents only lived a few blocks away, so assumed correctly that it would be inconvenient for Song May to deliver the package—for a reason other than distance. It took all of her discipline not to pry, but from her own past experiences during the Cultural Revolution, she knew it was better not to know certain things. Ignorance was often the key to self-preservation in China.

"Everything's fine, Auntie Liu. Please just make sure they get this, they should be by shortly. Now, I really must go." Auntie Liu stepped from behind the counter and the two women hugged for longer than they normally would, both certain it would be the last time they would ever see each other.

222

Song May left the store fully trusting Auntie Liu to deliver the package. She marveled at how little she could accomplish without the assistance of good friends. She was at times almost helpless without them. Her entire plan depended on unconditionally trusting the people closest to her, none of which were related by blood. She had told her parents to arrive at Auntie's kiosk promptly at 3:00 p.m. Their flight departed at 7:00, and she wanted to make sure they made it. It would be rush hour and it wasn't uncommon to get stuck in the middle of a two-hour traffic jam on Beijing streets at any time of day.

Song May wanted to make sure that Peter was out of the country or close to it before she met with General Wang, so she delayed her meeting with him for 36 hours. She was five minutes early. General Wang had not been on time for a meeting since Song May had started working on the project. Not once. But on this occasion he was waiting for her and greeted her with a nod in the reception area. She followed him into his office and sat down, for the last time she hoped, in the same place she always had; in one of the tacky, red, velvety chairs situated across from his desk. The General slowly sat down and waited for Song May to begin.

"Mission accomplished, General Wang; the boy is dead."

"He is dead?" The General was incredulous.

"Yes," she said convincingly. "My plan didn't go as smoothly as I would have liked, but I managed to track him down."

"Pursuit in a high-speed chase through the streets of Beijing ending with a major crash in a residential neighborhood is far from smooth; it is cause for your dismissal."

Song May started to defend herself. "Yes, I believe he was trying to flee the country, but—"

The General didn't let her finish. "Comrade, your work was sloppy and uncharacteristic. That boy should have been dead days ago, but instead you waited until he felt the wolves surrounding. Your high-speed chase and subsequent crash was witnessed by many, including an American who reported to the U.S. Embassy that he saw a white male running from the scene of the accident being chased by a Chinese woman. The Chinese man who you shot was also an American businessman. The Standing Committee is breathing down my neck demanding answers as well as my throat and the Americans, as you can imagine, are demanding a full and transparent investigation. Despite your success, I'm afraid your actions may cost you dearly.

"I understand, General," Song May responded. "If you remember I suggested we deport the teacher months ago."

"Yes, yes, comrade," the General sneered at Song May's defense. "Unfortunately I have neither the time nor the patience to consider what should have been done months ago. Your assignment in this project is, as of right now, terminated. You will cease contact with any of our spies overseas and will have no connection to the Academy in any manner whatsoever. Your escapade last night combined with other indiscretions committed by your colleagues have spooked the Standing Committee enough for them to order all corporate infiltration activities in the U.S. to go into complete sleeper mode until advised otherwise. This development is most unfortunate for both of us." The General looked at Song May in disgust, blaming her completely for the project's demise.

"Yes, General. Will that be all?" Song May had no reason to push further with her defense. She simply needed the General to believe that Peter was dead and that she was still on board.

"The Party Secretary would like to see you in his office tomorrow at 10:00 a.m. I believe he will discuss reassignment with you. That will be all, comrade."

"Thank you, General."

"Comrade Chen, one more thing." Song May was halfway out the door before the General called her back. "I'm curious. The Chief of Police informed me that the boy's body has not yet been found. Where may I ask, is it?"

"I was worried that we may have been seen in the chase," Song May explained, "so I waited for the boy to return to his apartment. I killed him at the entrance of the building and disposed of his body in a dumpster."

"I see. The Chief of Police informed me that the entire building and surrounding area was searched; perhaps the garbage was picked up that morning. Thank you, comrade."

As Song May left, the General picked up the receiver to his phone and his secretary answered. "Yes, General Wang."

The General commanded, "Miss Tsai, I need to speak with the Chief of Police and the Party Secretary immediately."

Chapter 39

The journey to Laos was thus far uneventful. The sweater-filled van passed through three checkpoints without incident. As Song May had told Peter, Chang knew most of the soldiers along the route. The soldiers were mostly from the countryside. Innocent kids who had joined the military for lack of other jobs and because the army gave even the lowliest of privates a sense of power and prestige: something most of them had never felt before. Over the years soldiers had come and gone, but with each new crop, Chang established the necessary relationships to ensure that his business ran smoothly. He did this primarily with money—bribes. Nothing major, but enough to keep the soldiers happy. It was a cost of doing business and saved Chang from any unnecessary aggravation. Though the soldiers abused their limited power at times, forcing Chang to unload his inventory and wait hours, they rarely did. Over the past five years and hundreds of trips, Chang had been delayed in this way only twice. Since it was now the policy of the People's Liberation Army to encourage trade and free enterprise, most of the rank and file privates didn't dare upset the flow of commerce. Sometimes Chang brought a bottle of spirits or some tea that could only be found in Beijing for the officers in charge of each post, but generally he simply greased their palms and continued on his journey.

Chang was distinctly conscious of avoiding a search on this particular run, so he doubled the bribes just in case. After driving for forty hours with only a couple of catnaps, they approached the border—and for the fourth time Chang looked down at Peter who was leaning against the passenger seat trying unsuccessfully to get comfortable enough to fall asleep. He tapped Peter's leg until Peter looked up and acknowledged him.

"You go, we Laos soon!" Chang yelled as he first pointed to the mound of sweaters in the back and then to the road. Peter had expected that sitting in the middle of a scratchy pile of half-polyester/half-cotton sweaters would be worse than it actually was. His greatest concern was how he would breathe, but just after Chang ordered Peter to go to the back right before the first checkpoint, he pulled out a small bag and handed it to Peter. Inside was a package of straws, not the thin kind you get at the local McDonald's, but the real thick ones used for shakes and slurpies. When Chang saw that Peter realized what they were for, he looked at him and smiled, showing teeth that were badly in need of a dentist. The straws turned out to be invaluable, without them Peter would have suffocated.

It was about a half-hour wait at the border. Most vehicles entering Laos were vans, similarly filled with goods to sell in the open market in the border town of Udomxai. The market had a huge demand for any type of clothes; shirts, jackets, sweaters, and pants were particularly big sellers. Sometimes importers from Vientiane, the capital, came up to the border and bought Chang's entire stock. He liked those days. During most trips though, Chang and his cousin had to apply expert salesmanship and low prices to clear their inventory. The Chinese were given visas for the day. They could choose to stay past their visas and remain the night, but the fines and bribes required for the Laotian and Chinese border guards upon returning were prohibitive.

Peter was getting restless and wondering how much longer until he would be free when he heard Chang talking with a border guard. The conversation seemed to be tenser than at previous checkpoints. Peter couldn't understand a word, but gathered that Chang's usual sweet-talking was not working. As each minute passed, Peter figured his chances of safely getting to Laos diminished. Chang clearly didn't know the border guard and Peter figured it was just his luck to run into the one soldier in all of China who was honest and incorruptible. He heard both men's voices rise in unison until both were yelling at each other simultaneously for what seemed like a minute, followed by absolute silence.

Peter heard Chang rush out of the minivan, and almost at the same time the side door opened and sweaters began pouring out. Chang rushed in front of the agent shouting that his whole inventory would be ruined, pushing his back against the sweaters to prevent any others from falling out—and to prevent Peter from being discovered. About fifty lay on the gravel road. Now Chang took a more conciliatory approach, suggesting that everything could be worked out. From his back pocket he pulled out five crisp $100

U.S. bills and nonchalantly handed them to the guard. It was his last-resort bribe if the smaller amounts didn't work. The guard looked at the bills for a moment as if to make sure they weren't counterfeit and then shoved them in his pocket. He looked at his clipboard for a minute, returned Chang's ID card, and told him to clean up the mess of sweaters and go. Chang pushed the sweaters back into the van and quickly closed the door. They passed through the border and cleared customs in Laos without further trouble. Chang drove through the dirt streets of the small border town and when he arrived at his cousin's house he called for Peter.

"You, out." Peter's entire body was drenched with sweat, his body still shaking from the stress. When he made his way through the sweaters to the front of the van he almost collapsed.

"What happen, border?" Peter pointed back towards the border and began speaking like Chang hoping it would help the two understand each other.

"He want money, Chang no give."

"Why no Chang? Why you big risk?" Peter knew it wasn't necessary for Chang to understand what he was saying; they both knew the topic of the conversation.

"He want too many, Chang say no, want give small. He open van, Chang say yes. I give $500. Now, I no profit." For Chang's limited English he conveyed what happened during his confrontation with the border guard with amazing clarity.

"I sorry Chang, I give Chang money, yes, yes!" Peter reached for his wallet in his front pocket, but before he could pull out the money, Chang lifted his hands pushing the wallet away.

"No, no, no, you need. Chang no need. Okay, okay, okay!" Chang yelled with surprising conviction, and before Peter could force Chang to take the money, he had jumped out of the van and was greeting his cousin and his wife.

After exchanging pleasantries and sitting down for tea in Chang's cousin's one-room house, the cousin led Peter to a small truck and pointed for Peter to get inside. Chang was following close behind.

"You go, he go city. Chang bye-bye."

"Thank you, Chang! You in America, you see me, yes?" Chang smiled and nodded his head confirming that he understood, and then walked to his van to prepare for his day in the market.

Chapter 40

If the Chinese Bureau of Economic Statistics could measure China's barter and underground economy, the official GDP would probably increase three fold. Song May was part of this barter economy and she used her connections and position in the Chinese Secret Service to help as many people as possible. Her salary was miniscule, but she never used her position for her own financial gain and only rarely wielded her power for personal uses. The only time she could remember taking advantage of her position was when she cut the line to be granted a beautiful apartment in the most desirable location in Beijing. It was intended for a close friend of the mayor, but Song May used her connections to obtain it. She felt intensely guilty for a couple of days, but she loved the apartment and justified her actions by convincing herself that it was part of her compensation as a poorly-paid government employee.

What Song May did use her connections for quite often though was to help others. She always went out of her way to help a friend. Besides old family friends, Song May's occupation made it difficult to get close to anyone, and she never felt comfortable about lying about basically her whole life. Though she realized the irony since her job was based on being someone else, playing roles, and lying, she felt uncomfortable having this charade pervade her personal life and so refused herself the joy of intimacy. She generally kept to herself, but her friends and acquaintances were many. Everyone knew she had a good position with the government and that she came from a good family. Many whom she helped had served under her grandfather in the military and were now retired, powerless former war heroes, but she also assisted people who just needed a hand. Most of her favors were minor. One woman who was friendly with her parents wanted a license to sell fruit at a busy section in the fruit and vegetable market; another wanted a taxi license so he could work two jobs. Requests of this nature were easy for Song May to grant. She enjoyed it and felt a sense of power that she managed to get things done that others couldn't. She did love the power, but it now seemed so fleeting. On one occasion, she helped an old family friend get a license to cross the border so he could sell kitchen supplies in the Russian Far East in a market about sixty miles outside Vladivostok. As she sat in a truck badly in need of new shock absorbers on a road in need of repaving, she prayed that she had built up enough good karma to make it safely to Thailand.

It was 8:00 a.m. on a cold December morning in Northern China and Song May was sitting in her friend's van with tea kettles, toasters, woks, pans, and a host of other items stuffed in the back of the truck. A favor returned.

She was carrying her Chinese ID verifying her citizenship and papers identifying her as a guest trader to the Russian Far East, all the information she needed to cross the border. She had a Chinese passport, but wouldn't dare use it in this situation since most ordinary Chinese citizens were still prohibited from having one. It would raise unnecessary suspicion at an obscure northern border. From there, she would make her way to the coastal city of Vladivostok and hop on a plane to Tokyo. She had a Canadian passport with the requisite Russian entry stamps as well as clothes and gear to make her look the part of a Canadian backpacker. If she had purchased the passport in the black market it would have cost her dearly, at least $100,000 U.S. and probably more, since she needed a Thai visa and a Russian entry stamp, which was notoriously hard to copy.

About seven years ago she had helped a man avoid the death penalty for murder. He was a good friend of her parents from the early days of the Cultural Revolution, and though she knew he was guilty of many crimes, he was not a murderer. At that time, Song May was considered a rising star and had the power to stay an execution. Her family connections and brilliant work with the Secret Service gave her the power to get her friend's sentence reduced to a minor charge, the Chinese equivalent of involuntary manslaughter. The man got five years and was now out forging passports and getting rich. Song May called in her favor and he happily complied.

She had decided on a Canadian passport because Canadians generally weren't scrutinized as closely as Americans, and it was a little easier to get. She had heard that over 100 genuine Canadian passports were recently stolen from a diplomat entering China and her friend was able to find her one. Essentially she could not possibly get caught as long as she didn't try to enter Canada, which she had no plans to do. It was a perfect fake.

She had her backpack hidden among the kitchen supplies in back and was now dressed as a peasant girl from the North of China accompanying her husband to Russia to sell their goods. She wasn't expected to meet the General Secretary until 10:00 a.m., so by the time red flags were raised, she'd be boarding a flight to Japan.

She took every precaution to ensure she wasn't followed and also reasoned that no one had reason to suspect that her loyalty had wavered. As far as the Party knew, Peter was dead, the leaks were closed, and the mission was temporarily halted. Damage controlled. Her parents were safely in Taiwan and her ties to China would be cut. The plan was almost foolproof. The border guards on both the Chinese and Russian sides were so used to seeing Chinese businessmen cross the border that they barely looked at their papers. Though the government miserly restricted overseas travel, they knew that almost no Chinese nationals wanted to remain in Russia long term. The cross-border trade brought reasonably-priced, good quality product into Russia, at least compared to Russian-made goods, and provided remote northern villages in China with a new, relatively-lucrative market. Trade had increased 1000% over the last five years between the two new capitalist societies.

From Tokyo, Song May would fly directly to Bangkok, Thailand to meet Peter. As she approached the border she allowed herself a moment to think about the prospect of never coming back to China. Song May was ambivalent. Her family would never be part of China again. The dynasty her grandfather had hoped to build in a 'new' China would never be. She would be the last of the Chen clan to call China home. She was going to miss her homeland and knew that not a day would go by that she wouldn't long to be back home walking the streets of Beijing, totally comfortable among her people. But, she was forced out. Things had changed. This wasn't the China she grew up in and the utopia that her grandfather envisioned was simply a figment of his imagination. But, China would always be her home and no country would be able to command the loyalty that her motherland could. She would now be country-less, a gypsy, with Peter as her only source of solace. She wondered if she were taking too big a risk. She suppressed her practical nature and prepared herself for the border crossing.

Hundreds of trucks packed with clothing made the crossing each day into Russia. The Russians were grateful, as they would never be able to get these items at such a reasonable price otherwise. The Chinese markets in Russia's Far East were helping to raise the average Russian's standard of living. The crossing had about a thirty-minute wait. Although slow on a normal day, Song May thought to herself that they were scrutinizing each vehicle a little too closely. She considered getting out of the car and running, but hesitated as she saw military personnel a few cars ahead.

As the military police approached the van, Song May knew her plan had failed. Three guards surrounded the car and asked for both her and the driver to get out. She had been followed.

Chapter 41

Peter had been waiting in Thailand for seven days. He had called his parents to tell them he was safe and purchased his plane ticket home. If she didn't show in four more days, he would have to return to America alone. If Song May didn't arrive by the seventh day, he was to send *The San Francisco Examiner* the letter that they wrote together at the apartment. He still remembered their conversation the morning before he departed for Laos. Song May told Peter about the entire operation, but as they were finishing the letter, she questioned whether she wanted to go through with it. She knew that the discovered agents would be violently interrogated by the CIA, spend their entire lives in prison, or, what she feared most, commit suicide. She pictured the unsettled souls of the agents following her around the world harassing her until her own death.

"Peter, I can't do this," she suddenly said.

"Can't do what?" Peter then realized what she meant and reassured her, "Song May we have to, this has to stop. It's the only way."

"These people trusted me; I knew every single one of them. Communicated with them when they first arrived in America and tracked them as they entered companies and worked their way up the corporate ladder. The bonds are unbreakable. We're going to have to find a better way."

"What do you suppose we do? If we don't break this case, the CIA will and they'll eventually find us. I'll probably get charged with treason. Song May, we have no choice," Peter pressed.

"Peter, whatever we do, I refuse to use these people as scapegoats. They played a part, but what choice did they realistically have? You do not understand the brainwashing and indoctrination that took place with these kids. They were trained from the time they were barely able to talk. They had no family; their only attachment was to country and to completing their mission. They had no self. Everything they did in their lives was calculated to put them in a safer and more secure position to carry out their mission. Not even the lure of a normal life in America could break the bonds between these agents and the Party. In a sense, rational thought was taken away from them, they were, and are, like machines. They are all victims."

"Song May, that is just too damn convenient. Do we blame the general because the troops killed innocent civilians? These are grown, highly intelligent adults who were able to make choices and who have not had any major influence from China for perhaps twenty years. They could have refused to continue, disappeared, and claimed they were unable to gain access to sensitive information. Pretended they were cooperating but delivered nothing. They were capable of rational thought."

"Some did rebel and disappear, but everyone who did was discovered and shot." A pleading tone crept into Song May's voice as she continued to speak. "You don't understand the pressure the agents were under to deliver. No, there was no direct contact and agents could disappear, but we seemed to be everywhere, a modern day Big Brother. I participated in this. We had agents show up at their houses unannounced, send letters threatening their lives. We broke them down constantly and then picked them back up with encouragement, words of loyalty, and love of country. Peter, this was all they ever knew. You need to understand the control we exerted. They had no choice and to make them pay would not be justice; it would solve nothing. They were pawns, can't you understand that? The powers in Beijing would not suffer. Yes, there would be loss of face, some would lose valuable stock from the bankrupted technology companies, and the diplomatic backlash would halt China's progress of entering the new world community—but essentially day-to-day they would not be affected. It will be another example of the people being sacrificed for the sake of the party. I can't, Peter, I can't."

Peter looked at the woman he loved and he softened at the desperation in Song May's voice. "Okay. Let's think of a better way. I don't know how we are going to be able to do it. We have to release at least the names of the agents who have already successfully transferred stolen technology to the Chinese companies. We can't explain the process and then not deliver the pot of gold at the end of the rainbow. Nobody would believe us, and *The Examiner* would never publish the story if they couldn't verify the facts. And, someone stateside has to be held responsible."

"Okay, I have an idea," Song May offered. "We explain step-by-step exactly how the Chinese Secret Service was able to so successfully infiltrate the U.S. companies on such a large scale. We start from the beginning. Explain how the children were forcibly taken from their homes and never allowed to see their parents again. Then we end by explaining how the Chinese companies were selected and who controlled them. We will not spare a single detail. It'll be the end of Chinagate and front-page news for weeks. *The San Francisco Examiner* will get to milk the exclusivity, and probes into the CIA's ineptness will keep the story hot. Every company will know what to look for in future background checks and current agents won't dare attempt to steal any more information. We'll provide a list of all fifty companies that the Chinese agents have infiltrated, but we'll give no names. I don't think the U.S. government will be able to bring even one successful case, even if the agents were discovered; the evidence is much too circumstantial and the agents were extremely careful to cover all of their tracks. For the students who are still studying, I will contact them right before I leave the country and let them know that their names will be released if they don't return to China immediately. As for the six agents who have already completed their missions, we will release their names. I agree with you, we have to. Peter, this is the only method I'll accept."

"All right, all sides accounted for," Peter nodded. "I only pray *The Examiner* doesn't hold the story."

Song May quickly shook her head, "This story will make a career, win awards; it's a guaranteed front page story. No reporter or editor with any ambition would hold it and risk losing exclusivity."

As Peter recounted that conversation and read the letter for the tenth time, he wondered what he should do. What if Song May was still in China waiting for her opportunity to escape? If the story broke, her chances of ever leaving China were lost—but Peter also

236

could not let the espionage continue. He hoped Song May would arrive soon.

Chapter 42

With her arms above her head and her wrists tied tightly together, Song May dangled from a rope in a semi-consciousness state; she had no recollection of how long she had been there and given up hope of being let down soon to return to her cell. The other end of the rope had been thrown over a crossbeam and tied to a hook in the wall. Her feet were about two feet off the ground. Song May's body was covered in sweat, blood, and water. She was naked.

"AHHHHHHHHHHHH, No, NO, NOOOOOOOOOOO!" If she weren't five stories below ground, her screams would be heard for miles. Song May had a very, very high tolerance for pain, but until now her threshold had never been tested. She didn't know how many more days she could survive, but she knew she had no hope of dying just yet; it wouldn't be that easy. Her captors would see that she lived, at least until they extracted the desired information.

A man about six feet tall with undistinguished features and wearing rubber gloves shocked Song May for the 20th time this session. He was a professional and had tortured hundreds of people, but rarely had he seen someone who could endure as much as Song May. In his perverted way he respected her tolerance, but it also made him that much more eager to break her. And he would break her, he thought.

In addition to an electromagnetic baton, he used an electric shocking device that resembled a clothing iron. He held the handle and applied the flat side to Song May's body. Each contact created such a shock that a welt immediately developed and blood streamed down her body. She had very few areas of skin left that did not have welts. As the torturer prepared for his next blow, the door opened and a man in military uniform, an officer, walked in smoking a cigarette.

"Take a break, comrade. A job well done," he said to Song May's torturer.

"Thank you, sir," he replied and exited the room. As the door closed, the man sat in a chair directly across from Song May; he was about three feet from her.

"Good morning, comrade. You seem to be acquiring quite a reputation around here. We are very impressed with your abilities to endure. I congratulate you." He laughed as he threw his Marlboro Light to the floor, pulling another from his front pocket and lighting it. "You have had a distinguished career with the Secret Service and we would like to offer you a full rehabilitation, but first you must tell us what we need to know."

The officer spoke calmly, almost in a pedantic tone as if Song May had been a naughty child. "Are you prepared to do that? I have in my hand a document signed by our President reinstating you; your record would be completely expunged. Let's end this. What can you tell us about the American? What does he know and where can we find him? We know you helped him escape."

Song May had so far resisted sharing any real information. She had made up stories, told countless lies, but was not sure how much more she could take. If she told the truth, they would execute her. At the moment that seemed preferable to the torture.

"Fuck you!" she yelled defiantly.

The officer stood and walked toward Song May. "We have been playing this game for seven days, are you aware of that?" He gave her a moment to answer. When she didn't, he removed his cigarette from his mouth and asked her, "Why must you be so stubborn?" He then took his cigarette and without any hesitation used Song May's stomach as his ashtray.

"FUUUUCCCCKKKKKK! You asshole, I'm gonna fuckin' kill you! FUCK!" Song May bucked, trying to kick the officer and barely missing as he quickly backed away.

The officer calmly sat back down, removed another cigarette, and lit it. Song May's back, chest, and stomach were covered with cigarette burns.

They had spent days going over the same subject. She had provided answers as convincingly as she could, but her explanations fell on deaf ears. She knew active spies in Thailand would easily find Peter, kill him, and destroy the evidence. She was completely unwilling to put Peter's life in jeopardy or take the chance of the program not being revealed to the world. They currently had absolutely no idea where he was and the story would break soon; she hoped Peter would follow the instructions she had given him.

Song May was becoming delirious and wondered if she was still capable of rational thought. Since arriving at the "rehabilitation center" in downtown Harbin, the closest major city to the Russian border, she had undergone countless sessions of electroshock torture. She had been beaten daily, her eyes so swollen that she could barely see and her jaw broken such that she could barely eat. She'd been suffocated, made to eat feces, and, besides cigarettes, she had also been burned with hot irons.

"My dear comrade, we have spent the last week closely tracing your last days of freedom. You were very busy closing all links to your homeland, weren't you? Your plan almost succeeded. Trying to send your parents to Taiwan was very clever. They could blend right in. And, I'm sure you have family who would have been able to take very good care of them. Again, it almost worked. Unfortunately for you, they were caught and will soon be joining you in our little sanctuary in the lovely city of Harbin."

"Liar, you are lying! They are safe, I made sure of that; you're full of shit!" Song May used her last bit of energy to gyrate her body to move closer to the officer; she wanted to break him in two. He couldn't be telling the truth, but how did he know so much? It was impossible that his parents had been caught, but she didn't know what to think. Her mind had grown fuzzy and she questioned her reasoning.

"Yes, comrade, it is very true and you will soon see them. We will bring them here to be close to you. If you think you've had it bad, just wait and see. They are also traitors and enemies of the state and we will inflict a "rehabilitation program" on them five times as bad as you've received. Do you want that for your parents?"

"You're lying, my parents are safe. They're free." Song May knew the torturer's techniques; he had to be lying, but after a week of abuse she couldn't be 100% certain. She could endure her own pain, but her parents would not survive one day of torture—she could not let that happen.

"I will give you a day to think about things, I expect a detailed description of everything you know. It would be difficult to see your aging parents tortured, no?" The officer stood and called for the guard.

"Take her back to her cell, handcuff her, and shackle her legs to the bars. Do not let her sleep."

The soldier untied the ropes and Song May's near lifeless body fell to the floor.

Chapter 43

Dear Jane,

Before you continue reading know that I loved you and have always loved you. What I've done to myself was the only way; any other solution would have resulted in a life more miserable than I could bear. What you'll read in the papers is mostly true, and I will not let the blame fall anywhere but on my own shoulders.

What is not true, at least for me, was the life of lies that the agents led to preserve their "covers." I lied to you from the day we met and pursued you, initially, as a way to blend more completely into the fabric of middle class America, but the love I developed was real and the life we had was my real life and everything else was a life of lies and deceit that I was unable to break away from. You and our children were the center of my world, the reason for my being, and you, Jane, were the love of my life.

On the following pages I'm going to tell you what happened to me from the time I was a child. I hope it can begin to explain why it was impossible for me to completely sever my ties with my mother country. I hope you will forgive me someday. I'll be with you always.

When I was three years old, six men from the Chinese Secret Service came to my house in a small farming community in Sichuan province 2000 miles from Beijing and took my brother and me away from our parents. We were taken to a secret facility in Beijing. The Chinese Secret Service scoured the country, accepting only the perfect candidates for a special training program. We were identical twins. That was the first criteria. No one was able to tell us apart, not even my granny who raised us from the time we were born. I remember nothing of my brother and only remember this particular day because it was so traumatic. Now I can't tell if everything I remember is true or imagined, but the details are too vivid and exact to allow me to believe that. Anyway, my brother and I were both identified as exceptionally brilliant children. I didn't know this at the time, but during training I had been told almost every day that I was specially selected from a pool of the brightest children in China. A test had been done, but it wasn't needed; we were both speaking, reading, writing, and doing basic math by the time we were three. I was supposedly the perfect candidate. The third criterion was that each child had to be extremely dexterous. Again my brother and I were exceptional. You remember how easy it was for me to pick up almost any sport? We were accepted into the program.

My parents were just coming back from the field as the men led us to the car. I can still picture my mother crying, trying to break free from the two men restraining her. I was sent to a special school where I began my life in the Chinese Secret Service and I later learned my brother was immediately shipped off to America. He was raised by two Chinese Secret Service agents acting as exchange students at a university on the west coast. He lived a normal American life as far as I know, quickly forgetting any Chinese he had learned and becoming as American as any other middle class kid. I never saw him again. When he was 12, he returned to China and was killed. The agents acting as his parents became my parents, but in effect had no influence over me. We moved to a new city and I continued the life of my now dead brother. It was a sick, but very successful program. From the minute I arrived in Beijing as a three year old, I began training to be an agent. The best teachers were brought in from the top universities to teach us every academic subject imaginable. We concentrated on Math, Science, and English. By the time I left Beijing for America to assume the life that my identical brother had been living, I spoke English as if I had lived in the States my whole life. I had no accent and was well versed in all of the cultural nuances and slang of the average American twelve-year-old boy.

I think back now and I'm amazed at the amount of knowledge I absorbed. We were trained in the martial arts, I was a black belt before I was ten, and from a very young age learned how to be calm and confident in the most stressful situations. I was trained to be a machine. Indoctrination sessions were weaved into our daily instruction. We were broken down just as if we were in boot camp and underwent severe psychological conditioning. I was in a class with about ten other children. The pressure to outperform one

243

another was intense. I slept an average of four hours per night for a period of nine years. You can't imagine how easy I thought life in America was compared to my life in Beijing. We were children of the Communist State, had no other loyalties, and were willing to die for our cause without hesitation. When I got to America, life became easy for me externally; I was finally able to apply all that I learned.

Of course I realized that all of my training had a purpose. At first I was worried that I'd be discovered, I didn't know what to expect, but my training was so complete that it was impossible to differentiate me from any other American suburban kid. The "parents" of my brother kept a detailed journal of his first twelve years, who his friends were, his teachers, coaches, his habits, his quirks. A day-to-day account of his whole life, right down to the most mundane. I assumed his life in a new city so as not to raise suspicions. In college, I once actually ran into an old friend of his, but he couldn't tell the difference. I frequently look back on those years and cannot fully believe how easily I acclimated into my new life.

I lived without worry right through high school, not grasping the burdens I would have to face. I simply enjoyed living in a society that awards and honors exceptional behavior. I was smarter than all of my classmates, more mature, and supremely confident. I thrived in America to such an extent that I never could have imagined just what life would be like here, outside the high walls of my training facility. The exhilaration of realizing that my mission was proceeding according to plan and the rush of being respected and admired by my peers was beyond intoxicating for a twelve-year-old kid. I lived my life like any other carefree teenager; that was my assignment. My caretakers had very little control, but they were able to exert pressure on me when needed by reporting inappropriate actions to headquarters. I was constantly made aware that I was being watched, that my actions were always being monitored. At times a supposed 'uncle' would show up at school or at my house and interview me for an hour, then abruptly get up and before leaving say, 'We are watching.' I also got phone calls from former instructors who would grill me over the phone until I finally broke down in tears. It wasn't until I graduated from university and went into complete sleeper-mode, isolated from any contacts from Beijing that I was able to totally break free from the constant indoctrination. But even then I believed I was being watched.

From the day I fell in love with you, not a day went by that I didn't think of escaping, of telling you what I was going through. I thought of a hundred ways to run, but after the kids were born, I was trapped. It was all part of the grand scam. I'm amazed at how such an inept government managed to run such a flawless operation. At the most inexplicable times they subtly let me know that they were there and that my family—you and the kids—would be killed if I strayed from my mission. It was never direct, but there was an unmistakable presence. They found my weakness and exploited it.

I don't know if they realized it, but their threats were unnecessary. As much as I wanted to run and knew rationally that I should at least attempt to escape, I couldn't. The mission was important, it had to be completed, I had no choice, and there was no way to control the absolute necessity to finish what I had trained my whole life to do. I always dreamed that once I sent the company's secrets and I accomplished what was expected of me, they would let me go. I'd be free to live a normal life in America with you and the kids. There is nothing else I wanted or wished for. For years I felt in total control, I was able to handle everything. A beautiful wife and family, living the American dream, climbing the corporate ladder, serving my homeland, and achieving my objective for the Communist Party. The stealing of secrets simply became another task that I did with the same proficiency that I accomplished everything else. For years I thrived in this precarious equilibrium, each day inching closer to delivering the sensitive proprietary information from Sageware that the Standing Committee in Beijing so eagerly craved.

I never knew for certain what 'they' would expect from me after I sent the corporate secrets, but I knew that my life as a Chinese Secret Service agent would end forever. I can't imagine how you must feel right now. I want to say I'm sorry, but it's useless at this point. What we had together, our accomplishments, our family, was real; it was the only thing that mattered in my life. Our life was not a lie, you weren't part of my cover, my love for you was true. I don't know what you're thinking right now and I can't imagine what you'll have to go through over the next six months, but it's better than the alternative. I spent countless sleepless nights thinking of every possible scenario and ultimately the only solution was to end my life. You must think I'm a coward, but there was no other way. I have no other choice.

I started this letter two months ago and never got further than 'Dear Jane,' the only impetus now being that I now know the end. Until today I still hoped that the problem would disappear, that we'd be able to live our lives and be free from the powers in Beijing forever. I now know my fate. I'm sitting in a hotel room in Cambridge, about a 10-minute walk from campus. I am almost positive that in a couple of days someone will break the Chinagate story wide open, exposing the entire operation in minute detail. I will be listed as one of the spies. Please believe me and please forgive me. I hope that one day you will allow the kids to have positive memories of their father. I'm going to be leaving you all alone to raise the kids, deal with friends and family, and face the scrutiny of the press. I know I'm a coward, but the thought of returning to Beijing is impossible and continuing to live in this world without you and the kids is unfathomable. I won't go to prison. I'm taking the easy way out and you'll have to deal with the fall-out—I'm sorry. Will you ever forgive me, will you ever look at our time together as memorable, as time well spent, as the best time of your life? I hope so. Our marriage and raising two wonderful children with you have been my greatest successes. I love you, Jane, know that I do and that every day spent with you was perfect. I'll be watching over you and the kids.

Love,
Scott

As soon as Jane saw the police at her front door, she knew. Scott always called, he was too regimented not to let her know exactly where he was at any given time, he was the most disciplined person she had ever met; spontaneity was not in his vocabulary. When he didn't return the night before, she had immediately begun preparing for the worst. She brought the kids to Granny's house and followed the police officers to the county morgue to identify Scott's body.

He had been found in a hotel, hanging from the shower.

Upon leaving the morgue she drove directly to Cambridge and found Scott's note hidden under the same study carrel where they had met so many years earlier. She read the letter over and over, tears running down her face uncontrollably, unable to begin to comprehend what would happen to her and trying to understand what the last ten years of her life meant. She was numb. Jane didn't know what to think. *How could he do this?* "It was all a lie, the last ten years of my life have been a front for a Chinese spy, how could he do this to me and our family?" she said to herself. *What a goddamn coward.* "Love? Love? How could he be talking about love? How could there be love? He was living a double life! And then he kills himself and makes me clean up the mess, that's not love. Love is sacrificing for the other, sharing, being honest, through thick and thin, he doesn't—didn't—know the first thing about love," she said, grief mixing with anger. "He had control, he could've told me, he could've not married me, divorced me, come clean. There are a hundred things he could've done to let me know, and now he's saying it was love. No, he was serving his own self-interest. Did he even consider me and the kids and what we now have to go through? Why didn't you stick it out? We could fight this together, that's love. Not apologizing, saying it wasn't your fault, that's not love. You asshole." She put her head on the desk and began crying anew.

"Why did you do this, why did you leave us? We need you more now than we ever did. Did you ever really love me? Did you?" After about 20 minutes she left the library and began walking back to her car. She started reeling off a list of things that needed to be done before the story broke. "I need to take the kids out of school and put the house up for sale, I need to tell my parents, I need to get our finances in order, I need to be strong, I need to be strong. We are going to get through this; we're going to make it," she said out loud as she walked through campus.

She didn't have time to think about what had just happened, her kids would be depending on her; she would have no one to lean on. She knew sometime soon she would have to look back on everything, properly heal so she could move on, but there was no time for that now.

"We're going to make it," she kept repeating to herself out loud as if she could somehow convince herself it was true. She reached into her purse and pulled two valium from a prescription she had filled a few weeks ago, started the engine to her car, and headed north to her parent's house.

Chapter 44

Song May sat in her cell, hands cuffed and legs shackled to the front bars. She had been there for twelve hours, unable to go to the bathroom. Only five prisoners were in the entire building and none on her wing, so it was quiet, especially at night. Bright lights shined in her cell making it almost impossible to sleep. If she did succeed in dozing off, a guard passed by her cell every thirty minutes and woke her. The guards were generally younger and sympathetic to Song May and the abuse she was taking. Most would try to sneak her food, give her ointments for her wounds, or try to talk to her.

The guard who worked the graveyard shift was especially thoughtful. He had seen her the first night looking as beautiful as any movie star he had ever seen and he was immediately smitten. The guard, short and homely, was from the country, barely eighteen, and a virgin. A naïve, shy, young boy who could be easily manipulated. Song May had been seducing the boy from her first night in the cell; she knew he might be her only way out.

As the rest of the prison slept, the two talked. The boy, scared at first, became more brazen with each day, risking certain punishment, but determined to help Song May survive.

"Hi, Song May, how're you doing tonight?" he asked her.

"Not so good, barely surviving. I don't know how much longer I'm going to be able to make it. Tonight might be my last night on this earth," she told him, an attempt at manipulation, but also possibly true.

"Don't talk like that, you have to stay positive." He tried reasoning with her, "Why don't you tell them what they want to hear, why so headstrong? Life would be easier if you did. They might even let you out."

"If I tell them what they want they will kill me," Song May explained. "At least now they have to keep me alive. Soon it won't matter, my knowledge will be meaningless." Now she laid it on thick, "I will die in here a broken, ugly woman."

"Song May, you're not ugly. You're the most beautiful woman I've ever seen. I hope one day to marry someone as pretty as you," the guard blushed with this admittance.

"You're sweet, but I can only imagine how horrible I must look with all these bruises and broken bones. I'm thankful for not having a mirror in my cell. Wun Hway, can I ask you a personal question?" she asked him.

"You can ask me anything you want, but I don't know if I'll be able to answer," he responded.

"What do you want to do with your life, what do you dream about?" she asked him.

"Haven't really given it much thought," he told her. "This is the first job I've had other than working the fields and the first time I've ever left my village, if you can call a three-mile bus ride leaving. I guess I'm pretty happy to have a paycheck."

"You must dream of something," Song May pushed him, "something you want more than anything else. Maybe you want to live in Beijing, go to university, travel to America. If you had one wish, more than anything else, what would it be?"

"I don't—I don't know if we should be talking so much. I could get in trouble. I should go check on the other prisoners," Wun Hway was clearly getting nervous.

"Wun Hway, please don't leave me. I don't know how much longer I'll be with you. You're the only person I can tell my secrets to, I'm losing hope and you're all I have left."

"You're gonna be set free one day, Song May, you just need to tell them the truth. Don't give up; they'll let you out soon."

"Wun Hway, just look at me, look at my half-naked body shackled to these bars. I'm cold, sick, hungry, and losing my desire to live. I don't know how much longer I can survive even if they don't kill me." Song May started to cry uncontrollably, another manipulation but easy to do given the last several days of her life.

Wun Hway stood there in shocked silence for a moment; he didn't know what to do. "Song May, Song May, please don't cry. I'm sorry for not being more understanding. I can't even begin to imagine the hell you're going through." He reached his hand through the bars and began stroking her hair. As he continued, she cried louder.

"I'm never going to get out of here!" she wailed. "I have no hope of survival." As Wun Hway continued to gently stroke her long, unwashed, black hair, she grabbed his hand and held it. "Wun Hway, you're the only friend I have left, you're the only one who will listen." Her crying continued.

"It's going to be all right, Song May. It's going to be okay," he feebly attempted to calm her. Song May continued crying and the two of them remained silent, hands embraced, until Song May finally started to calm down.

"Wun Hway, will you tell me your dreams?" she asked sweetly.

"Okay, Song May. One day I hope to marry and start a family. Maybe I'll find a wife as perfect as you."

"You're wonderful, Wun Hway."

"I've always dreamt of one day moving to the big city and working in construction. I've always been good with my hands."

"I bet you are." Wun Hway blushed and they both laughed.

"Wun Hway, you could do anything you want, I believe in you. I bet one day you're going to be a big boss and build huge skyscrapers that dot the Beijing skyline."

"Do you think so? I'm just a boy from the country with no education, I don't know if I'll ever be brave enough to leave my village. I don't know if I have what it takes."

"You can do it; I have faith in you." Song May made Wun Hway smile. "You know, I have a lot of friends in Beijing. I could help you, we could do it together, Wun Hway."

"Do you think so?"

"I know so. You're going to be great one day; you're already great." She began gently rubbing his arm through the bars and slowly they both moved their faces close to the bars, their lips touched, and they kissed. As their lips parted, Song May spoke sensually to what she hoped would be her next conquest.

"Wun Hway, can you come into the cell with me? I want to be with you tonight." They looked at each other for a second and Wun Hway turned away and looked down the hall. Nothing was there to explain his gaze, but Song May could sense that Wun Hway was getting cold feet.

"I don't have the keys to get into your cell, Song May. Only the captain has the keys."

"Wun Hway, I want to be with you tonight. I've never been with a man before and if I die tomorrow, I want you to be the one. I love you Wun Hway. Make love to me."

Wun Hway's mind was racing, this couldn't be happening. He couldn't believe his good fortune, but also couldn't believe it was coming to him when he had to take such risks to obtain it. His first chance at popping his cherry! *What to do? Isn't this a no-brainer?*

"I don't know if I can get the keys." He was sweating. Maybe he could get the keys, he thought. He was as hard as a petrified tree.

Song May pressed on, "I'm sure the captain must be asleep by now and probably three sheets to the wind. Wun Hway, this may be our only chance to be together. Don't you want to be with me?"

"Wait here," he told her as he left her cell.

Wun Hway slowly walked down the hall, careful not to make a sound. It was quiet. Very quiet. The guard in the other ward had fallen asleep long ago. Wun Hway slowly opened the door to the captain's office. He was lying on his back on the couch, the TV blaring, and an empty bottle of whiskey at his feet. He was snoring. The keys sat on his chest.

Wun Hway slowly walked up to the captain and called his name—no response. He reached down and took hold of the key ring with his thumb and forefinger. As he lifted the keys from the captain's chest, they jangled and the captain stirred. Wun Hway stood motionless, holding his breath. The captain began coughing and at the exact moment he opened his eyes, Wun Hway grabbed the empty whiskey bottle, wound up, and connected with the captain's head. The bottle shattered into 100 pieces and blood gushed from the captain's forehead. Wun Hway thought only momentarily of the repercussions as he ran out the door. The problem was, he was thinking with the wrong head.

When he got back to Song May's cell, his confession spilled out, "The captain may be dead. He was about to wake and I clocked him with a whiskey bottle. He's bleeding pretty badly; I think I killed the captain." Wun Hway was shaking, the moment that Song May had created was gone.

"You did that for me, no one has ever sacrificed so much for me. Wun Hway, I'm going to make it worth your while," she said sensually. I can't wait to be with you, Wun Hway. Do you still want to make love with me?"

With those words, Wun Hway opened the cell door. As he fiddled through the keys trying to find the right one to free Song May's shackles, she began to move both of her handcuffed hands up his leg and to his loins. As she did this, the keys dropped from Wun Hway's hand and he sighed. Men are so weak, thought Song May. After unlocking her leg shackles, the two began to undress. They kissed passionately. Wun Hway was in the throes of ecstasy and

Song May moved around him and began caressing him from behind. As she moved up his back, she adroitly placed her hands around his neck and before Wun Hway knew what hit him; he was dead. Song May cracked his neck; he didn't feel a thing.

She looked down at Wun Hway and wanted to feel guilt, but she couldn't. She simply couldn't conjure up any feelings resembling remorse. She needed help. She took Wun Hway's pants and undershirt and put them on. She'd look out of place, but not completely. She took the wallet out of his pocket, grabbed about $4 and left. The prison was small, like a county jail. It had no alarms. She casually unlocked and walked through a number of security doors and within five minutes was feeling the night air. It was 3:30 a.m. She had very little time.

She walked with a limp and had expended almost all of her energy on Wun Hway. Song May found a pay phone and called a number she had memorized.

"Hello," a groggy deep male voice answered the phone.

"I need your help."

Chapter 45

On a Tuesday, twenty-four hours before Song May's escape, Peter
Fed Ex'd the story to Bill O'Malley at *The San Francisco
Examiner*'s Hong Kong office. Song May had given him the name
of the reporter and paper to send the information. He hoped she
knew what she was doing. In the letter, he said he would give them
twenty-four hours for due diligence and if they didn't go to print
by Thursday, he would give the story to every major paper and
network in the country. This offer was a very short exclusive. Peter
was ready to call his own bluff and start sending information out in
the morning. He had spent the last two days finding out the
numbers to CNN, Reuters, and AP, as well as the major networks.
He found out where all of their local Bangkok offices were located
and had copies of all the spies' information and the companies they
worked for in America. Song May had helped him sort the
information and organize it before she left.

As Song May was escaping her cell, Peter was lying in bed
restless. He prayed that *The Examiner* would run the article. He
didn't want to have to go to Plan B, and if they balked, he
wondered if the others would as well. Peter knew they couldn't
logically sit on the story, it was front-page news for months and to
break the story on the biggest economic espionage case the country
had ever seen would be a major coup for any news organization.
But as the deadline approached, Peter felt as stressed as if he were
walking into his first college examination.

As important as it was to publish the truth about the espionage, the
pit in Peter's stomach from not knowing what had happened to
Song May was the main culprit for his lack of sleep over the past
several days. He had delayed sending the story for almost a week,
hoping she would show up, but as the two-week mark approached,
he could wait no longer. He had to act. He still wasn't sure if this
was the ultimate act of betrayal. He wondered if she were in the
same position, would Song May hold off until she knew he was
safe or would she be pragmatic? He now found it hard to justify his
decision. Was breaking the story more important than her safety?
Was she acting the role of the martyr or did she really want him to
do it? If she died, was it to be her legacy that the spy ring was

uncovered? Peter still did not have any answers. He prayed almost every second of every day that she would show up. He was lost without her, and regardless of his parents imploring him to come home, he wasn't ready to give up hope. It was 6:00 a.m., the internet cafes would open soon and Peter was hoping to log in to find that the article had been published.

Chapter 46

SPIES IN AMERICA

Chinagate: The Greatest Economic Espionage Case in History Exposed
By Bill O'Malley

The headline ran across the entire front page of *The San Francisco Examiner* with the article filling the rest of the page and two others inside Section A. Another article on the coming demise of the six Chinese companies, the lawsuits that would subsequently be filed, and the imminent downward spiral of the Hong Kong Stock Exchange was featured in the business section.

The futures markets had to be temporarily shut down in Hong Kong as the market was expected to immediately drop 15% once it opened the following day and the six Chinese companies were expecting to open 90% lower than the previous day's close. The tech heavy NASDAQ, which had been in a lull the past year, was up 10% in heavy trading and the six U.S. companies that had been duped were up significantly.

Silicon Valley was in a state of euphoria. Companies were shutting down and throwing parties in celebration of the end of Chinagate. Bars and nightclubs were being booked for private events. The mayor of San Francisco declared victory on the steps of City Hall. Soap operas were interrupted so the President could make an official announcement on the end of Chinagate. He praised law enforcement for their diligent work and thanked Bill O'Malley for his award-winning investigative journalism. He vowed the rest of the agents would be caught and tried as spies and promised retribution against the Reds in China. The Valley had been suffering from an identity crisis and questioning whether it could remain the center of the tech universe, an insecurity that had not been seen since the early 80s. Now all was right again, America's technical superiority reinstated. Seattle and every other tech-heavy city were also in various states of elation.

The Examiner tripled its normal run in anticipation of high demand, but by 9:00 a.m. not one newsstand in the entire city had a copy. Its servers had been down for almost an hour with a ten times increase in traffic to the paper's website. Experts were saying that the story circled the globe faster than the Blaster virus of 2003. The TV networks started running the story almost immediately, providing updates on arrests, ongoing investigations, and interviewing the CEOs of the six companies.

The mood at Sage was beyond ecstatic. Employees were almost giddy as they watched the company stock price rise from the single digits to levels not seen since 1999. Music blared from supped up computer speakers, champagne and boxes of liquor were delivered for an impromptu party. Colleagues were making out in the halls and twenty-two year old graduates of Stanford and Cal Tech were high fiving after checking their online portfolios. People were even talking about the future. Their paper millions restored and faith in the American work ethic renewed. David Biddleberry was making the rounds, providing interviews on CNBC, CNN, and FOX. He had won again. His once good friend Scott Chen was dead and not a tear was shed.

Bill O'Malley was a worker: nothing he accomplished came easy and all of his success was well earned. Luck was never something he thought about, unless at the racetrack, but when it came his way he never dismissed it as the fruits of his hard work. He took it completely at face value, as a lucky break. Being at the right place at the right time, stumbling across a Pulitzer-Prize-winning story, receiving the perfect tip. It happened rarely, but when it did, it was usually monumental.

As he sat at the Kings Arms in Hong Kong waiting for Tommy Anderson, he was still mystified at how the biggest story in the last twenty years had landed on his desk. He smiled as he sipped on his beer, recounting the events of the last forty-eight hours.

It had all started with a seemingly innocuous Fed Ex package that contained a gold mine. It was reputation changing, a break that only comes around once in a lifetime. In the package were the names of the Chinese agents of all six companies that had had secrets stolen, a list of every company that agents had infiltrated, and a complete twenty-five page description of exactly how the system worked. He sat at his desk for hours poring over the documents, in shock at the complexity of the operation and the patience of the Chinese. He read the description like he would a mystery novel, a page-turner that he was unable to put down. As he began imagining the front-page story, he started to sweat, strategizing how he would approach Hank Applebaum, the Editor-in-Chief. *The Examiner* would certainly print the story, but he worried about Applebaum's conservative tendencies. He spent the rest of the day verifying facts, confirming that the agents did work at the six companies, and researching the rest of the named companies looking for trends on how close they were to launching new products or introducing groundbreaking technology. He was convinced of the authenticity of the information. He reread the instructions of the letter and knew that if he did not convince Applebaum in one sitting, the story would be gone. He set up an appointment, had every document scanned and sent to Applebaum's office, and called him thirty minutes later.

"So whatdaya think?" O'Malley asked Applebaum.

"Is this some story you wrote during fits of insomnia? This cannot be true," Applebaum responded in his true conservative fashion.

"It is true, we both know it's true, so let's take a small, calculated risk and print it," O'Malley pushed.

"Any corroboration, have you done any fact checking?"

"All six people mentioned do work at the named companies, the other companies that are mentioned are in the advanced stages of groundbreaking product development. They were all pretty suspicious of my questions, especially with all that's happened. We have enough to take a chance; it's not rock solid, but someone will break this story and we'll be left high and dry. We have nothing to lose," O'Malley pressed on.

"Except our reputation," Applebaum scoffed. "It's too risky, let's call this guy's bluff and hold off for a day."

"If we don't go to press tomorrow, it's too late. Let's run with it. goddamnit."

O'Malley was only slightly surprised when Applebaum eventually came around. *The San Francisco Times* had been eating *The Examiner*'s lunch recently and this story would be a huge circulation boost. Both men agreed that the same morning the story went to print, a copy of the documents would be delivered to the FBI and CIA.

"Mr. O'Malley, basking in your glory, I see," bellowed Tommy as he approached O'Malley at the bar.

"I'm in such shock over what's happened over the last twenty-four hours that I don't even feel like drinking. I'm on a natural high." O'Malley laughed, downed his pint of Guinness and ordered two more.

"So, I guess your conspiracy theory had some merit to it. How the hell did you put the pieces together?" Tommy knew Peter had dropped the story in his lap, but he wanted to see if Bill would fess up.

"A lucky break. I found my own deep throat."

"Four arrests, two suicides, proprietary information found on three of the suspected agents' home computers, leads on infiltrations in the other companies you listed, a 30% one-day drop in the Hang Seng Index, six bankrupt Chinese companies, offers to write a book based on your article, movie offers, a possible Pulitzer Prize—fuckin' a, did you get laid as well?" Tommy joked.

"I'm not gonna lie, it feels good." O'Malley for the first time in his life was enjoying the moment. He wasn't thinking about deadlines, missed opportunities, or his alcohol problem; he was relishing in the fact that he had made it. A career-changing story. He had achieved success and for the first time he had thoughts of creating a legacy. He had already done interviews with CNN and Fox and his cell phone was filled with other invitations. "It feels very good. So, what brings you down to Hong Kong?"

"Well, I came down specifically to see you. I'm being sent home, reassigned to headquarters. The CEO wants to bring in new blood to run the business. It's been a nice run, but I'm ready to head home." Tommy was actually being demoted. He blamed himself for what transpired on the streets of Beijing and the death of Winston Chang. He second-guessed himself constantly, wondering if he should have told Peter that he was working for the CIA. Perhaps he would have been more loyal. In the end, the case was cracked, but a veteran agent sacrificed his life. This one would stay with Tommy for years to come.

"Well, I may see you stateside," O'Malley bragged. "CNN has made some inquires as has CNBC. I may be going big time."

"With your mug, don't count on it. Have they seen what you look like?" Tommy ribbed him.

"No, trying to keep them in the dark as long as possible." The two laughed and ordered a final round.

"Congrats on breaking the biggest news story of the 21st Century." The two men lifted their fresh pints and drank in honor of Bill O'Malley.

Chapter 47

"General Wang, thank you for seeing me on such short notice."

"Yes, Party Secretary, how may I be of assistance?"

"Comrade, as you know, the situation in America is very grave indeed. We made some mistakes and we let our arrogance and greed get the best of us. How have we let a perfectly planned mission be destroyed in a matter of days? How did this happen?"

"Well, Party Secretary, I think we have had some bad luck. There seems to have been some leaks and betrayals of the Motherland. We are currently dealing with the problem."

"Comrade, shouldn't this problem have been dealt with or been noticed ahead of time? Surely there were signs." The Party Secretary's voice was beginning to rise.

"Yes, well," the General shifted in his chair, "we wanted the mission to continue since we had built a very successful momentum."

"General, who, may I ask, are you referring to when you say 'we'?"

"With great respect, Party Secretary, the major decisions were made by the top members of the party." The General had nothing better to say, as he wasn't prepared to take total blame himself quite yet.

"Comrade, am I correct in my interpretation that you are blaming the members of the Standing Committee, the President, and the Prime Minster for your ineptness? Are you insane? Do you know what is happening in America? We have spent over 30 years building a strong relationship with America and you have managed to destroy years of goodwill in about two days. Have you been reading the briefings, do you know what the hell is happening?" He was silent for a moment waiting for the General to answer and then continued. "You were in control of every facet of this project.

You managed the program, supplied us with briefings and reports, provided updates on the progress. It is obvious that you candy-coated these reports and now everything is ruined. Yes, you are quite right, comrade, we are to blame. And do you know why?" he paused momentarily. "Because we trusted you. I am still trying to figure out how someone could be so stupid. General, are you prepared to answer that question for me?" screamed the Party Secretary.

The two men sat in silence, the Party Secretary in utter frustration and the General too scared to make a peep. After a few minutes the Party Secretary continued. "General, it is going to take quite a long time to repair our relationship with America. We are, of course, claiming ignorance, but the evidence is quite overwhelming and I'm sure with enough pressure, our agents will begin to talk. This situation is undeniably terrible. General, you are being reassigned. Many areas of the province of Tibet have had uprisings. We have a small regiment there that we would like you to head up. You will leave at once."

General Wang immediately pleaded with him, "Party Secretary, please, I have not been in the field for twenty years and the winters in Tibet won't be good for my arthritis. Please consider my years of service and loyalty to the country. Please, Party Secretary." General Wang's begging was unbecoming of a general and the Party Secretary looked at him with disgust.

"That will be all, comrade. Good day."

Chapter 48

It had been eight days since the story broke, but Peter still could not resign himself to the fact that he would never again see Song May. He reassured his parents that he was okay, but day after day he remained in Bangkok, hoping his prayers would be answered.

At 3:00 a.m. on a sweltering hot night in Bangkok, he heard a slight knock on his door. Peter awoke instantly and called out, "Who's there?" Although he should have been frightened that perhaps the Communists had tracked him down, all he felt was hope. He opened the door slowly and was instantly filled with emotion, relief, and shock as he looked at Song May's battered face.

They stood in the door silently, looking at each other as if for the first time. It had been almost three weeks since they had seen each other and both had nearly lost hope. Both refused to let the moment pass and as tears began rolling down their faces and sobs turned into cries and cries turned into laughs, they intertwined, kissed softly, and hugged. They remained motionless in the doorway kissing, hugging, and whispering into each other's ears until Song May had to sit down. Peter gently led her into the small room and as they sat on the bed, the soft uneven mattress almost swallowed them. Peter was terrified to hear what she had endured.

"Am I still beautiful?" asked Song May with a vulnerability Peter had never heard from her. Song May's wounds had barely started to heal, her eyes still black and blue, her nose and jaw broken, and her cheeks, though the swelling had gone done, still looked like a chipmunk's. So self-conscious about her looks, she'd looked in a mirror only once since she had escaped. She still wasn't sure if the beauty she once possessed would ever return to her.

"I'm searching my soul to find something perfect to say. I thought I'd never see you again. You are beautiful. You're beyond beautiful. You're perfect. I don't want to lose you. I couldn't ever imagine that I could have so much love for one person."

"I love you, Peter."

They embraced and lay in bed for hours, sometimes silently and then speaking non-stop until sunrise. When Song May calmed down, she told Peter some of what she went through, sparing him the details of the worst of her nightmarish experience.

She explained how Charlie had come through again, taking her cross country, getting her a Canadian passport, and paying the border guards $1000 USD to get her into Vietnam. After her escape and *The Examiner* story, the whole country was put on alert. Her picture had been seen by everyone with a TV set or who read a newspaper. Charlie had risked his life to see her to safety.

Song May interrupted herself with a start, "*The Examiner*? Do you have the story?" Peter showed her *The Examiner* and all of the subsequent clippings. He kept the story of the suicides and arrests from her, not wanting to create too much trauma too soon.

Song May was relieved. It was over. It was truly over. It was time to start her life anew.

Peter said he wanted her to see one more article. He showed her the front-page article from the Hong Kong Post. They were rich. The Chinese company stocks had tanked and all six had already declared bankruptcy. Peter's father had liquidated all of their positions and they had reaped a sizeable profit.

As the sun rose and Song May and Peter lay on their backs facing the ceiling, Song May looked at Peter and asked, "What's next?"

He looked at her resolutely, "I have a plan."

Chapter 49

Peter stared at Song May walking across the beach in her black string bikini as if he had never made love to her. She looked beautiful and walked confidently yet pensively as the midday sun illuminated her tanned body. After a week in Thailand, they flew from Bangkok via Mexico to Barbados and had been recovering at the beach for the past three months.

Song May had been to the doctor to fix her nose and jaw and to repair some of the burn marks on her skin. Some of her physical wounds would never heal and they were daily reminders of her tortuous days in prison, but she was looking as ravishing as she did when Peter first saw her. She slept a few hours each night at best and woke most nights screaming from nightmares. She had no idea when her nightmares would subside and avoided sleep like a child waiting for Santa Claus on Christmas Eve. But with each week that passed, she slept a little bit better and a little bit longer.

Peter waited until he felt Song May was both physically and mentally strong again to give her the articles about the agent suicides and arrests. Song May had known all of the agents and had worked directly with some of them. She knew this was an inevitable outcome of the revelation of the espionage, but in lieu of remorse she felt relief.

As Peter finished slathering himself with SPF 30, he joined Song May for a swim in the warm waters of the Atlantic. They were together and living in the moment. They spoke infrequently about the future, promising to talk about it *mañana*.

THE END

About the Author

Shawn Lipton speaks fluent Mandarin Chinese and has spent time living, working, and traveling in China and Taiwan. Shawn went to Taiwan as a recent college graduate to teach English and quickly fell in love with the Chinese language, culture, and people. An initial plan of spending three months saving money and then continuing a backpacking journey through Southeast Asia turned into 2.5 years in Taiwan and another year traveling in Asia. Shawn is also the author of *50 Proven Networking Tips for Career Development Success*.